Instant Mystic

Gail Gray Helm

Instant Mystic

Gail Gray Helm

Morning Glory Press

Buena Park, CA 90620

gailgrayhelm@gmail.com

ISBN 978-0-9964430-0-5

Cover design by Victoria Markle
Keystroke Graphics
vickydmarkle@aol.com

Morning Glory Press
Buena Park, CA 90620
Printed in U.S.A.

Table of Contents

Explore the Places in Instant Mystic

If you are vacationing or live in Southern California you might like to visit places mentioned in this book. Little India is on Pioneer Boulevard in the city of Artesia between Artesia Blvd. and South Street. There are many fine restaurants, splendid jewelry and sari shops, and the grocery stores are fascinating. A further plus is that it will save you an eighteen hour flight to India! Udupi Palace is at 18635 Pioneer Boulevard, Artesia, California. In that local vicinity, don't forget to stop by and see the Cerritos Public Library at 18025 Bloomfield Avenue, Cerritos. Considered one of the world's most beautiful public libraries, the library houses an aquarium, a collection of splendid art and of course the T-Rex in the children's section. Seal Beach is a great old-style Southern California beach town. Walt's Wharf restaurant is located at 201 Main Street, in Seal Beach.

Long Beach boasts beautiful beaches, great museums, old California ranchos, and perfect weather for exploring. *Retro Row* is on 4th Street between Junipero and Cherry. Joe Jost's Tavern is located in Long Beach at 2803 E. Anaheim, and has been serving Long Beach folks since 1924. The Library: A Coffee House,3418 E. Broadway, also in Long Beach. On your adventures Long Beach look south to the *Queen Mary*; a trip aboard will transport you back to the 1930's. Thanks, to the previously cited restaurants for their permission to be used as settings in *Instant Mystic*.

Thanks

I am deeply grateful for the friendship and support of Jeanne Warren Lindsay who has inspired many as a teacher, writer, editor, publisher and mentor. Without her encouragement this book would not have come to fruition. Thanks also to Phyllis Merys and Marjorie Robertson for their initial confidence in this story and Barbara Vangsness who was a diligent and kind copy editor. Vicky Markle designed the marvelous cover, helping readers know *this* book by its cover. Thanks to Pat Alviso and Jeff Merrick for all things nautical and to Steven and Michael Derryberry, my 'beta' readers. Damaris Gonzalez helped me with idiomatic Spanish. Additionally I would like to acknowledge Padmini Prabhakar, Librarian II of the Cerritos Library, and Janice Dawson, President of *The Friends of the Cerritos Library*, the organizers of '*Mystery on the Menu,*' which gave me the notion that writing fiction could be good clean fun.

For the world's coolest husband, Steve
and my son Michael,
who lives and breathes ideas and words

Gail Gray Helm

Mango Lassi

Cool fingertips gently stroked the arch of his brow then softly traced the edges of his lips. He was safely in the arms of her love. Suddenly sound ripped through the walls shaking them and pulled him from sleep. Adrenaline surged through his body demanding that he run and hide. Still caught between realities, he tried to drag her features from the edges of dream and memory, but the struggle pushed the vision of her farther away. The crushing machine sounds of the garbage truck ground him into Wednesday morning and the cogs of his consciousness sped him forward into day. The memory of her face eluded him once again.

He walked to his kitchen, opened his small old refrigerator and looked pensively inside, hoping a delicious breakfast might just await him. No such luck. Instead he grabbed a white paper carton seeping orange stains and wolfed down *baingan barta* leftover from Sunday night in Little India. The curried eggplant was slimy and unctuous. He should have thrown it out in this morning's trash instead of making a garbage can of his stomach. Too late. He gulped down some *mango lassi* and hoped that the magical compensatory live yogurt cultures might kill whatever weird stuff was growing in the eggplant. He peed, pulled on some board shorts and a very faded T-shirt with a murky photo of Sting that said *Spirits in the Material World* across the top, and walked outside to look at the surf.

He owned one of the last 1950's stucco cottages left on Ocean Avenue in Seal Beach. He was surrounded by overbuilt beachy McMansions and it appeared that he might become the only holdout to smallness and simplicity. The faded flat roofed white house was vaguely boat-like in style with funky portholes in the kitchen. He exited toward the ocean through a glass door to a tiny backyard with an old brick patio set in sand. Ice plant and a few succulents survived the salt air. In the corner next to a hibachi three surfboards leaned against the edge of a planter. One was a translucent aqua short board with a small design of a dancing Zen skeleton in black. The second was an old sand colored long board with a Dewey Weber sticker on it. Both were layered with rivulets of wax and sand. The third, propped up against the wall, was a stand up paddle board with a carbon fiber paddle in its case. He looked down from his little cliff at a dull gray Pacific weighted down by a heavy leaden sky. A snarky little breeze and messy small waves were all that greeted him. No surf, no sun, no excuses to keep him from getting to work.

He went back inside and sat down at the old oak table that served both as dining table and desk. He looked out at the ocean through a large picture window hazy from salt and sea air. It needed to be washed again. He sighed. On the screen of his laptop waited a translation for a client whose professional documentation, academic records, and curriculum vitae were in *Hindi*. The finished translation would prove up the client's bona fides for a multinational corporation based in Melbourne.

Dev had discovered his unique facility for acquiring foreign languages when he was a kid. He had moved so frequently and needed to adjust so rapidly to different speech that an innate ear for language developed into a real talent. Speech and meaning just came together for him without much effort. Just as some musicians can play anything by ear, pick up any instrument and learn it quickly, that is how he acquired languages. He could read and translate ancient *Sanskrit*, spoke and wrote *Hindi,*

Bengali, Gujarati, Punjabi, Urdu, as well as unrelated *Telugu* and *Tamil*. He also read and spoke Tibetan languages and English and French. Being a polyglot allowed him to readily earn a living and meant that there were always new people to talk to and learn from. Reading and writing were more challenging, but they were fun and games for him. He enjoyed them much as other people liked to do sudoku or crosswords. Currently he was teaching himself Arabic and sometimes went to a mosque in Orange County to listen or chat with locals who spoke the language. He found their written script the most visually striking among the languages he had learned. Like Japanese scrolls with masterful brushstrokes, *Arabesque* was extraordinarily beautiful to see, even if you didn't know what it said.

His translations completed, he gathered the papers together and put them in a manila envelope. He would drive up to Little India to take the documents to Jay's law office. Jay would write the attorney cover letter and seal the documents with an *apostille* certifying their legitimacy to the receiving foreign corporation.

He belched and tasted the sour remnants of the tired eggplant. He needed to put something decent in his stomach. He grabbed the documents and decided to stop at Lupe's Café for breakfast on his way up to Little India.

La Ropa Vieja

The wooden palette she held was covered only in grays. Gray with a tiny bit of cadmium red to warm it, greened out grays, grays that were greige, putty grays, lavender grays, mushroom grays. An oil painter's secret was that if you saved the old paint from your various palettes you would end up with gray when you mixed them together. Each time she finished a painting she would mush the remaining paint around with her palette knife and scrape the resulting gray leftovers into a baby food jar and store it in her freezer. This painting consisted of palette debris from at least a dozen paintings. The knife quickly pulled spackle gray oil paints across dried out tropical impassioned Frida Kahlo colors—juicy mangos, quetzal blues and tart jungle greens. She painted over an old canvas she no longer wanted to complete, letting just whispers of the jungle peak through. She looked up at the textured nearly non-objective grays of the large painting. She knew it would probably be hung by a decorator above some rich guy's stainless steel mantel in Bel Air. They would probably never realize that what she had really painted was a blown up hyper-realistic detail of some old rags. *La ropa vieja*, she giggled to herself at the unintended joke, *Hijole!* She looked at all the varieties of gray on her palette and wondered if the layers of *gringa* gray covering up a very Mexican tropical painting had some psychological significance. But the thought of *ropa vieja* had her jonesing for just that dish with its ragged shredded pieces of beef, caramelized onions and peppers. She needed to take a break from her tedious self criticism and get something to eat. Fresh flour tortillas warm with lots of butter, like a *guera* white girl, to scoop the juicy meat up. She put down her brush, looked out the window at the ocean, and it was as gray as her palette.

Her studio-apartment was upstairs over her gallery and shop. She snuck down the tile staircase through an archway on the side of the old Spanish Revival building, avoiding the entrance of *El Corazon en Fuego*. For a long time, despite the shop's name, her heart hadn't been on fire for her business of Latin American handicrafts and local Latino art. She thought that the only fire in her heart was from indigestion; maybe she should just call the shop *Heartburn*. She laughed to herself realizing that her gray mood was probably just hunger. She relaxed a little knowing her manager Jennifer was running the shop contentedly without her. Lupe's little café was just a few blocks away.

It was still breakfast time and when she arrived the café was packed. She grabbed an empty stool near the end of the counter, and stationed herself between a giant glass jar of a pickled *escabeche* of carrots, radishes and jalapenos and a messy pile of this morning's *L.A. Times* and *Long Beach Press Telegrams*.

"Hi Lupe, I'm starving. You don't have *ropa vieja* do you?"

"Not on the menu, but we can just use *machaca,* fry up some onions and peppers and put it together for you."

"That's great. You got any coffee left?"

"Yeah, but it's kinda gray."

"Well, that's just pretty much par for the course this morning."

Lupe said, "That bad huh? I'll brew up some fresh."

She studied a tired looking radish floating forlornly in the pickle jar.

Lupe returned with a thick cream colored mug, set it down and then grabbed the newspapers next to her from off the counter. "Welcome!" Lupe said to a newcomer as he entered the small café. "Come on in, I'll make some room for you over here!"

A slender tanned man with straight brown hair pulled back in a neat ponytail sat down next to her. Lupe started to bring him a menu, but he said, "No, thanks. Just some coffee and *huevos rancheros* over easy please."

"Sure thing."

He sat on the green leatherette stool and swiveled towards her. "Morning," he smiled, "okay if I sit here?"

"Sure, it's fine," she replied and was startled to see his eyes, gray ringed with much darker gray, somehow disarming against his tan face. She thought this must be what people see when they look at my blue eyes – they are taken aback because they seem out of context.

"Man, this June gloom gets old fast," he said as he sat down.

"Yeah," she said, "it's May, so I guess it's actually May gray. People who don't live at the beach always expect great warm weather now and in the summer, but it's most splendid in late autumn."

"I know; when I first moved here there was heavy marine layer for months. When it finally lifted I could see Catalina Island so distinctly that it looked like I could walk across the water to it. But I guess I'd need a boat just like everybody else."

She laughed, "When you do take a boat, make sure it's the Express, those slow boats are murder! Speed trumps nausea. I think the best time here is between Halloween and Thanksgiving. You know that on a couple of days in the fall, it's so crystal clear you can see all the way to San Nicholas Island."

"I'd like to see that; it must be fifty miles away!"

"I'd love to go there. My favorite book when I was a little girl was *Island of the Blue Dolphins*. It's about a native girl who lived on the island all alone. They say she's buried at the Mission Santa Barbara."

He imagined her as a little girl, with her small sweet face and serious eyes. He said, "I've always wanted to go to the

Channel Islands. Once when I was flying to Asia, it was so clear that as we headed west over the ocean we were still low enough that you could see the islands, with golden cliffs and turquoise coves fading out to the darker blue Pacific."

"Yeah, I think that some of the islands are a state park. I'd like to visit. I've camped on the far side of Catalina and it gives you a sense of how the California coast was before we screwed it up. Where did you go in Asia?"

"I don't remember that time. I've been quite a few times."

"Business?"

"No, mostly because I lived in India some when I was younger."

"Oh you're Indian? I couldn't tell – your coloring and features – I was uncertain."

"I'm kind of one of those guys who's a chameleon." He didn't share with her that in fact he didn't know *what* or for that matter *who* he was. "Everybody thinks I'm one of whatever they are. It's quite nice – kind of an American Express face – accepted everywhere."

She wasn't sure she felt accepted anywhere. She had tried to be a regular white girl in high school, then in college tried to be a Latina. Now she was just trying to be herself, not anyone else's, or even her own expectation of what she ought to be.

Lupe, plates stacked along her arms, brought their food, more fresh salsa and chips, and refilled their heavy mugs with fresh coffee.

"Thanks Lupita," she smiled. Her hand cradled the mug, embracing its penetrating warmth. She turned to him and said, "I think sometime I'd like to go to India—maybe Goa—it used to be a Portuguese colony, right?"

"Yes, it has beautiful beaches and lots of hippies and expats."

"My dad,"she said, "was Dutch and Portuguese. His father's family owned a big dairy and his mom was the daughter of one of the milkers who came over from the Azores like many of the Portuguese people who settled in Dairy Valley. I learned to speak a few words of Portuguese from my grandma."

"Really? *Isso e grande!*"

"You speak Portuguese?"

"No, just 'Where's the bathroom, Hello and Goodbye.' But your Portuguese wouldn't do you much good in Goa. Maybe old timers still speak it, but Goa became independent in the early 60's and the island is a state in India. The official language is *Konkani* but most official business is done in English, maybe some in *Hindi*. You'd be fine there with your English. You know, I've never heard of Dairy Valley. Where is it?"

"Oh it doesn't exist anymore; all the dairies are gone. But it became incorporated as the city of Cerritos, you know right next to Artesia."

"No kidding! I didn't know that. I'm on my way up to Little India in Artesia right after breakfast. I didn't know about the dairies."

"When I was little there were still some dairies left. The people who bought new fancy houses with cathedral ceilings suffered from the flies and the cow stink. Cerritos means little hills in Spanish. There aren't any hills, let alone little ones, around there. My dad used to laugh at the fancy name and say the only hills there were the enormous piles of cowshit!"

He laughed and smiled at her. There was something so expansive and kind about his smile it made her feel like the beach – warm sand and the endless stretch of the Pacific. She was shocked at all the feelings that smile opened up in her.

"My name is Dev," he said as he extended his hand, "Yours?"

"Mine's Adrianna Beatrix Margarida Reukema." Her smile dimpled with the seeming silliness of her moniker. "Both grandmothers," she explained, "but Adri is okay."

"Well Adri, it's Dev Tagore. Do you like to eat Indian?"

"Yeah, but I'm kind of full right now." Then quickly, not wanting to lose this opportunity to be with him again, she said, "But I really like *mango lassi*!"

He smiled.

Good & Plenty

Jay was dressed in an impeccably tailored sharkskin suit. "Hey Dude!" he said as he high-fived Dev. Radiantly white cuffs shot from his sleeves revealing wine colored star ruby cufflinks and a matching ring all set in 22 carat gold. Like many Indian men he wore a colored stone ring guaranteeing good fortune auspiciously in harmony with his horoscope. Jay's gems were very much the real deal.

Jay's office seemed coordinated with his cufflinks, decorated with deep cabernet velvet couches, accented by pillows of mustard seed colored gold brocade. Surprisingly, the effect was more opulent than garish, indicating to his clients that he was successful and that if they used him as their attorney, so would they be. Dev handed the documents he had translated to Jay and the bill for his services. Jay sat down at his ornately carved desk to write him a check.

"Tara wants money again," Dev said.

"So what's new with her? That's all she ever wanted from you or any other man. In spite of what she calls herself, she ain't no Buddha of Compassion!" Jay said, looking at his friend and shaking his head seriously.

"Now, now, Jay, be nice. They say the Buddha nature lives

in all of us. Yours may be slinking around in the shadows of your murky soul, lurking there and waiting to sneak up on you sometime and surprise the hell out of you! Listen though, I have this idea I want to run by you. I've been thinking that I can send her some rough material. It'll be kind of novel trying to smuggle diamonds into India instead of the other way around. If I mail her rough stones they should be easy to hide because they won't look faceted or glittering when they go through X-rays. She can just get them cut in *Surat*. Ironically, one will probably end up back here in the three carat engagement ring of some Orange County ingénue. The idea of that kind of tickles me."

Jay said, "Don't tell me anymore—I don't want to know—talk about my soul!"

Dev said, "That's a crock! You're curious about everything. Right now you're simply dying to know how I'm going to smuggle them out."

"First," said Jay, "I'm sad every time she manipulates you. Second, I figure you're using someone as an intermediary in Vancouver or Antwerp – maybe both, and then they relay messages back and forth to India for you. I know you must use one or more intermediaries to still have contact with Tara without her being able to locate you. I know she would have her temple dogs after you if she had even a good guess about where you are."

"I hope you're right about me keeping one step ahead of her and all the others trying to find me. Please don't feel sorry for me because if I keep her solvent, I figure maybe she, or her minions, or any of the rest won't come knocking at my door."

"That makes sense, man, but you need to be careful." Jay wanted to lighten up on showing how he worried about his boyhood friend, and so, smiling broadly, he said, "Did you hear that story about the guy that Interpol was sure was smuggling diamonds hidden in the cast of his broken leg? They had a doctor come in and cut off the cast, only to find there were no stones in it. Then the guy demanded his own doctor come to the airport and replace the cast. The doctor had the diamonds hidden in the dry plaster, then he mixed it up and put on a new cast.

Interpol didn't even X-ray it, they just put him on the plane."

"That took some balls eh? Kind of like in the *Purloined Letter*, hiding in plain sight— just like I'm doing." Dev exhaled and gazed down at his hands. It sounded too much like a sigh to him. He continued teasingly – knowing it would piss off his friend. "My plan is to mail big rough octahedrons, you know the raw diamonds that look like two pyramids stuck together top to bottom, in with some dollar souvenir fluorites that have exactly the same configuration, some cheap agates, tiger's eyes and amethyst crystals. Then pack them in with a Toys R' Us rock tumbler and a kid's book called *The Magnificent World of Rocks and Minerals*."

Jay put his fingers in his ears, hummed loudly, and said, "Jeez Dev, I don't want to know. I'm an officer of the court!"

Dev said, "Of course you do and now you'll go home to your Bixby Knolls mansion and ruminate and plan and figure out even better ways to smuggle diamonds. Not only that, you will have to tell me eventually because you won't be able to keep your devious cleverness to yourself."

Jay said, "Okay, I give. You know me way too well and it's not really a mansion."

"Yeah, so you always say. Listen Man I don't want you to worry about me. If they haven't figured out where I am yet, they probably never will. As for the smuggling, you have to admit it's a good bit of fun."

Jay looked at his friend and smiled and said, "I am ashamed to admit it, but I would like to be a fly on the wall when Tara gets that package and tries to figure out why the hell you sent a bunch of rocks to her."

Dev said, "You know it won't take her long, she could be a certified gemologist. But enough about her. How about you have dinner with me at *Udupi* Palace tonight? You should know though, that I have an ulterior motive. I met this girl who seems special and I want to give her lots of breathing room. I'll seem more trustworthy and respectable if I bring my fashionable well-heeled lawyer friend along with my ponytailed self."

"Why don't you just cut off that nasty rat's ass, you dork?

Next thing I know you'll be nurturing dreadlocks looking like some kind of *Rastafarian Saddhu*."

"I cut my hair off for such a long time that now I revel in the freedom of my hairiness."

"Well you look like a poor hippy surfer."

"Well yeah—that's kind of what I am, but unfortunately I'm a crappy surfer."

"That may be true about the surfing, but 'poor' stretches credulity a bit, Dev. And regarding your poverty, just out of curiosity, how many diamonds do you have stockpiled?"

"I thought you didn't want to know! But just so you know, the old man put away a few kilos and a bunch of antique pieces that are magnificent. Why, you need some money, Jay?"

"No! Thank you very much. But I guess you can afford to buy me dinner!" He looked his friend in the eye and couldn't hold back his curiosity about Dev's invitation. "You never asked me to meet a girl before – I just figured it was due to your old monkish ways. So, Pinocchio, do tell, what's different this time?"

Dev reached over to an ornate filigreed small covered silver bowl. "I just have a good feeling about her, familiar and comfortable, like meeting an old friend when all the years just fall away. So, just roll on over to *Udupi* around 7:00." He took the lid off the bowl expecting to find *mukhwas*, the traditional Indian breath freshener and digestive comprised of fennel seeds and tiny pastilles of white and pink sugar. Instead he saw large shocking pink and white capsule shaped candies that looked like huge vitamin pills.

"What are these?"

"Try some."

Dev took a few and bit down. They were crunchy sugary outside and gooey chewy licoricey inside. They tasted just like *mukhwas*.

Jay laughed and said, "They're *Good & Plenty*! They are quintessentially American but taste like home."

"They say home is where the heart is, but I'm still not sure just where that is."

Gypsy Tart

Tara punctured the tin of evaporated milk and poured it over the dark *muscavado* sugar. She began to whip them together and to weep. She wept for herself and the harder she beat the mixture the harder she cried. She was making what everybody back home in Kent called Gypsy Tart. She remembered her grandmother saying you had to beat it until you thought you could no longer bear it. Now she was nearly old enough to be a grandmother too. The horror of that made her beat the gooey dark sugary milk even harder. Her beauty, her mystery and her cleverness were her only assets. The goddess used those assets to give her power and attract her devotees. But the goddess in her was waning. As her beauty faded so did the goddess. Dev's reflected light had for many years provided substance to her mystery and a sense of significance to her endeavors. Then he disappeared. No one knew where he was, although she knew they were looking for him. She had paid people to try to find him too. All she was sure of was that he was alive because he sent her some money now and then.

On her legal records, Tara was Mary Smith. Her Gypsy name was Mara Spiroski, the same as her grandmother. It was only later, when the goddess inhabited her that she became

Tara. Her mother had died in childbirth and she lived with her father much of the time in his Volkswagen camper van. Her grandparents still lived in a *vardo*, the old fashioned kind of Gypsy wagon that the English Romani people cherished. She stayed with her grandparents when her father felt inclined to get rid of her for a few months to go pick fruit, train hops, or visit women or whatever he did when she wasn't around. These were the happiest times for her.

Her grandmother had been born in that *vardo*. Dark red and round topped, it had little shutters and scrollwork designs all painted white with a small smokestack peeking through the roof. You entered it by climbing a small curving set of steps which were removed when the wagon was hitched to the horses. There was a small platform extending out from the door where a lantern was hung, which was a wonderful place to sit and whittle or shell peas. To enter, there was a Dutch door and once inside, the *vardo's* woodwork was fitted as tidily as a boat's. On the left was a cast iron stove set around with deep green tiles and on the right a table and benches. The rest of the interior was composed of cabinets, all of which were painted in various shades of yellow with touches of gilt making them appear opulent and golden. A few of the cabinet doors were mirrored and on each of these there had been painted nosegays of violets and red polka-dotted mushrooms. She remembered that sometimes when she was very little, they would bring her up into the bed nestled high above the cabinets where she would sleep wrapped in a flowery quilt, but usually she slept under the stars as did they, only using the little bender tent if it rained.

Her grandparents taught her to trap rabbits for beautiful Poacher's Stew, always with the wild mushrooms they had gathered in the forest. Her favorite thing had been hunting for mushrooms in the damp meadows in the early morning dew or in the woods with the light slicing low through the trees, illuminating her search of the forest floor. She learned to carve little flowers and mushrooms out of wood to sell along with the daffodils, bunches of violets and watercress they picked from the hedgerows. Sometimes too, they would catch hedgehogs, what her grandmother called *hatchi-witchi*, and draw them and singe their spines off in the fire then roast little chunks on a spit. But usually on the fire there was a just a pot of what Romany people called Joe Gray, simply sausages, onions, potatoes and a tin of tomato sauce. On chilly evenings sitting by the camp fire, they would study the stars, and even that humble stew went down a treat.

But Gypsy Tart was a rare and wonderful extravagance. It only had two ingredients, condensed milk and the dark molassesey rummy *muscavado* sugar. Here in India it was easy to find *jaggery*—palm sugar—pressed into cylinders, and occasionally if she was lucky she could purchase the much darker sugar of her childhood. It was a dish that Kent was famous for, but she knew others in the Home Counties south of London enjoyed it as their pudding too. The smell of the sugar caramelizing in the oven would take her back to her grandmother's *vardo*, which was perhaps the closest thing to a home she had ever known. Sadly, throughout England the *vardo* and the gypsy horse had become a thing of the past. The magical Gypsy wagons became playthings of wealthy collectors while Gypsies and Travelers chose to live in the more modern rolling luxury of motor caravans.

She looked out the window, her arm tired from beating the milk. The rhododendrons were in bloom, a blaze of pink against the dark mossy green of the forest background. She could see there was still much snow left on the Himalayas. She had been sleeping outside lately, but it had begun to drizzle, and June would bring on the rains of July and August. She longed to be moving on to somewhere where you could always sleep outside and walk through meadows forever. She still had seven diehard acolytes at the house. It was located a few miles outside of *Dharamsala* on the road to *Dal* Lake. The house and land were big enough to convert into a profitable guest house or small resort. She could turn it into a high end spa with *Reiki* and meditation for those wanting the experience of a spiritual journey without the hassle. Little Lhasa was full of fancy herbal tea shops, yoga studios and various and sundry purveyors of

Buddhist baloney each promising that for a sum you could move closer to spiritual attainment.

She took the blind baked crust out of the oven and lowered the temperature to gas mark 4. She was tired of beating, but knew it took a full fifteen minutes to make the texture perfect. She had beaten away all the tears and was thinking about Dev. She had never really considered why he had disappeared, being rather more concerned about its effect on her. She had written him a letter carefully designed to cajole him back into the life he had led before. His only response was to send her money through an intermediary. He undoubtedly assumed she still had followers and supporters. He never believed in the goddess, thinking it was just another Gypsy con; but for her it was the only thing that gave real meaning to her life. She hadn't performed any rituals and shared them with her believers in nearly six months. The extraordinary and magical way she had conducted her life seemed to be disappearing. If it were only a Gypsy trick she would know how to make it reappear; but she didn't, and yet knew she must try once again.

She filled the pie shell with the glossy sticky sugar mixture. Then as she turned and bent to open the oven door, one of her acolytes entered the kitchen. He said, "Oh Goddess, please let me do that for you. I could never forgive myself if you were burned!"

Dosas

Dev drove Adri up to little India in his faded blue Volvo station wagon. She looked at Pioneer Boulevard, the main street of little India, with new eyes. She recognized the old drug store which had been Standards Sweets and Snacks for most of her life with a *mandala* design on the sandstone brick front. The old Artesia Dutch Bakery was gone, now replaced with a glamorous looking marble façade, and where the feed store had been there were a dozen new townhomes. Yet the street to her eyes was a combination of California cow town plainness with an overlay of glamour. New little areas of 21st century styling were interspersed with the old. Indian jewelry stores were laden with the golden opulence of jewels fit for a maharini; one, High Glow, had a tower comprised of harlequin sheets of glass, its gradually shifting lights creating a moiré of different colors in the early evening light. The sari shops seemed alive with silks in vivid colors that were almost lurid to a western eye. Advertisements in storefront windows for eyebrow threading and *henna* wedding tattoos abounded.

Dev pulled around behind the restaurant and walked Adri through the back door. The waiters, dressed in wine colored shirts with '*More Sambar!*' written on the backs, greeted Dev by name and pointed them to a table by the window. Seated there, Adri noticed a tall elegant Indian man in a suit who smiled and waved at them.

Jay was anticipating meeting Dev's date. It was a first. He wasn't sure Dev ever dated, but Jay imagined whatever his romantic life, he would have kept it very private. He was curious to discover the kind of woman Dev might be attracted to. She was petite, dressed in a white on white embroidered blouse and dark narrow jeans. Her blue eyes were serious looking and her shiny nut brown hair was simply knotted at the nape of her neck. She wore no makeup and the only embellishment on her person was a heavy silver cuff on her wrist.

He stood and said, "Hi Adri, I'm Jay Mehta. I hear you like Indian food."

"Well I like what I've tried which are mostly *samosas* and a couple of kinds of curry, oh and *mango lassi*."

"Well you have a treat in store. This is Southern Indian food and is all vegetarian. The specialties here are *dosas* which are these marvelous giant Indian pancakes. I think you'll like them."

"I'm pretty sure I never met a pancake I didn't like, but what's the '*sambar*' written on the back of the waiter's shirts?"

Dev said, "It is a savory vegetable broth served almost as a condiment with most things on the menu. How about Jay and I just order for you, of course making sure you get *mango lassi*?"

Their waiter was new to Dev and Jay. He said he was from Nepal. He was smaller than the other waiters and extremely courtly in his manners.

Adri asked, "Is Nepal where the Dali Lama lives now?"

Jay said, "No, he escaped from Tibet, but now he lives in *Dharamsala* in the north of India. It is one of what the British during their occupation called a Hill Station."

"Right, both Tibet and Nepal are up in the Himalayas, I got them confused. I remember my grandpa had all sorts of cool stuff in the garage. One of the books was *The Boy's Book of Wonder,* from maybe 1940, and it had a photo of the little Dalai Lama and a story about him. I remember he had on a funny pointed hat."

Dev explained, "He still would have been in *Lhasa* in Tibet then. The Chinese invaded Tibet in 1949 and his Holiness escaped to *Dharamsala* in 1959. He was just a teenager. He has been living in India since then. The Tibetan government in exile is located in *Mcleodganj*, the old name for the hill station which is kind of a suburb of *Dharamsala*. There are so many Tibetans there that many refer to it as Little *Lhas*a. Europeans and Americans flock there too, some in pilgrimage, others out of a kind of romantic curiosity."

"Have you heard the Dalai Lama joke?" They looked at her, surprised. She said, "So it goes like this. The Dalai Lama walks into a pizza joint and asks the guy to make him 'One With Everything.' Well, apparently the joke's been around for a long time, but recently some Australian reporter told the Dalai Lama the joke. The Dalai Lama just looked at him clueless. He didn't get it at all."

Dev and Jay looked at her pretty much the way the Dalai Lama must have looked at the reporter when he had told the joke. Bewildered, astonished, what was the look on their faces? She scrunched up her lips and drew air in through her teeth realizing she may have offended them or just told the joke badly. She knew she sucked at telling jokes. Feeling nervous and worried that she had made a stupid gaffe, she said, "I don't suppose the Dalai Lama orders a large pepperoni very often. Probably not a lot of Pizza Huts in *Dharamsala*!"

Dev laughed and he and Jay began to relax. Then Dev said, "Why can't the Dalai Lama vacuum under the sofa?" Adri looked at Dev waiting for the punch line. "He has no attachments." He met her eyes and smiled in a way that told her that she was okay with him.

Jay said, "Dev knows the Dalai Lama."

Dev gave Jay an extremely withering look, and said, "Lots of people have been fortunate enough to meet his Holiness. I am just one of many thousands."

Jay looked at Dev, "Sorry, Pinocchio." Then he turned toward Adri and said, "I have a friend who went to visit Lhasa which is now part of China. It has been heavily colonized by lots of Chinese, but visitors still want to see the old Tibet. My friend was wearing a T-shirt with an old photo of Groucho Marx on it, you know in his funny round glasses. Chinese soldiers started hassling him because they thought that it was a photo depicting the Dalai Lama. It would be more amusing if it wasn't so tragic."

Dev looked a bit uncomfortable and excused himself to wash his hands before dinner. After chatting a little with Jay, she asked him why he called Dev 'Pinocchio.'

"Oh, it's because all he really wants is to be a *real boy*." Then Jay began to sing, in his very cultured accent, "I've got no strings to tie me down," his hands partially in the air bobbing around like a puppet on a string.

Dev returned to the table and joined in the song. "Hi ho the merrio, there are no strings on me." Adri giggled, astonished to see these sophisticated men acting like fifth graders.

Dev explained to Adri, "When Jay and I were little, we spent summers together in Belgium. I was living in Antwerp and Jay came to spend time at his great uncle's house. His folks, besides wanting to get rid of him for a while, knew that if he learned French, German and English, it would help him in their jewelry import-export business in the future. His great uncle was sort of my adopted uncle *cum* godfather. He loved having both of us around and was wonderful to us. He took us to the films to see *Pinocchio*. So, you see, Jay has been calling me that for a long time." Dev turned toward Jay and raised one eyebrow and continued, "But he better watch what he says or he'll be growing big long donkey ears!"

Their brotherly taunting had relaxed Adri and she began telling them about her sister Paloma and her nephew Ray. The waiter arrived, carrying astonishingly large incredibly thin golden crispy pancakes rolled around a filling of potatoes cooked with chiles, black and yellow mustard seeds and onions.

Dev said to her, "I hope you don't mind if we eat with our hands, it's what we are accustomed to. For some reason it just tastes all that much better that way." He pinched off a bit of *dosa* and dipped it in his bowl of *sambar*.

"Yeah I know, it's like eating pizza with a fork, it somehow distances you from the experience. It certainly doesn't make you one with the pizza!"

Dev smiled at her attempt at vamping on the earlier joke. "Here, try a little of the mango chutney. It may take a little getting used to."

She tasted it and sucked in her cheeks and squiggled up her eyes. "Oh, my God, that's like Tide and Drano combined!"

"Ooh sorry, Jay and I love it. Perhaps you'll enjoy the mint or tamarind chutney better."

"The dosas are great, but Dev, do you mind if I order another mango *lassi* to wash that soap suds chutney down?"

"Most certainly. If that would make you happy it will make me happy too."

She shyly leaned her shoulder gently into his and said, "Then another lassi please."

Juicy Fruit Gum

Jimmy Dracos hung up the phone and swiveled his chair toward Gary, the fresh hire. "O.K. Kid I've got work to do. I've got a lead on a guy who comes up on the Special Interest Alien list. He's a Canadian citizen with Permanent Resident status here. His birthplace is listed as Vancouver B.C., but we've an alert that the birth certificate may be falsified. It looks like the parents on the birth certificate are bullshit too. His father is listed as Rabindranath Tagore, occupation 'poet.' The guys in D.C. tell me that's the name of some famous Indian writer, long dead before the guy could have even been born." Jimmy didn't tell Gary that there were no guys in D.C., and certainly no directive. He was working off a tip from Maxine and he was hoping it would pay off for him big time.

Jimmy continued, "He hit the radar because he has been attending mosque or some Islamic learning center in Orange County. He has a LLC called Kaliglot and he translates documents for a lawyer in Little India. Apparently he's been brushing up on his Arabic and chatting up the Pakis. So now we need to find out what he's up to."

"So what did they say we're supposed to do?" Gary asked

"Not we. Me. You need to stay here and concentrate on this

week's shipping manifests, especially the ones with Argentine registries. You know, the usual stuff. I've got an address on him in Seal Beach and I'm gonna check it out."

Jimmy drove his new red Camaro away from the small satellite Homeland Security office near the convention center in downtown Long Beach. He headed East on Shoreline Drive and continued on to Ocean. He curved past the old Victorian mansion that was now the Long Beach Art Museum. Debbi always wanted to go there. He thought it was too late now for Valentine's and Mother's Day, maybe for her next birthday. It was June now, and as always, the gloom had arrived. On his right, people in jackets walked their dogs along the bluffs. The oil platforms a few miles out in the gray Pacific looked almost pretty and somewhat fanciful veiled by the marine layer. He passed the fancy houses on his left. He always looked for the one with the statue of the Virgin Mary in a little grotto. She was still there and he crossed himself as he passed her. He heard that the house was a monastery or something for Buddhist Monks now. Weird. He swooped up past the Belmont Pier so he could catch Second Street to get over the bay to PCH. Maybe he'd hit the Belmont Brewery on the way back for a sandwich and a beer. They had a great view and heaters on the patio.

He loved that he could talk and drive with the hands free thingy on his new car. Jimmy dialed Sue on his phone. They chatted about the Dodgers. He had met her a few years before at his son's Little League games. She was a few years behind him in high school and remembered him as the BMOC, varsity everything. They had made out a few times in the parking lot when their spouses hadn't been at games. She had great tits and wanted to stay married, so he was just the guy for her. They could have conversations laden with meaningful sighs and a little heavy breathing over the phone, then go on to talk about baseball. It was a non-marriage made in heaven.

Jimmy's cell phone rang as soon as he hung up. The ring tone was *My Girl* by the Temptations. It was Jimmy's wife.

"Hi Babe. What's up? No I didn't hear the call waiting. Sorry, it was Bruce talking about a new Beer League Baseball team. What time are they coming over? Yeah I'll check the spelling on the cake. What kind of ice cream? Chocolate mint chip. Got it. See you later. Love you Babe."

He parked a half a block away from the address on Ocean and called Maxine. "Hi Maxie, I'm near Tagore's house. Anything else I should know? Yeah Baby, I miss you too. Are any of the agents in your unit active on this yet? Cool! Maybe I'll get my big break, actually *our* big break. Gotta go Max, love you, you're the best."

Dev Tagore's house was a modest one on the beach side of the street. There was no car in the driveway. Jimmy had a couple of plans on how he could scope the place out. The beach wasn't usually populated by guys in suits unless they were realtors or Jehovah's Witnesses. So he pulled a *Watchtower* magazine out of the glove box he'd saved last Sunday when they came knocking on his door. He'd told them there were already too many JWs to fit into heaven, so he didn't have a chance, but he'd like the magazine all the same! He also had a brochure from a local realtor. He stuck them both in the inside breast pocket of his jacket, just in case. He figured they would come in handy if somebody was home at Tagore's place.

He looked at the plain small house and realized realtors were probably trying to buy this shithole all the time to fix up. Tagore probably had one of the best lots in Seal Beach. He needed to check the deed and see who owned the house. Probably some friggin' towel head.

As Dracos walked down the block toward Tagore's house, he fantasized about how he'd finally make it on board at the F.B.I. He was supposed to be researching some ships under Argentine registry for possible weapons smuggling into the Port of Long Beach. But the kid, Gary, was good at the stuff they were legitimately supposed to be doing. Jimmy had promised Maxine if he could catch a terrorist, it would change everything for him. He told her if he became a huge hero, the money would follow and he could leave his wife and they'd be able to travel and buy a boat and a place at the beach. He realized that he'd probably never tie himself to anybody but Debbi. She wanted to be tied to his star too. She had a big investment in him, twenty years, plus all the work she had done getting him through college. She had supported him, written all his papers, and even today composed almost all of his reports. She was shy, but enjoyed basking in the glow of his limelight. When their son was little she had literally caught Jimmy with his pants down and didn't leave him. She said if she ever caught him again she'd kill him. He believed her too.

He didn't sleep with all his women, he just enjoyed the game. When things got carried away, he told them he promised his mother on her death bed he wouldn't cheat again and he couldn't break his word to his mother. He did swear that to his mother, but he didn't say he wouldn't fool around in other ways. Bill Clinton did it and Hilary stayed. Besides if Debbi asked him if he was sleeping with somebody he didn't really have to lie. He was a terrific liar, but Debbi knew that. His fantasies warmed him as he decided against the F.B.I., it would be much bigger than that. He'd be offered book deals, shots on the Today Show, the Late Night circuit. He figured he could parlay the fame into at least small parts in movies or maybe run for office. It worked for Sully when he landed the plane in the Hudson; the nation revered him. Jimmy thought, I'm way better looking and more charismatic then he is.

Jimmy reached Tagore's house and walked down the walkway alongside of the garage. He casually peeked in. There were a couple of bikes, a wetsuit and a beach towel hung over a clothesline, a kayak, paddles, and some skis in the rafters. Nothing else except an old washer and drier. It was the least crowded garage Jimmy had seen in years. He knocked on the door. Waited and rapped more loudly and waited. Nothing.

There was no answer, no vehicles around unless a kayak counts, just sports equipment. Dev Tagore's stuff didn't seem to fit the profile of a terrorist, unless maybe he was going to try to paddle his kayak up to the Queen Mary and blow it up. Then Jimmy realized the beach boy shit might be a cover worthy of Mohammed Atta.

Jimmy walked down the side yard toward the beach side

of the house and on to a small brick patio, with a couple of surfboards leaning against the wall. Maybe this guy truly is a beach boy terrorist. The glass door was ajar and a cocoa brown cat with blue eyes sat on the threshold.

Jimmy said, "Hello! Hey, anybody home?" then more loudly, "I didn't get any answer at the front door when I knocked, anybody home?" Jimmy pushed the door open further. The cat ran off into a bush. "Yoo-hoo, anybody home?"

The neat little kitchen had a porthole window over the sink to the side yard. On the green and white Formica counter there was a small old brown teapot. There were no dishes in the sink, but little saucers were on a placemat on the floor with food and water for the cat. On the counter, there was a juice glass with a small bouquet of leaves and a sprig of Queen Anne's lace. In the living-dining area, Jimmy noticed an old table by the picture window with a laptop and a bunch of papers spread out around it. Some of the writing was in script he didn't recognize. There was a new looking couch and two straight backed dining chairs. On a shelf made of bricks and boards, fifty or so books were lined up neatly. He began to move quickly through the small house. One bedroom was completely empty. The second had a single bed covered with a thin cotton Indian bedspread, another dining chair and a small chest of drawers. Jimmy rifled through the drawers but found only underwear, shorts and socks. He glanced at the bare walls, then looked under the bed and checked the closet. He found one jacket with nothing in its pockets, three pairs of Levis hung over wire hangers, six T-shirts and a couple of pairs of shoes.

Jimmy returned to the living room and thought that either this guy was a decorating minimalist or was living like some kind of monk. There was nothing much to search. He didn't even have a T.V. The place was so empty it made Jimmy anxious. He thought he'd be bored out of his gourd if he lived like this. He pulled out a yellow pack of Juicy Fruit gum from his shirt pocket and extricated two pieces. He folded them both in half, put them in his mouth and deposited the wrappers back in his pocket.

He walked to the makeshift bookcase and began to look at the books. The ones in English were mostly related to religion or philosophy. He couldn't even guess what language some of the books were written in. He thought he recognized Arabic; he'd seen it in history books and it was kind of pretty. He thought he'd recognize Korean because he saw it all over town, mostly circles and straight lines—but there was nothing like that here. There were some novels by William Gibson, Elmore Leonard and Tom Robbins. His finger traced the spines as he tilted his head to read the titles. It stopped on the title, *Quran*. Jimmy knew that was an alternative spelling for the *Koran*. His finger passed the *Quran*, and the next title was *Holy War on the Homefront. The Secret Islamic Terror Network in the United States*, and next to it, one titled, *Dying to Win. The Strategic Logic of Suicide Terrorism*. Jimmy felt a tide of cold fear rise through his body. With the fear came certainty. Jimmy knew this guy was the real deal.

He continued to look at the books. There was a thick Japanese style comic called *Summit of the Gods*, and even a *Green Lantern* and *Silver Surfer*. Next to the comics and shoved far back was a book called the *Diamond Sutra* that seemed to be out of place. He lifted it out to try and figure out what it was about and behind it saw hidden an ornately formed silver box. He pulled the box out from behind the book. The hinged lid was tessellated with a whirling pattern of tiny cabochons of deeply colored stones. It looked ancient and the rounded stones didn't look like glass, probably tiny emeralds, sapphires, rubies and diamonds. The workmanship was astonishing, certainly worthy of a museum or a rajah's palace. Jimmy had never seen anything like it. As he gazed at the surface, a pattern began to form and then emerged. It was a swastika.

Jimmy couldn't figure out why the guy would have some Nazi treasure. He opened the box. It was lined with softly faded slightly tattered embroidered silk. It held three small keys and maybe ten of the biggest diamonds Jimmy had ever seen, enough to fund a whole lot of death and destruction. Suddenly anxious, he figured he'd better get the hell outta Dodge.

About five minutes after Jimmy left, Dev walked up the slope from the beach. He put down the small aqua board, unzipped and rolled off his thigh length wetsuit, grabbed a towel and wiped himself down. He shook his wet hair which sprinkled the cat, who appeared to be highly offended.

"Sorry Pabu." He picked him up and began to stroke him. The cat greeted Dev with a sable colored paw touched lightly to Dev's lips. He carried the cat in through the glass door rubbing the side of his chin, telling him he was a good boy. Immediately he noticed the house had a different smell. It wasn't closed up stale or beachy musty, it smelled kind of flowery sweet and artificially fruity, like chewing gum.

Man of La Mancha Cheese

They drove down a street just a few blocks from Little India in Artesia. Adri had now been on half a dozen dates with Dev and recognized she had fallen in love for the first time. She felt anxious when she was with him, afraid she might blow it, sure that she was an insignificant ninny and he would realize it at any moment. At home she thought of him incessantly, fantasizing romantic scenarios all the while deliriously happy and simultaneously semi-deranged. The feeling was so new and extraordinary that she couldn't get away from the all encompassing feeling sufficiently to analyze it. She just knew she had it bad and feared he didn't have it at all.

Adri pointed to a large California ranch style house, pale green with redwood trim at the end of the street. The house spread low across a large frontage and Dev thought it must look exactly as it had when it was built in the early 60's. The shingled roof was elevated across a driveway connecting it to what must be the garage. Adri said, "Just turn in the driveway, go through the windway and park in the back yard."

Dev said, "I've never heard the term 'windway'—I know *port cochere* and carport."

"I don't know—maybe it's just a Southern California

term—I know that's just what we always called it. But I'm glad to help the linguist learn new vocabulary." Adri gave him a taunting smile.

He smiled at her but said nothing. As usual she doubted his reaction and nervousness festered in her because she was taking him to meet her sister. Was it too soon? Then her self-doubt expanded so rapidly that she began even doubting her doubts. Just as she began to drown in misgivings there was a sudden 'whoosh' in her head. Her nervous system hit some sort of overflow and suddenly all the mental crap was flushed away. Relieved, she became conscious that she might not always suffer from this lovesickness.

She said, "I hope my nephew Ray is home. You'll love him. I don't know whether I told you this. Stop me if I have. Paloma is my half-sister. Her dad was a real bastard, so when she was old enough she came to live with us. I idolized her—and still do. She married her high school sweetheart, Ray's dad, Alex. He was a killer guitar player and my sister is a wonderful singer and keyboard player. They started a rockabilly band which had some local hits. Alex had that crossover gift from music to math. My sister was teaching music in Long Beach and Alex was doing post graduate studies at UCLA. My dad, my sister's stepfather, owned the dairies and various properties and so he hired Alex to do accounting. Alex had his own hours, good pay and could work on his studies too. Anyway, to make a long story short, it turned out that he was defrauding the businesses. He was bleeding money out of the companies and putting it in offshore accounts. When it was discovered, he split to *Mazatlan* in *Sinaloa* where he had family. Paloma and I think he did it just to see if he could. After that we three made our home here together. About two years ago I bought my shop and moved out, but I'm over here all the time."

Dev asked, "Is Alex in contact with you guys at all?"

"Paloma took Ray to see him a couple of times when he was little and then she got scared he might kidnap him. She lets him talk to Ray on the phone. I think they talk pretty regularly."

"Isn't there extradition from Mexico?"

"My dad died right after all of this. Alex was gone and somehow I thought betraying the people who loved you and being away from your child was punishment enough. I suppose there is still a warrant out for his arrest. We just don't talk about it."

As they pulled into the drive under the roof, he saw a backyard that was probably close to an acre. Directly behind the garage there was a small orchard with a half dozen orange trees still regaled in big amber globes of fruit. Right behind the house was an oval dichondra lawn ringed by roses in the blaze of spring's first blush. Further back he saw a woman kneeling, working the furrows of a vegetable garden. They pulled into a paved area between the back of the garage and the little orchard. As they got out of the car, Dev noticed the woman rise from her digging and turn towards them.

Adri said, "Hi Pal!" and her sister waved and began brushing dirt and embedded grass from her knees. Her smile was dazzling, movie star white through velvety Revlon red lips. She wore a 1940's styled white sun suit dotted with cherries. As she stood, the sunshine seemed to burn through the gloom spotlighting her. The effect was reminiscent of a *Look* Magazine publicity photo of Rita Haworth relaxing in her sunny Hollywood home.

Adri said, "Isn't she glorious?" As Paloma came towards Dev she brushed her hands off, reaching out to shake his. Deep rich red rose tattoos vined up her left arm encircling her shoulder then cascaded across her chest with an iridescent blue-green hummingbird coming in for a landing over her left breast. Closer in the sunlight Dev could see that there were small lines around Paloma's eyes and that her shoulder length burnished black pageboy was likely dyed. The sunlight revealed the ten years she had on her little sister. The sisters kissed each other on the lips, hugged, then held each other's hands tightly. The older sister was taller and uncompromisingly glamorous, the younger sister, demure and less studied in her look.

"Dev I want you to meet my big sister Paloma. She has been my best friend, my little mother, and everything good in this life."

Dev loved Adri's naïve enthusiasm and lack of typical social reticence in her introduction of her obviously beloved sister. There was a sweetness and lack of guile in her that he found endearing and made him feel a tenderness he wasn't used to. Paloma squeezed Adri's hand and then broke away.

Dev said, "I'm so pleased to have this opportunity to get to know you. Wow this yard is huge! I see you have orange trees and what is that tree over there?"

Paloma said, "Quince. Adri's grandparents planted this yard with an apricot, one pretty lousy apple, a plum and a lemon. There is a pomegranate too, and of course lots of oranges. The rose garden is over fifty years old. It's a pain in the butt to prune but the roses are splendid. I am setting some pumpkins and *calabazas* for next fall right now and working on getting my beds ready for vegetables."

Dev said, "I have no real yard, just some succulents; nothing much grows right by the ocean. I'd love to give you a hand in the garden some time, dig and trim trees and maybe do some stuff you don't like to do. I like working hard outside."

Paloma smiled and Adri said, "She grows wonderful heirloom tomatoes too. If you want to work hard in the garden then you definitely get to share the fruits of your labor. Those old orange trees bear fruit like liquid sunshine and the apricots are indescribably delicate and so lovely with their little sun-kissed spots and freckles." The image of the apricots made Dev imagine Adri's dainty shoulders, warm, soft and perhaps freckled like the little apricots in the sun.

Adri interrupted his reverie and said, "I make a mean *bruschetta* from my sis's tomatoes, but my apricot jam and quince paste are divine if I do say so myself!"

"Adri is the cook and I'm the farmer. Come on in and we can have some of Adri's delicious preserves on something with tea or coffee."

"Tea, thanks," said Dev.

They walked in through a sliding glass door into what Dev expected to be a standard mid-century ranch house. Instead he was astonished by walls of deep densely pigmented fuchsia. The fireplace, once local flagstone, was now completely encrusted with layers of gaudy costume jewelry, bottle caps, tiny plastic animals and assorted toys. The effect was startling, amusing and surprisingly pretty. The few pieces of furniture were massive dark Spanish colonial pieces, with the exception of an Empire Style mahogany sofa covered in pale lavender velvet. There were two high backed spindled throne-like Spanish Revival chairs with deep turquoise velvet cushions. A large coffee table was fashioned out of a door to which hundreds of foreign coins had been affixed. Dev recognized big Australian copper pennies with kangaroos, familiar Indian square and fluted edged coins, a few old silver dollars, Indian head pennies, and some silver coins with holes in the middle he didn't recognize. In the far corner of the room was a black grand piano wearing an embroidered Spanish shawl with long silken fringe, looking like the instrument of a gypsy queen. ,

The only painting in the room was what appeared to be an enormous seventeenth century antique oil painting in a splendid ornate gilded frame. The tableau consisted of three women and a small solemn faced boy. The women posed in elegantly draped tight-bodiced dark velvets with golden lace. The boy held a crucifix and rosary and the youngest of the women held a small black and white spaniel.

On the long library table was a beautifully carved wooden case with glass on three sides. Inside the case was an ornate filigreed silver sunburst, a cross radiating out from its center. In the foreground were antique ivory figurines of the same family as in the portrait, their surface crazed and aged by time. In the front of the case was what looked like the rosary in the painting with a plaited lock of hair and a small open locket with a sepia photo of two girls. The cloth behind the sunburst and small figures appeared to be feather work of most astonishing iridescent jungle colors, hummingbird blues, parrot greens and corals, with long feathers which looked like they might be *quetzal*. He thought these must be treasures of the family who was portrayed in the oil painting. In the other corner was a T.V.

with a wii plugged in, an assortment of big velvet pillows strewn on the floor, athletic shoes, a backpack and some textbooks thrown down nearby. Dev was astonished and enchanted. The room was quite lovely.

"What a unique surprise this room is. You have an amazing eye, Paloma, and a beautiful home."

Paloma said," It's not my eye, its Adri's and so is the house."

Dev looked surprised and turned toward Adri. She grimaced and said, "Only because she won't take it! This is the house my grandfather built in 1961. I lived here with my dad after our mother died. Because she lived with her own father, we didn't get to be together that often when I was really little. But after our mother died and Pal was older she came to live here and has lived here ever since."

Dev said, "The painting is magnificent. Is it from Spain? It looks like a Velasquez, but I know that would be quite impossible. Maybe it was by one of his students?"

Paloma said, "Go look at it up closer."

Dev went nearer the painting. With a sharp intake of air his breath made a small gasping sound. Two of the women in the painting appeared to be Adri and Paloma. "Are these your ancestors, or are you some extraordinary resurrection of these women?"

Adri began to giggle, her face flushed. Her sister said delightedly, "Adri painted it. It's our mother and us and my son when he was little. Ray is now fourteen, a freshman in high school. Adri created the *nicho* in the carved case on the library table too. She carved the figurines and made them look like ivory and did the feather work. The rosary and locket belonged to our mother and her mother before her; the little photos are of us."

Dev, impressed and surprised, looked at Adri and said, "They are magical; your talent is quite extraordinary."

Adri blushed even more. Dev noticed as the color rose in her cheeks she did have tiny sun kissed freckles like an apricot.

She was pleased that he recognized something deeper in her.

She was so nervously in love with him that she felt silly, overly chatty, and a little idiotic around him most of the time.

Adri said, "Well you know magic is all about illusion; its intent is to mystify and confound." She wondered to herself if that was also true of the magic of falling in love. Was Dev the magician or was she just so hungry for the experience that she was willing to suspend her disbelief?

Paloma said, "The whole family did the fireplace together. Ray had a thing about his toy farm animals and then we stuck in some of his Lego creations. Adri and I realized we didn't want to get rid of our childhood treasures, so you'll see our dolls, lots of little girlie glass animals, Japanese miniature food items, board game pieces, troll dolls, Disney stuff and our little handicraft creations."

Adri came closer to the fireplace and pointed at an old Nehi grape soda bottle cap. "We found dozens of these in the garage where my grandpa had piles of cool junk. That's where we found a lot of the coins. We collected all the jewelry at flea markets and garage sales. We started it when Ray was little over a Christmas holiday when Pal was still teaching music at the high school. Anyway, we don't work on the fireplace much anymore, but it's still open for renovation anytime someone wants to stick something else on there. Just like we will stick more coins on the coffee table if we go somewhere new or someone brings us something back from abroad."

Dev said, "Next time I'm oversees, I'll bring you some interesting coins." He turned to Paloma and asked, "You don't teach music anymore?"

Before Paloma could respond, Adri excitedly jumped in and said, "Now she's a music producer. Pal's trying to keep blues and rockabilly alive. There was a resurgence of interest in the blues a decade ago. Long Beach had quite a few cool venues, but *Blue Café*, *The Blue Dog* and *Cat Man Blue* are all gone. We still have great local radio, KJZZ on the Cal State Long Beach campus with a program called *Nothin' but the Blues*, and there's one local Blues Festival in Long Beach. But all these great players need producers and promoters to keep the art form alive.

Now it's easier to arrange a European tour or one in Japan than one in the States."

Dev smiled at Adri's enthusiasm and said to Paloma, "I don't know anything about American music, or any music for that matter, but doesn't music fashion change just like hemlines and hairstyles?"

Paloma replied, "Yeah, big band was replaced by rock and roll, then rock had all of its various permutations. Now even some hip-hop lovers reminisce about 'old school rap,' and are always 'sampling' older R&B. So you're right, music styles and preferences are in constant flux. But I think of it as a continuum and the blues is the root of the American musical tree."

He heard commitment in Paloma's voice. "I'd like to learn more about American music. I hope you can share your knowledge and maybe some CDs with me."

Adri smiled. "Oh I think Paloma can fix you right up. Wait 'til you hear her play piano. She sounds like the rockabilly incarnation of Professor Longhair!"

Paloma laughed and said, "Thanks Sis, I wish."

Dev had no idea what the reference was about so he smiled, shrugged and put his palms up out to his sides in the universal sign of 'beats me.' Both sisters laughed. Paloma patted him on the arm and said, "I'll go make us all some tea."

Dev turned to Adri and took her hand. The sisters seemed as layered and surprising as the fireplace. Adri looked at him with such depth and vulnerability that it worried him. He needed to be careful around her. She tilted her head up expecting to be kissed, but Dev resisted. Not wanting to reject her, he touched the back of his index finger lightly to her cheek and said, "I think your artwork is powerful. I'm impressed with its depth and its mysterious yet amusing quality that I can't quite put my finger on. I like that it continues to intrigue me."

She said, "I have felt very lost about the direction of my art recently. I'm stumbling and have lost not just my edge but my confidence. So it's important to hear that, especially from you."

He said, "Lately I've been a little lost about the direction my life should take too." He immediately regretted his words.

Her head jerked back slightly in surprise. "Wow, that's something I didn't expect to hear. You seem so composed and together that I'm taken aback by even the notion that you don't have it totally together! It's not like you've shared much about yourself or for that matter anything at . . ."

Just then Paloma returned from the kitchen carrying a silver tray with an ornate silver tea service. Dev, relieved to not have to respond to Adri, took the heavy tea set and put it down on the coin encrusted table.

"Enjoy! I put out some crackers, Spanish *Manchego*, a Maytag Blue, some California *Chevre* and some of Adri's quince paste." Dev took a piece of cheese and cracker and put a slice of quince paste on top as Paloma poured his tea.

He said, "In Pakistan, I've had quince *murabba,* a kind of jam. This is delicious, thicker than what I had there.

"In Spanish," Paloma said, "it's called *dulce de membrillo*. Adri and I always like it with *Manchego*. We call it Man of La Mancha cheese, because that's the region it's originally from in Spain."

Just as he started to take a bite, the front door slammed and a very skinny young man ran into the room. He had on black and white leather shoes in a 1950's style you might have seen on Carl Perkins. They looked huge and clunky against his spare frame. The geeky effect was exacerbated by heavy black framed Foster Grants overwhelming his rather delicate features. The look was topped off by a high glistening rather rigid looking black pompadour. If the kid was trying to get noticed, he surely would. He looked like a life size Buddy Holly bobble head.

"Ray! Come here and meet our friend Dev."

His face was much browner than his mother's, but he had that same great white smile. Dev was glad the kid didn't have braces, since that would make him look even more awkward and geeky.

"Hi man!" Ray stretched out his fist to bump a hello to Dev.

Adri said, "This is my nephew Stevie Ray Ayala."

"Jeez Tia, don't use the whole stupid name!" He said to Dev, "My parents were drug addled idiot music fans and named me after Stevie Ray Vaughn. It coulda been worse; if I'd been a girl they would have named me Ma Rainey or Big Mama Thornton! I'll tell you I've had some crazy shit to put up with because of that stupid moniker. That's a helluva thing to do to a kid. Just call me Ray." He put his hand out again for Dev to shake. "Hey are you trying out some of my aunt's Man of La Mancha cheese? Isn't it wild my aunt owns all those dairies and cheese factories and shit?"

Adri winced. She didn't like people to find out she was wealthy, especially guys— most especially not this guy.

Ray continued, "This cheese is really good but it's made from sheep's milk. I think that's kinda nasty; I just can't get the picture of little Bo Peep milking her lambs. Anyway Bro, that's why I call her my *Tia Queso*, cause maybe someday she'll leave me all the factories and then I'll be the big cheese." Adri grabbed him and struggled to tickle him.

He freed himself from her grasp and said, "Nice to meet you, dude."

Instant Mystic Chai

Clouds scudded gray and darker gray randomly revealing jigsaw puzzle pieces of clear starry sky over the Pacific. At the entrance to the pier, a bronze seal greeted them, his head shiny and golden from the caresses of visitors. Adri reached over and rubbed the sculpture's nose affectionately. She and Dev strolled past the landing stairs where tenders docked to take workers to the oil pumping islands. It was a long pier, lined with stainless steel sinks for cleaning fish and a little shack for selling bait and fishing licenses. They circled around to the end and looked out to sea. A single night fisherman shared their view out to the Pacific. The ocean smelled alive with the night.

Dev said, "Seal Beach and Long Beach are about the same latitude as Tokyo. I think I can smell the cherry blossoms."

She giggled, "I think maybe it's the sushi or sashimi; it's pretty fishy to me." He put his jacket over her shoulders and stood close behind her.

They looked out through the low clouds on the horizon. He pointed to the artificial oil drilling islands in the distance. Clouds hung low, but they could see they were lit with blue, orange and pink lights. Dev said, "Aren't they bizarre? They tried to make the nation's third largest oil field look like *Cancun*.

Did you know they extracted so much oil that in the 1950's Long Beach had sunk 29 feet? Then they started pumping water back in to control the subsidence. Imagine what a tsunami might do."

She said, "What I'm most afraid of is a terrorist attack. Wilmington, San Pedro, Long Beach—the oil, the port, it would be an incredible disaster. Just a shipping strike at this port put a major dent in the American economy. I think a major attack might bring the West Coast to its knees."

Dev continued to look out to sea. After a few moments, he turned her around towards him and took both of her hands in his. "Your hands are cold." He held her hand gently and said, "I like your hands. They're delicate and move gracefully yet with purpose."

She looked up at him filled with wonder and expectation. She realized she was gone, smitten, totally gob smacked in love with him. He just looked at her and smiled that certain smile. She was giddy, tremulous and waiting to be kissed. But no kiss came.

He said, "Come on, it's chilly, I need to get you home." He took her arm and led her back toward the beach. They drove toward her place in Belmont Shores. The bars and restaurants and streets were still alive with college students from Long Beach State.

"You want to stop for a drink or some coffee?" he asked.

"Sure, but I have a coffeemaker in my shop. Then you can get a good look around the place."

They went around the back of her shop and she used the keypad to shut off the alarm. The back room had a little wrought iron bistro table and chairs. There was a small sink and counter and on it a coffeemaker, a tiny fridge and a microwave. She rinsed out and filled an electric kettle and it began to purr.

"What's your poison? I can make you a filtered decaf or regular coffee, or I have a bunch of different teas."

He noticed a can labeled *Instant Mystic Chai Tea*. Beneath the words smiled a little Buddhist monk sitting in full lotus with a cup of tea in his hands. The steam from the cup of chai rose and circled his smiling face like a halo. Dev said, "Did you know that chai is just the word for tea, so to me this label reads instant mystic tea tea. It's a little disconcerting. "But I think I'd like to have a cup of this tea tea."

She giggled, "Oh, I didn't think you'd want that ersatz imitation of the real deal."

"Well," he said, "It intrigues me—instant karma—instant mystic. I could use a little readymade mysticism right out of the package. Will you join me so we can both be transported to *Shangri-la* in a sip?"

"I saw that movie, *Lost Horizon*, right?"

"Yep. I think it had much to do with the romanticizing of Tibetan Buddhism in Western Culture. People here don't think about the peasants whose daily drudgery makes a life of spiritual devotion possible for those who live in the lamaseries. In truth it is quite medieval and not so romantic for many."

"I didn't know. I love going into the shops in Little India; the goods and craftsmanship are beautiful. But last time I went, I noticed some high school girls buying purses and bracelets with colorful depictions of Hindu gods on them. You know the elephant one?"

"*Ganesh*."

"Yes, and *Shiva*, I think. Anyway, I thought it was sort of sacrilegious. It seemed like it could be pretty offensive if you were a believer to see a little blonde with your god on her purse because she thought it was cute."

He said, "Yes, I think you're probably right."

She scooped beige powder from the can with the smiling monk into mugs, poured in the steaming hot water and added a little milk. She said, "It's better with a little milk to cool it down." She stirred it round and handed the swirling frothy cup to him. "Come on, let me show you around the shop."

Glass counters surrounded an ornate antique cash register in the center of the shop. Silver jewelry filled them. Some pieces appeared to be antique, others contemporary and bold. The walls were hung with brilliantly complex colored weavings and paintings.

"All the jewelry is from Latin America and I only carry silver. The price of gold is prohibitive and it's really not a good fit for the theme of the shop. All of the pieces are handmade by artisans. Much of it is from *Oaxaca* and *Chiapas*.

"What are those?" He pointed to high shelves along the perimeter of the shop lined with what looked like brightly colored little altars or shrines, many of which seemed to have sculptures of skeletons.

"Oh they're *nichos*, little Day of the Dead altars. They are a kind of shadow box or diorama with costumed *Calaveras*—skeletons, doing the every day activities of life. You'll see doctors, mechanics, taco vendors, even brides and grooms. They are traditional in Mexico for celebrating the Day of the Dead, All Saints Day. You know, the day after Halloween. Even in pre-Colombian Mexico skulls were significant, like crystal ones; the Toltecs even had pipes that were skulls. Pretty spooky those old Mexicans."

"Skulls are objects of great veneration in Tibet too. They don't picture skeletons in ordinary daily activities, but meditating on your own death and decay is one of the tools of their Buddhist practice. It is supposed to help you prepare for death."

"No thanks. That sounds super creepy to me. I like the amusing Mexican ones though. I try to find musicians for my sister because she has been in a bunch of bands."

He said, looking around, "It's a great shop, Adri."

She smiled. "I'm lucky there's enough money and demand in this neighborhood to allow me to bring in high quality imports. I can pretty much run the shop as I see fit; my inventory seems to sell rapidly. I own the building and because I live upstairs, my overhead is minimal."

"How do you get all these different goods? Are they all from Mexico?"

"I go to Mexico, Guatemala and sometimes Peru a couple of times a year. It's fun but hard work to find new things. Paloma goes with me when she can and Ray too. Those times are the best because the adventure isn't daunting, just exciting and fun."

"What areas do you like best?" he asked.

"Oh I like the old colonial cities and I like to be up in the hills where there are lots of birds and cooler breezes. I haven't been lots of places yet. I haven't traveled out of the Americas, but I have a serious case of wanderlust. I'm excited visually by different cultures; everything from clothing to architecture is a feast for my eyes."

"I kind of feel that way about languages. It's pleasing for me to study and practice and listen to tapes, but to talk to people, to hear the cadence and music of their speech is delightful to me. Their gestures and expressions make the words come to life."

"I have one fulltime employee, Jennifer. She manages the shop and there are a few part-timers. It works out well for me. I have time to paint and not be worried about the day to day stuff. It also frees me up to go on buying trips, but I would love to visit just about anywhere."

"Yeah, you mentioned Goa."

"That would be nice. How about you? Are you originally from India? You have a little accent, but it's like your looks, I can't quite put my finger on your background."

He said, "I have lived many places and speak a few languages, but my accent is probably mostly mid-Atlantic; certainly English is my first language. My birth certificate is Canadian and my mother put 'Unknown' down for my father. So I'm not even sure about that part of my ancestry. More and more I have come to believe that I'm not Canadian and spent my earliest years around Southern California. That is one of the reasons I came to this area. I'm trying to unravel my early past."

"Really! Is your mom still alive? Won't she help you?"

"I'm not in contact with her." Suddenly his face grew cold and seemed very far away. "Listen, I have an early morning tomorrow, so I think I better hit the road."

"Oh." She looked at his mug and he hadn't touched his tea.

Crunchy PB&J

The brown paper package arrived in *Dharamsala* at Tara's door. There was no return address but the postmarks were from Vancouver B.C., so she knew it must be from Dev since all of her recent contacts from him came through the mail from Canada. Occasionally he called her. Each time it was from different cell phone numbers. Her detectives had not been able to find him and she knew others besides her wanted to find him too, but nobody had.

She began to rip the parcel open, but stopped when she saw the way he had addressed the label. It was to *Baby Smith* in care of *Mary (Tara) Smith*. When she saw the address she felt sick rise in her throat and her hands began to tremble. They had lied about the baby. It wasn't true what they believed. She would have never done what they suspected of her.

She sat down holding the package on her lap and stared out the window toward the woods. Dev was many things but she had never known him to be cruel. She was stunned that he would try to hurt her so. As she sat holding the parcel, her body began to rock gently back and forth like a child comforting itself.

She remembered how alone she was when she first came

to the States from England. She had met an American guy in London and he wanted her to come back with him to California. She was happy to oblige as she longed for sunshine and a way out of a country that hated people like her. She stayed with him only a few days after her arrival at LAX and then ditched him and struck out on her own. She began to travel the west coast beach cities that first summer, from Laguna to Venice. She would lay an Indian print bedspread on the sand, put out her crystal ball and lay out a spread of Tarot cards in the Celtic Cross and easily make a hundred bucks a day. She avoided being close to piers and concessions where shopkeepers and cops might catch on to her. She never stayed long and moved from beach to beach. She worked her little cons, always finding men willing to put her up for a week or two and give her money.

It was during her second summer in California that she met him. It was the Tuesday after Labor Day and the weather was brilliant. School was back in session and there were few people at the beach. She laid out her spread a dozen blocks north of the Hermosa Beach Pier, close enough to the Strand wall that she could be seen by a curious passerby but far enough back from the life guard stand that they would pay little attention to her. Unbeknownst to her, he'd been watching her from the deck of his house and became curious.

He walked across the sand towards the spread she had laid out in the sand and said hello. She just figured he was another mark. He was tall and handsome, probably in his very early twenties. He pointed across the Strand to a little blue house, its white deck coming out from a second story overhanging a sandy yard. The railing of the deck was festooned with ropes and fishing nets studded with blue and green glass floats. On either side of the white staircase hung blue life preservers, and in the center, mounted above the railing, a ship's wheel. The house looked happy and like it might sail away.

They began to chat and he listened to her carefully. He didn't look at her bosom or ask her stupid questions. She remembered he called the day 'sparkling' which was the perfect description, and then he asked her if she wanted a sandwich. She was hungry and she watched as he ran up the steps of his house, returning quickly with a tray with two sandwiches and two glasses of milk. The sandwiches were peanut butter and jelly warm from the sun on soft white bread. She remembered that her hand was sandy and some of the sand clung to the peanut butter and she awkwardly spit the gritty bite out on the sand.

He said, "Personally I prefer smooth peanut butter to crunchy!"

She was grateful that he made her laugh instead of letting her feel embarrassed. They chatted easily for a while and then he asked her if she was from Kent.

"How in the world would you know that?" she asked

"Well you said, 'I was *naff* good at school' and your accent sounds like Kent. Besides it appears to me you're a Gypsy and many English Gypsy folk live in Kent."

"How do you know that? Have you been there?" she asked him.

"No, but I'm interested in languages. That is what I study. What do you call your handbag, not a pocket book I bet."

She looked suspiciously at him. "Well I might just, but my grandma called it her money purse."

He clapped his hands and smiled and asked, "Do you say 'mabbled' for when things are all mixed up and confused?"

"People study this? I can't imagine why. I thought people studied foreign languages."

"Yeah," he said, "your English words are unique to Kent. But people study Gypsy language too. People used to think the Gypsies came from Egypt and that is where the name 'Gypsy' came from. But you folks call yourself Rom and linguists refer to your language as Romani. It has always been a great mystery who the gypsies are and where they came from. But the study of linguistics has pretty much nailed down that your people migrated from Northern India, maybe around Kashmir about a thousand years ago. So they were not Egyptians, rather speakers of what is now ancient Sanskrit. Sanskrit had three genders, the feminine, the masculine and the neuter. And while modern Indian languages have lost the genders, they remain in Romani. But I don't want to go on and on and lose you. I'm very interested in Sanskrit and the history of Indo-European languages, as they are our mother tongue."

"We Rom came from India? I'd like to know more about that, I'd like to go there. Would people there think I was one of them? Do I look like them? Is that where cashmere sweaters come from? I don't know where India is on a map. I don't know much about such things as I am not smart. I wasn't regular going to school and never went after my first form. But I want to know a lot of things and go to new places."

"Intelligence is not necessarily related to education, you know. Lots of educated people just appear to be smart, but really don't think for themselves." He smiled at her. "I study linguistics. I have a knack for it like you do for reading the cards. The first time I knew about the peculiarities of the Kentish dialect was from reading the *Pickwick Papers*. Dickens' character, Samuel Weller, is a classic example of the unique forms of English found in Kent."

She said, "Are you calling the way I talk peculiar?"

He laughed. "Oh no! I think the way you speak is a charming part of who you are and where you come from. Please come up to the house and I'll show you on a map where India is. You can meet my mom; she would like you very much. You can stay to dinner, and if you need a place to spend the night, we have a little guestroom with a separate entrance downstairs."

No man had ever invited her to meet his mother. She was grateful because she wouldn't be expected to sleep with him, but she was nervous about meeting some guy's mother. But in fact, his mother Peg had been kind and welcoming. She made her feel safe, just like she felt when her Gran had been alive. Peg was small but strong, her eyes the color of blue willowware. Her tanned lined face was still lovely, framed by hair that gleamed silver white in the sun.

She remembered she fell in love with both of them and the life they had. She realized now that it was the happiest time of her life. She was pregnant by Thanksgiving and they got married at the old courthouse in San Pedro with his mum and his best friend Tom as witnesses. They ate at Papadakis Greek restaurant nearby. She remembered the belly dancers, the owner kissing her, and that she was happier than she had ever been in her life to have a family and have his baby on the way. Driving home it was misty and the Christmas lights glowed softly. But that was long ago— now she looked down at the brown paper package in her hands. They were shaking, the veins distended and corded and she noticed a flat brown age spot like her Gran used to have. Then she remembered the betrayal of her husband and mother-in-law, and what she had done because of how they hurt her.

She said aloud, "I would never ever do what they believed of me to my own child."

Baba Ganoush

The little café was off Brookhurst in Anaheim. It was private, off the beaten path, the *Halal* food was good and this was a convenient place for them to meet. Mansour was later than usual, so Dev ordered some *baba ganoush*. He was probably being immoderate in his love of *aubergine*, which wasn't like him. He dipped freshly baked still warm pita bread into the smooth lemony eggplant. The Americans had given the shiny purple plant an ugly name. In Sanskrit it was *vatingana*, in Arabic, *albadingen*, which eventually morphed in French to *aubergine*, the word they also used in England. But in California, asking for *aubergine* just mystified people. The foods he loved best, eggplants, potatoes, peppers, tomatoes were all 'nightshades,' high in alkaloids. The traditional *Ayurvedic* physicians of India warned that these were too warming for persons of his body type and should be avoided.

These weren't like the alkaloids in *datura* and *belladonna,* all of which Tara had probably tried. Tara, like Alice, had been lost in her own wonderland. The guide through her alternate universe was the white dotted red fairy tale mushroom, *amanita muscaria*. She had met up with her own 'hookah smoking caterpillar' sometime before Dev had arrived on the scene, and like Alice she was not herself. Or at least he assumed so, since he'd never known her before the time she had gone through her own personal mushroom focused looking glass. He realized he didn't know her very well at all. She had kept so many secrets from him. He was sick of secrets.

Dev heard the little bells that hung from a cord on the door jingle. He turned expecting to see Mansour, but it was a nice looking man, not very tall in a dark suit and red tie. He wasn't Arab or Indian, maybe a Turk or Greek, probably a local businessman missing Mediterranean food. The man sat near the door and didn't look at Dev. The only other customers were the two older gentlemen near the cash register who had finished their meals and were lingering over *demitasse* cups of coffee.

Dev returned to his musings. He wondered why it was so easy to think about eggplant and so hard to think about the problem of Adri. He didn't know what to do about her. He had given her the sickness of a hungry heart and yet he spent his time thinking about eggplant. It had gone too far; it was inevitable that she would be hurt. It had not been part of his plan to hurt her.

Jimmy Dracos had followed Dev Tagore to the restaurant. The little joint was too far away from the Long Beach area to drive to just to get a good *falafel*, so he was suspicious. He looked at the two old guys in the corner with long beards and weird doily looking crocheted beanies on their heads. Their hats looked like the old fashioned lace doilies his grandma put on the arms of her chairs. Tagore was faced away from him eating some kind of dip. He figured he was waiting for someone because when the waiter talked to him he had gestured toward the door.

The waiter brought Jimmy a menu, but he said he'd just have a *falafel* and a Diet Coke. He pulled out his phone and texted Maxine that he was 'thinking of her,' just to kill some time and look busy. He could see Tagore's back. His ponytail camouflaged what was written on the back of his green T-shirt. The door behind him opened, ringing the little bells. Jimmy didn't turn to look, pretending to concentrate on his phone. But as Tagore shifted his torso to look at the newcomer, his ponytail moved and Jimmy could read 'Visualize Whirled Peas' across his shirt. Jimmy could imagine peas in a blender. It took a few beats before he got the joke. The irony of the message horrified him. He started to hate Tagore. A terrorist with such cynicism and contempt for humanity must be stopped.

A young bearded man walked to Dev's table. He too had on a beanie, but not of the crocheted old lady lacey variety. His was brownish wool and looked like the kind of knit cap any kid might wear. He was dressed in jeans and leather work boots. The young guy told Tagore in English he was sorry he was late, but that he got held up at the jobsite. That was the last of the bulk of the conversation Dracos understood. The men now began to speak in what he assumed was Arabic. The two of them looked like a couple of dudes in their early thirties that still smoked a lot of weed and had been the best skateboarders in the neighborhood. They didn't look like terrorists; they looked like they should be out in the street playing hacky sack. It was a pretty good cover look he had to admit. But after the bombings at the Boston Marathon, he knew better than be fooled by a perpetrator's appearance alone. The waiter brought him a *falafel* with shredded cabbage and pieces of some purple pickled stuff. He drowned it all in *tahini* sauce and took a bite.

When the waiter returned with his Diet Coke, Jimmy said, "Hey, this is really good. What's the crunchy purple stuff?"

"Oh sir, this is pickled turnip colored pink from beet juice."

Jimmy said, "Wow, no kidding! I'm Greek and we don't have that stuff but I like it. We have a sauce kind of like this with little bits of cucumber in it we call *tzatziki*. They're real similar, you ever had that?"

"No sir, but I know much of the food is similar all around the Mediterranean Sea."

"Hey, is that Turkish those guys are speaking? It sounds kinda familiar, but I don't quite recognize it."

The waiter said, "No, sometimes we get Turks in here, but those gentlemen are speaking Arabic."

"No kidding? Well it's all Greek to me."

The waiter looked blankly at Jimmy and said, "No sir, it is the Arabic as spoken in Egypt. I am from Egypt. This is how we speak."

"Well thanks for the info. I like to learn about other cultures. The *falafel* was so great I want to bring my wife and family here. What you got for dessert? Something like *baklava* maybe?"

"Yes sir, of course one *baklawa*. Our name is very similar sir. We use pistachios. Do Greek people do this—with cinnamon or maybe rose water?"

"Yeah we have the kind with pistachios or maybe walnuts I think. Yeah and some coffee too."

"Yes sir, very happy to bring that to you."

The waiter disappeared into the kitchen. Jimmy watched Tagore and the other man and listened to the tone of their conversation which seemed mostly friendly. As the waiter returned with his dessert and a tiny cup of strong coffee, the men began to talk quietly and more seriously. He recognized some phrases in English. He distinctly heard 'Disneyland Hotel' and then he heard 'Queen Mary.' Jimmy felt chills shimmer down his spine when he realized his hunch about these guys was for real. These guys were going to blow up some popular tourist destination. Jimmy watched as Tagore brought something to the top of the table. First he gave the guy an envelope which the young man folded and stuck in his pocket, and then Tagore pulled from the pocket of his T-shirt a small package of folded paper. As the young man unwrapped it, Jimmy saw it glint. Then after the paper was removed, Jimmy saw what looked like a really big ass diamond. Tagore spoke very formally to the young man and the young man seemed to bow his head down. Jimmy Dracos had a fertile imagination, but he didn't think for a second that this was some kind of gay wedding proposal.

Jimmy got up and walked past Tagore and his comrade, navigating boxes and stacks of supplies back behind the kitchen on the way to the bathroom. He wanted to see Tagore's face without being noticed. He had never seen him up close and personal and the idea was both daunting and thrilling. He went in the tiny bathroom, washed his hands, smiled into the mirror checking his teeth for debris, combed his hair, straightened his tie, shot his cuffs, and pulled two sticks of Juicy Fruit Gum from his shirt pocket. They were warm and flexible as he folded them in half and put them in his mouth. He headed back out by Tagore's table. He looked casually at him and Tagore turned toward him. Tagore's gray eyes fixed on Jimmy for an instant. Jimmy could have sworn he saw storm clouds moving within the man's eyes. Unnerved, he turned away and rushed out the door, the little bells jangling his exit.

Red Licorice

Paloma and Ray were spent. Back from the beach, they both stretched out on the lavender couch foot to foot. Tired and relaxed after sunning and swimming they chatted in a languid calm. They had spent all day at Dev's house meeting Jay for the first time. They were chewing on leftover red licorice vines that were warm, stretchy and limp from sitting out at the beach much of the day. They felt just like the red licorice.

Paloma said, "When I was little, your Uncle Victor and I would try to fill these up with the powder from Pixie Stix. I liked red licorice with the lime green Pixie Stix. It would take us forever to fill them up but not too long to eat 'em."

"Why are they so flexible?"

"I think they have a bunch of glycerin in them."

"It's probably a good thing Uncle Victor didn't know that. He'd probably hear the word glycerin and think nitro! I can imagine him trying to create a red licorice Molotov cocktail. Probably try and fill them up with gun powder and light them. You think he still has enough weaponry for a small militia in his basement?"

"His new wife was freaked out by all his guns. Vic told me that she said to lose the guns, or she'd leave him."

"You think he got rid of all of them?"

"Well, he said she came unglued when she found a Glock in the glove box of his car. She asked him if he was licensed to carry a concealed weapon; of course he wasn't. He said that after that happened, she left and went to stay at her mother's. He told me he got rid of them because he wanted her back."

Ray looked at his mother and shook his head. "I don't know. He showed me some of his guns once. He laid a bunch of them on the bed all neat and orderly. Maybe he would rather have a wife in his bed than all that rigid techno looking metal. I hope so. He had me hold a Glock 29 or something. No wonder his wife freaked out, it was a disturbing looking piece. Even the names of his guns are sinister. You know, Glock, Luger, Ruger, they all sound like the last names of Nazi S.S. officers." Ray smiled at his mother and laughed a little. "Well they don't *all* sound evil. The Russian ones sound like ballet dancers—you know—Kalishnikov, Baryshnikov; and the Italian one, Beretta, sounds like a good name for a fast car. "

"You never told me about the guns, Ray." Paloma shuddered, and crossing her arms across her chest, rubbed her hands up and down on her upper arms.

"You cold, Mom?"

"I could see the bed all spread out with guns and him showing them to you. It gave me a chill. I think your uncle Vic did some bad things when he was young. He was so pissed at our mother that he let himself get jumped into a gang. I heard he did some ugly stuff. I used to wish he would get caught, but he never did."

"I think he was disappointed in me. I didn't like the guns, he knew that. He wanted me to think they were cool and— I don't know, maybe— sort of *bond* over the guns."

Paloma looked into her son's warm brown eyes. She saw tenderness in them, a vulnerability, that made her heart hurt. She said, "I hope his wife will be good for your *tio*. He hasn't been very happy. Maybe she can help him set aside some of his anger and bitterness. But I don't know, she seems pretty high maintenance, boats, cars, exotic vacations. It could be stressful to live up to her expectations."

"Mom, she seems pretty nice. Maybe with his new wife and his new cool restaurant, he'll leave the *macho* crap behind him."

She said, "I hope so. They seem to be making and spending money hand over fist. That probably makes him happy. Her too. My brother has always been so pissed about money—because Adri and I inherited from Mom and Phil and he didn't."

"How come your mom didn't leave her son money?"

"Oh, honey. Mama died long before Phil did, and it was Phil's money anyhow. But it was probably because Vic didn't want anything to do with our mother after she left my dad."

"Shit Mom, I can't imagine not wanting to see you no matter what you did. I still want to see my dad, even though I know he stole money and abandoned us. I don't get it."

"Victor thought he was abandoned by our mother. But she had to leave, she had no choice. I think if she hadn't, at some point my father would have killed her."

"Why? Why was he so mad at her?"

Paloma's expression was flat. She looked down and said, "No reason at all. She was his scapegoat. He just liked to hurt her. I can't tell you how awful it is to see your mother beaten by your father, when you are just a little kid and you can't defend her. You feel so responsible somehow."

Ray's mother rubbed the knuckle of her thumb back and forth across her lower lip. He said to her, "I'm so sorry, Mom."

She looked up at him and smiled a little and shaking her head said, "Thanks Mijo, it's okay now. Really. When my mom finally left, my father portrayed her as a wanton woman abandoning her kids. The courts gave him custody and in the beginning we only got to see our mother one weekend a month. It was heartbreaking for me and for your uncle Vic too. Later Phil's lawyers got us more weekends, but sometimes Vic would just refuse to go see her."

"Why?"

"He just chose sides and let his anger fester. He's still mad at me for picking mom and Phil over him and our shitty dad. I decided I would never allow myself to take my father's abuse any more. Phil was so good to me and he would've been good to Vic too, if only Vic had allowed that to happen. I'm glad our father left him the restaurants and everything after I moved out. I didn't want anything from that son of a bitch anyway."

"Is that why he doesn't come around much? We go to see him at his restaurants, but he doesn't usually even show up for Christmas and Thanksgiving."

"Yeah, we try to keep him in our lives. But he treats Adri practically like a stranger, instead of our sister. It's just wrong to treat your little sister like she isn't blood. Adri always acts like everything is okay though; I guess she does it for me and to honor our mother. I hope it will be better now that he has a wife."

"Hey Ma, let's take Jay and Dev to Vic's new restaurant. I would like him to meet our new friends and I bet he'd love to show off to them."

Paloma smiled at her son. "You are such a nice guy. I'm so lucky."

They were quiet for a while, and then Paloma rubbed her big toe gently on the bottom of her son's sandy foot, and asked, "Hey you, what do you think of Jay?"

"He and Dev seemed to be such good friends, you know, buddies. It's interesting the work they do together as a lawyer and translator of documents."

"You think that's interesting?"

"Kinda. I was impressed cause Jay is so intelligent. He was dressed pretty fancy for the beach though. The watch he had on didn't look like the fake Rolexes I've seen. It looked like a real something and he had on a really expensive sweater. I was relieved he wasn't wearing a Speedo like a lot of foreign guys do. They're just too weird. I guess probably ritzy guys in India don't go to the beach much."

His mother said, "Cartier and cashmere." She sighed and continued, "But what did you *really* think about him?"

Ray responded "Oh. I did think he was an interesting mix of foreign and American, and he was nice to us, and I liked that. What I appreciated the most was that he and Dev seemed to be almost like brothers. The way they treated each other reminds me of how you and Aunt Adri are together, except of course they didn't go on about all the girlie crap like you guys do. Why do you want to know?"

"He asked me out on a date. I thought I'd go, but my motives are a little nefarious. I want to know more about Dev and make sure he's not gonna hurt my little sister."

"I think you should go out with him cause you like him, not for Adri. Are you attracted to him? Because he sure couldn't take his eyes off your *chi-chis*!"

"Wow!" Her head shot forward with surprise. "I thought he was pretty polite and I did have on a bathing suit and as you well know I don't hide my assets. That's pretty normal for guys, *mijo*. You're getting older and we can talk like this now; but I wouldn't start dating unless you were cool with it."

"I know. He was cool—it's cool. I just get a little weary of guys looking at your boobs."

"Weary! Well you don't say." She squeezed her lips together tightly realizing she had never considered his comfort with her overt femininity.

"I would think you'd be pretty used to my style by now."

"Yeah, I am."

"I have always dressed this way, but honey I would gladly change if it makes you uncomfortable."

"I don't want you to change the way you dress. It's part of who you are. Just like right now I'm doing a retro kinda rockabilly thing like Pop did, when you guys were in the *Vato Tacos* band. But it gets pretty old when men are so absolutely smitten with your looks. You're still my mother after all. You'd be beautiful no matter how you dressed, but I have to admit it sometimes gets pretty creepy for me. The weird part is that all they do is gawk and they never get to know you. I think your looks are intimidating. You never even go out with anybody. Do you do that on purpose, as a kinda boob barrier?"

"You're too much. I love that! You have to be the coolest kid ever. 'Boob barrier'! She started to crack up. "How about a bosom barricade?"

He snorted, "A booby blockade!"

She spluttered through her giggles, "My bulwark of boobiness!"

They both kept laughing and then, after, in the stillness that follows much laughter, he said, "Mom, that Dev guy is kinda different. Have you noticed that?"

"Well, he seems pretty quiet, but he's nice to your *tia*. I think I like him pretty well. But I'm gonna take a wait and see attitude. That's why I want to find out more about this mystery man. What did you think was so different about him?"

"Sometimes he seems very still. And I think he looks different, he sort of has a glowy look. And this is weird, but he smells kinda like flowers, but I looked in his bathroom and he just has Ivory soap. I once read that there is a sweet odor that saints have."

"Glowy! Well he is kinda pretty—you're not getting funny on me about your *tia's* boyfriend are you? Were you drinking some of that Indian beer with the kingfisher on the label that Jay brought? And as for saints, do you think all the people with Saint Christopher medals were still safe until some Pope deposed their protector from the canon of saints? Half of the so-called saints were probably child molesters if they're anything like the rest of the Church!"

He gave the bottom of her bare foot a quick kick with his, and said, "Wow, that was pretty harsh Mom. I guess I may have heard your opinion of religion about a hundred times before! So do me a favor—I'm not kidding and I didn't drink any of Jay's beer. Dev just seems different from anybody I've met before. He makes me feel safe and calm. We were sitting out on the surfboard just floating up and down with the swells and he seemed kind of radiant."

"You must really like this guy if you think he glows in the dark! I'm sure that it just was a trick of the light. And some people just smell good, probably because he's a vegetarian and eats a lot of fruit. Maybe it's just his shampoo. Lots of times shampoo can make you smell nice. They used to even have a shampoo when I was little called, Gee Your Hair Smells Terrific.

Stupid name—never tried it."

"That's so lame, Mom. You know what he told me?"

"What?"

"He said that he didn't know who or where his dad was and that he had no real history he could trust. That what he knew about himself might all be lies, fabricated. He wasn't sure where he was born even. He said he came here to figure that out."

"Wow, really? Did he say why he chose here?"

"He said he thought he remembered some stuff from when he was a little kid. I think he was trying to make me feel better, like we had something in common. He said he'd teach me to surf if I wanted and I could come to his house anytime to go to the beach. He said he liked our family a lot and I was really lucky to have such a great mom and a sweet aunt; and he hoped I knew that I was very fortunate even if I missed Dad."

"That was pretty nice. Do you miss your dad that much? It's not like he was ever around much. Damn it! I knew I shouldn't have taken you to see him in Mexico. It was so stupid of me. I think it made you miss him even more. It's hard to always know what is best and I've screwed up plenty. Ray, I'm so sorry for that."

"Ma, why are you apologizing? He's the one who stole money from your stepfather and he's the one who was such a *hijo de puta* that he took off for Mexico rather than face the consequences here and be a husband and a dad. I love him and miss him, but what he did to us makes me think he's a coward*!*"

"Wow, what's with the Mexican mouth? You sound like a little badass *vato*."

"I think that cussing in Spanish is more expressive of my true self."

She giggled, and asked, "And pray tell, sir, what precisely is the identity of your true self?"

"Well," he exhaled slowly, "I think emotionally I'm Mexican; academically I act more like my Asian friends." Then he became quiet and lowered his eyes. His mother waited for him to speak. He continued in a voice no longer clever or glib. "I'm a little bit scared sometimes—and sad too. I'm not sure I want to grow up."

She looked at his slender serious face. The overwhelming love and tenderness she felt for this funny perceptive man-child was almost more than she could bear.

Prosecco and Pee

Tara set the table meditatively with slow precision. With measured care she had already arranged the ornate silverware with the dessert spoon and cake fork placed above the plate, the deeply cut *Lalique* crystal champagne flute to the right of the dessert fork. The plates, laid on dark blue linen were the finest Royal Copenhagen porcelain, the pattern *Flora, Danica Fungi.* Triple banded with raised gold beading, a single perfectly hand painted mushroom was centered on each white porcelain dish. For each disciple participating in tonight's ceremony she chose a different species of mushroom.

The morning light, soft and buttery, came low through the French doors into the dining room and struck the prisms of the chandelier. She wondered how such low light could even strike the chandelier of the tall ceilinged room. Then she noticed that a beam of light was hitting the convex surface of the silver tea service on the sideboard and bouncing up toward the ceiling. Tonight the room would be candle lit and prismatic light would dance across its walls. When she served a ritual, she always set the table early in the morning so it would be ready when the sun set. She had fasted for three days, eating only fruit and spring water. She needed to make her body ready to be inhabited by the

Goddess so that her essence would be pure and palatable for her followers.

The first splendid mushroom plate she set down was a *Honey Fungus* emerging from a log. Next she placed the *Chicken of the Wood* with its coral-like folds ruffled and dark brown. The third plate was a charming *Common Ink Cap,* its crown flouncing gaily like the twirling skirt of a little girl, followed by the small smooth gray innocuous looking *Death Cap*. The final place setting was of her fairytale friend, the white dotted red Fly Agaric, botanical name *Amanita Muscaria*. She rubbed her thumb across the raised white dots on the brilliant red mushroom's head. Those white dots were actually remnants of what mycologists called the universal veil. The veil covered the head and gills of the mushroom as it emerged from the earth, then as the mushroom matured, the veil broke leaving the white dots. *What a fitting name*, she thought for the alkaloid which allowed the veil between her and the Goddess to be lifted.

She kissed the plate before she centered it between the ornate sterling flatware at the head of the table where she, as the Goddess, would sit this evening. Her disciples would be allowed a glimpse behind the veil when they drank of her essence. She looked at the table indecisively. She had not decided on a centerpiece; she thought perhaps just the large Cristophle candelabras with something between them. Between them, she placed her most recently acquired oval serving dish of Royal Copenhagen. She had paid the equivalent of nearly $10,000 for it and had it shipped from Europe as a gift to herself. The mushroom on it was called *Barrister's Wig* because it resembled the silly wooly wig worn by British lawyers. American lawyers didn't wear wigs. It made her recall America and the early days of her marriage. She began to wonder if he had divorced her. By now she imagined he well may have, but she wasn't sure. He had every right she supposed.

After her son was born they had lived in Boston in a dingy cramped apartment while her husband finished school. He was completing a doctorate in South Indian Studies at Harvard. Being cooped up with her seven-month old son during a Boston winter gave her cabin fever and a depression so profound that her husband sent her back to his mother's house in California. Perhaps she would be happier by the wide open broad beach and boundless sea. Peg had missed the little boy terribly. It was decided that her husband would return to California for the summer, before he would have to be away from them one last time while he did his final field work in India.

She remembered how carefree she had become when she could run along the sand, dig for sand crabs with her little boy, and watch the dog chase the seagulls. In the late afternoon she and Peg would cook dinner together and dine watching the sun set over the various moods of the Pacific. After the child they both loved had gone to sleep, she and Peg would read or embroider and chat. Mary felt loved and safe and at home.

It was Peg who thought it would be healthy for her to spend time with people her own age. She really only knew Tom, who had been the best man at their little wedding. He was still at U.C.L.A. and was a botanist specializing in cultural uses of fungi. She knew something about the Gypsy uses of European mushrooms since hunting them had been what she and her Gran had most loved to do together. So she became a willing and enthusiastic student of his knowledge of mycology and shared what folk lore she knew of forest plants with him. In the spring, Peg encouraged her to go on a weekend mushroom hunting trip to northern California with him and some students. Peg thought they were hunting truffles and delicious Shaggy Caps and asked them to return with enough mushrooms to make a *ragu*. But her mother-in-law didn't realize that Tom and his students as ethno-botanists were more interested in the shamanic uses of mushrooms than their culinary delights. It was there, on that weekend, that she evolved and became Tara.

She remembered how wild and unburdened she felt searching the shady forest as she had done as a child. It was exhilarating when they found the dowdy *Psilocybin*. Tom was a longtime aficionado of the effects of *Psilocybin* or Magic Mushrooms. He described to Mary how this entheogen had been used ritualistically for thousands of years in shamanic cultures in both the Americas and Africa. He explained that Mexico alone had over fifty species of this fungus and that it was found to a lesser degree throughout the world.

As they scoured the forest floor he taught her about various fungi and she told him Gypsy stories and names of those mushrooms she recognized. As they hunted, he told her that other plants, that were not fungi, like *peyote*, *datura* and even unprocessed tobacco, had been used by shamans with similar effects. Throughout the world these substances had been used for visions by shamans who would believe themselves inhabited by spirit guides from a reality outside of time. Tom asked her if she would like to try mushrooms with him. She remembered that she told him she had never taken drugs, and only had a glass of wine once in a while, so she didn't think it would be a good idea to start now.

But just then, as the sun was lowering and on the forest floor, lit by a shaft of golden light she spotted the beautiful waxy red polka-dotted mushrooms of fairytales. These were her favorites and had even been painted on the cabinets of her grandmother's Gypsy *Vardo*. Excitedly she told Tom that these were the toadstools she loved. She remembered that as a child she dreamed she would play under their giant red and white umbrellas.

Tom said they were called *Amanita Muscaria*, common name, Fly Agaric. He explained that they had a reputation as being poisonous, but perhaps that was to flies, not people. He said the white and yellow types were highly toxic, but that the shiny red with white polka dots had been used in shamanic cultures for millennium. He explained that in European folklore they were associated with witches and some investigators suggested women who used these mushrooms experienced hallucinations of flying. He continued to tell her that the single most fascinating use was by Siberian shamans. He said they would ingest the *amanita muscaria* and experience its unpleasant side effects. After the shaman had digested the mushrooms, he would urinate and his followers would drink his urine! His body having processed the alkaloids, the urine provided a deeper spiritual experience with none of the uncomfortable side effects for those who drank it. Tom said the urine would often be recycled up to a half dozen times, still having its psychoactive properties. Tara remembered that at the time she thought that was the most disgusting and bizarre practice she had ever heard of, not realizing that she would do the same for her own disciples scores of times in the future.

Mary had become fascinated with the subject of India and Hinduism ever since her husband told her that the study of the Gypsy language proved that her ancestors' origins were not from Egypt, as so many people falsely believed, but from India. So she was spellbound when Tom said that some researchers believed the red *amanita muscaria* mushroom was the one mentioned frequently in the ancient texts of the Hindu *Rig-Veda* as *'Soma.'* Tom said that the *Rig-Veda* mentioned the drug in many hymns including the *Soma Mandala*, in which it is referred to as the 'one-legged thunderborn.' This was because at the onset of its effects upon the consumers of the red mushrooms, they experienced a roar like thunder. This crashing report as loud as a thunderbolt was considered the herald of the god's arrival. Tom said that in the *Rig-Veda, amanita muscaria* was even referred to as the 'God of gods'!

She recalled that after Tom's description of the little shiny red mushroom's effects, he had taken her hand and looked seriously at her. He suggested that since she had a deep affinity for the cute little polka-dotted fellows, perhaps her unconscious wanted her to open doors to deeper understanding by experimenting with them.

That night as Tom and his students sat around the campfire, many of them ingested the psilocybin mushrooms. Mary was excited by the stories Tom had told her and figured if she just ate a few of the little red ones they certainly couldn't do her too much harm. She asked Tom what to do. He said she could just eat a couple or make a kind of tea. He warned her that they would be bitter and she would probably throw up. She went to her collecting bag and took out a couple of the little shiny red mushrooms. On close scrutiny she could see the little white remnants of the 'veil.' She threw them in her mouth and choked them down followed by a slug of whiskey that Tom handed to her. The burning whiskey taste seemed to overwhelm the bitterness.

She sat and watched the fire against the darkness until the flames quieted to embers. Suddenly a profound nausea came upon her. She moved away from the fire to a grassy area and threw up repeatedly. She was cold and tired so she got in her sleeping bag. She tried to get warm, but chills became shudders, and shudders spasms. After what seemed like hours of fear and regret, she broke into a heavy sweat and finally fell asleep.

The tremendous deafening crash of thunder came at the same instant as a white light more brilliant than a magnesium flare. From within the brilliance appeared a terrifying and beautiful green skinned goddess riding a golden elephant. The dazzling structure atop the elephant in which the goddess rode was a small golden *vardo* covered in sparkling ruby polka dotted toadstools. The goddess reached her arm down toward Mary and smiled. She in turn reached her hand up toward the golden crowned goddess. Their fingers touched and Mary ceased to exist.

Tara could still remember the vision and the touch of the goddess which forever changed her. Her thoughts returned to the task at hand and she turned and carefully picked up the ornate silver tray with the tea service from the sideboard. It was heavy and she moved carefully as she took it to the kitchen and placed it on the counter. She put on the kettle and took out an antique tea caddy filled with powdered *amanita muscaria*. When the kettle boiled she poured a little in the silver teapot and swished it around and then dumped it in the sink. Then she opened the tea caddy and looked at the shriveled and dried remnants of the once brilliant red toadstools and smiled. She scooped out a heaping spoonful and put it in the teapot. She poured the boiling water over the powdered toadstools.

Now she would suffer terribly for the goddess and her disciples. She would be filled with the wholeness and power of Green Tara. Tonight in the dining room alight with candles, their light dancing through the prisms of the chandelier, her disciples would toast the goddess and drink her essence from crystal flutes topped with sparkling *prosecco*.

Blow Job in a Shot Glass

Paloma wore a fitted red sheath exposing voluptuous curves he had never seen outside the movies. Jay was glad that in spite of her wicked looking five inch heels he was still slightly taller than her. She looked like a goddess to him. What made it worse was that she was smart, funny, talented, wonderful to her family and totally capable of taking care of herself. He couldn't imagine what he had to offer her.

For the past three years Jay had been having an affair with the jaded wife of an elderly wealthy Palos Verdes investment banker. They had sex every Thursday after which she took her mother to dinner in Little India. She smelled of the Dunhill cigarettes that she always extracted from her gold cigarette case and lit up after they made love. He hated the smell but enjoyed getting laid without any effort or commitment. She was world weary and cynical about life, politics, and just about everything but sex with him. During sex she was passionate, inventive and enthusiastic. When her orgasm had resolved itself, she lit up and inhaled. Then she was just a drag.

His parents had died in an auto accident in Mumbai while he was in law school at Boalt Hall in Berkeley. It had left him in shambles for a long time. Having Dev around was a great solace to him now. They shared memories and their friendship brought light into a life that had often been dark and lonely since his parents died. He had filled his life with busy law practices, the one in Little India which was only open one or two days a week, usually by appointment, and a partnership in downtown Long Beach focusing on international trade. He had inherited his Great Uncle's home near Virginia Country Club in Bixby Knolls and liked to golf. He had the freedom to travel at will, buy art, drink fine wine and sleep with pretty girls on occasion. Because his parents were gone there had been no pressure on him to marry. Yet he found he wanted more than sex with Paloma. It was a first for him. All of a sudden there were these two lovely sisters. One head over handlebars in love with his best friend Dev and he seemed to be falling in love with the other. He wondered if anyone had noticed.

He had watched Paloma with her sister and son. The little family they had created for themselves seemed joyful and sustaining. He wanted to have that too. Jay was a rational and patient man. He decided he would take his time and try to build a kind and supportive relationship with her and with her son. Dev and he had been on half a dozen outings with the three of them and each time had been better than the last. Their friendship had been growing in a very natural way. He hoped this first date without the others wasn't a mistake. His fantasy was that Dev would love Adri and Paloma would love him and (of course) they all would become one big happy family. He was amused at the banality of his fantasy, but he had never wanted anything more.

Paloma had never before been to the cocktail lounge on the Queen Mary before. It was a clear night, with a cool breeze off the ocean and traces of twilight still visible in the western sky. She knew she looked fabulous in the red dress. She always turned heads and enjoyed it, but tonight she felt awkward and ill at ease. She had not dated since Ray's dad had stolen her stepfather's money and fled to Mexico. Not one date. Her rationale for going out on this date with Jay was to play Mata Hari and try to find out about the mysterious Dev. She wanted to protect Adri whatever the cost. She thought the cost might be sex with Jay. The trouble with that was that she liked Jay a lot. She thought if she could seduce him she might be able to extract information about Dev. Something was going on with that guy that was far too secretive and weird. Adri was so bananas over him that she couldn't think straight or protect her own interests. Adri always referred to her big sister as her 'little mother' and Paloma agreed that since their mother died she felt more like a mother than a big sister. Pal didn't know what Dev was hiding. a wife, illegal activities, a gender reassignment? She had no clue, but the guy's history was a mystery and Paloma didn't like it one little bit.

They passed between the classic Art Deco maroon and aluminum torcheres of the Queen Mary's Observation Lounge and sat at the semi-circular rosewood bar. A huge horizontal frieze behind the bar pictured a long circle of dancers holding hands circling faster and faster. Society women in diaphanous gowns, their skirts swirling about them, soldiers dressed in khaki uniforms, sailors smiling at young girls in knee length skirts all spun around the painting in mad abandon. The bartender appeared and Jay ordered a Maker's Mark, neat. The bartender turned to Paloma and she said, "I'll have a Blow Job." His eyebrow shot up and he said, "Certainly Miss."

Jay watched Paloma's beautiful cheek redden as she stared straight ahead. He wondered what was going on and why she would try to shock him. The bartender brought Jay his bourbon and for the lady a tall slim shot glass with layers of white and beige liqueur and a towering peak of whipped cream about six inches high on top. Jay waited and didn't say anything. Paloma stared at the painting wishing she was somewhere else. She noticed that one girl in the circle of dancers had fallen down and lay on the ballroom floor with her skirt hiked up to her thighs. Paloma knew how the dancer felt.

She looked down at the shot glass and felt mortified. She had been reading *Cosmopolitan* magazine at the dentist's office and it described approaching the drink in a robust and sexy way. She just wanted to ask for a spoon or better yet just disappear.

Her drink just sat there, neither of them saying a thing. After a minute or two, the whipped cream began to lose its structure and dribble down the sides of the glass. Jay picked up his drink, downed it in a couple of gulps and put thirty dollars on the bar. "Come, my dear friend, let's go out and look at the splendid view." He took her hand and escorted her away from the now flaccid tower of whipped cream.

Out on the deck, Jay placed his hand on the small of Paloma's back and said, "Come on, let's go get some mushroom tacos at a little joint I like on Broadway. You look like you need a beer. *Dos Equis* dark if I remember correctly."

As Paloma was downing her third beer, she said to the waitress, "Mushroom tacos are delicious – go figure! Oh and I'll have another beer please." She downed the first two to try to take the edge off the shame she felt over the blow job fiasco. She was chilly in her sleeveless sheath and Jay noticed gooseflesh on her arms, so he took off his jacket and placed it over her shoulders. As he wrapped it around her she saw the *Armani* label, and as he stretched his arms around her, she noticed tonight he was wearing a Rolex and star sapphire cufflinks on perfectly white starched cuffs.

"I can't believe I'm out with a guy who wears Armani suits and a Rolex."

He looked hard at her and said, "I inherited the watch and cufflinks. They belonged to my great uncle who was so kind and generous to both Dev and I. He left me his beautiful home, paid for my education, but most significantly, he was the finest, most loving person I have ever known. He was an importer of diamonds and other jewels and owned businesses in India, Belgium and here in the United States. When I wear his watches or his jewelry I carry him with me. When I put on the cufflinks this evening I thought, 'Uncle, tonight you meet my new dear friend Paloma'."

Shame is not a pleasant visitor. Paloma felt it shriveling inside of her. In spite of her best efforts at self control, her eyes began to well up with tears. She met Jay's eyes and could feel the shame creeping into her cheeks and mouth and she began to sob. This shocked them both. Jay got off his barstool and went to her and held her and rocked her and patted her awkwardly. He laid down another few twenties on the table and said, "Come on, let me take you home."

Paloma put her head against the cool window of his Mercedes. She thought better of saying anything snotty about the fancy car. She was so self-absorbed that she didn't even notice when Jay turned left on Pacific Coast Highway instead of right. He turned on to Long Beach Boulevard and headed up to Bixby Knolls. At the top of the hill he turned into the Virginia Country Club area. She recognized the road and remembered that the beautiful old adobe, Rancho los Cerritos, was at the end of the road. The street was lined with majestic trees and dotted with graceful two story California bungalows and Spanish Revival homes. He pulled into the driveway of a deep forest green two story shingle style house. She said, "I thought you were taking me home."

"Well, this is my house. I guess I just automatically came this way. Come in. I'll make you some tea and we can talk."

They entered through an oak door with a deep beveled glass oval. She could see built-in bookshelves and a mantel beyond. He took her inside and she sat on a worn leather sofa which faced the fireplace. He bent down and turned on the gas fire and said, "I'll go make the tea." The room was comfortable and worn. The walls were covered with California plein air oil paintings, scenes she recognized of Monterey, Laguna Beach and Yosemite. She wondered if they were inherited from his uncle or if Jay had purchased them.

He returned with two big mugs, and said, "This will warm you. It is my family's blend for *chai*. He sat down on the couch next to her. The *chai* tasted spicy and a little astringent, bracing and comforting at the same time.

He put a throw over her legs. Her eyes were red and swollen and her tears had left rivulets of dirty gray mascara streaking down her cheeks. Her red lipstick was just a faded stain. He said, "So what's up?"

She drank a little tea and cast her eyes down for a few

seconds. She looked up at him and said, "I was playing Mata Hari. I thought if I could seduce you I could get information about Dev. I don't want my sister to be hurt or used. He is too much a mystery. I don't trust him. It makes me feel desperate because I have never seen her so crazy in love before. I would do anything to protect her."

"Even sleep with me? Wow! That is desperate!"

She put her hands over her face and eyes, her head bowed. He waited.

She took her hands from her face and said, "Oh God. I haven't slept with anybody since Ray's dad left us. I like you very much. I admire the depth of your friendship with Dev and your intelligence and kindness. I'm frightened of your elegance; it is unfamiliar and foreign to me. I really don't want to seduce you. Maybe later on, if you forgive me, you might be willing to seduce me."

He smiled and said, "Oh I think that I will be more than willing. Let me tell you this about Dev. He has lived a very unusual life and even I only know a part of his story. But as far as I am aware he has not left a string of broken hearted women behind him. He has been here for a couple of years and has started a business, bought a house and taught himself to surf. Now he is keeping company with your sweet little sister."

She said, "She is freaked out because he hasn't tried to sleep with her. He doesn't reveal anything about himself. It's making her nuts and that is making me even more nuts!"

"Maybe he is being old fashioned. But whatever the reason, isn't it something Adri needs to address with him? Perhaps he believes she needs to be on a more equal footing with him. The fact that she is in love with him is more than obvious. My guess is that he senses her vulnerability and wants to wait. Maybe he is unsure himself. I haven't spoken to him regarding your sister as this seems a very private matter. But whatever is going on between the two of them, it seems to me it is theirs to work out." Then Jay looked at her and said, "Paloma, you're a mess."

She said, "I know. I'm an idiot. I can't believe I. . ."

"No, I mean your face is a mess. You have mascara

everywhere."

"Oh, sorry. I'll go wash it."

"No, I like it. You know you said you were put off by my elegance? Well, since you are the loveliest woman I have ever seen, I like you looking a wreck. You are much more approachable."

He traced his finger along the trails of her ravaged mascara. Then leaned in and kissed her dirty cheek ever so lightly. She looked directly into his large, kind brown eyes. He took his fingers and pulled her hair back from her ear and neck and began to kiss her in the soft curve that her hair usually covered. She shuddered and felt her body come alive. She turned her face into his and began to kiss him fully. The kiss that answered hers seemed to promise her everything and made her brave. She felt safe and opened herself completely to him.

The Whole Enchilada

It was one of those perfect California days, blue skies, scudding clouds, seagulls wheeling across the horizon, and a van full of happy day trippers. Adri, Dev and Ray were in the back seat singing 'Born to be Wild.' Jay, in the shotgun seat, looked a little terrified at Paloma's driving and occasionally grabbed for the chicken bar, which made Paloma laugh and drive even more erratically.

Their morning excursion had been to 'Retro Row' on East 4th Street in Long Beach where the women had gone shopping for vintage clothing, while Ray went in the barber shop to get a specialty hair cut. Dev and Jay accompanied the boy into a fabulous fifties style barbershop.

Ray had asked for a modified 'quiff' and suggested that Dev and Jay modify their look too. Jay settled for a businessman's haircut, while Dev watched and engaged the barber in a conversation about the origins of the word 'quiff.' The barber told him the there were lots of kinds of quiffs. The one like Elvis wore, psychobilly quiff, had a little standup 'mohawk' thing going on, and which was sometimes referred to as 'fauxhawk.' It was all pretty arcane and interesting. Jay suggested maybe 'quiff' was derived from a rude word about women's private parts; but the barber informed them that it probably was from the French word *coiffe* or the Dutch word for 'crest' which was *kuif*. Dev couldn't have been happier talking about word derivations, Jay liked his haircut, and Ray's final 'do' was sort of pointy and high on top and shaved on the sides.

The women had met them in the barbershop and showed them their purchases. Paloma had a jungle-printed sarong with a matching bolero, and Adri an old embroidered shawl. Lunch choices were discussed. Ray wanted to go to *Pike's* which was owned by the guy who was drummer for 'Social Distortion.' Adri voted for Greek food at *George's* or *Kafe Neo*. Dev said he loved this spinach turnover thing at *Baba Ganouj* in Bixby Knolls. Jay said whatever everybody else wanted was fine with him.

Then Paloma said, "I'm gonna make an executive decision and overrule everybody. I think it's time you guys meet our brother, Victor." The men looked at her a little surprised but nodded in agreement. She got out her phone and called Vic to see if he was at one of his restaurants. He said he was at the one in North Long Beach, so she told him to get ready to make his mean Margaritas for five as they were bringing company. So they all had piled in the van to go to Vic's.

As 'Born to be Wild' dragged on, Paloma asked, "How come nobody ever knows the words to a complete song, just the chorus? It drives me a little cuckoo." The singers became very quiet. She continued, "Sorry, I'm nervous; but I think it is important that I tell you guys a little family history before I introduce you to my brother. I'm not used to talking about it, but I want you to know this stuff." She turned her head towards Jay.

He looked at her and said, "Paloma, you don't have to tell us anything that you're uncomfortable with."

She smiled a little and reached over and touched his hand. She exhaled and said, "Okay, here goes. When our mom was in high school, she was in love with Adri's dad, Phil. My grandfather was very traditional and insisted she marry my father, Victor Senior. He was older, Catholic, and Mexican. He owned a couple of successful restaurants and that impressed my *abuelo*. He told Mom he'd disown her if she married that stupid gringo cowpoke. So Mom obeyed her father and married my father instead of Phil. Vic and I were born by the time she was twenty. She worked in Dad's businesses, kept his books, took his insults and endured his beatings. After a decade of this misery she got birth control pills and started taking anti-depressants. My father found the pills and then broke her arm and a few teeth. He hit me too. He hadn't done that before. That was the last straw. She grabbed Vic and me and ran away. We went to Phil's house and he hid us. She didn't call the police, but my father did and had Phil charged with kidnapping. Anyway, to make a miserable long story shorter, Phil and mom got married and spent a few years and lots of money trying to get the right for visitation."

Paloma looked at her little sister in the rearview mirror and asked her, "You okay, Baby?"

She said, "Yeah, I'm fine. Go on."

"I was aware of how my dad treated our mother, so he couldn't poison my heart, but my brother was younger and didn't understand. He felt abandoned by mom. My father instilled a ration of hatred in my little brother on a daily basis. Mom was so sweet and felt so guilty that after Adri was born, she just sort of faded away. Then she died when Adri was seven."

Everyone was quiet. Paloma continued, "Phil was good to me; I moved in the day I turned eighteen. He sent me to Long Beach State, paid for my music lessons, and even after my ex-husband had stolen money from him, he left me a sizeable inheritance. I adored him."

Adri spoke up. "So Paloma and I are trying to make sure we don't lose touch with Vic. He inherited the restaurants and just opened a new one. He has a new marriage and seems to be doing great. But I guess he never has been able to forgive our mother."

Paloma added, "Yeah, and I think he's made his bitterness all about the money. We are his sisters and at the very least we want to be his friend. That is why we go to his restaurant every month or so. We invite him for holidays and doings, but he usually says he can't make it." She pulled the van into the parking lot of the restaurant. It was nearly full. She said, "Looks like it's pretty busy today."

They went inside and were met by their brother. Vic was a tall broad shouldered man who was as handsome as Paloma was pretty. Paloma made the introductions and then Vic directed them toward a large booth with enough seating for all of them.

Vic said, "Cadillac Margaritas for everybody but Ray. *Mijo* I'll mix you up a cherry coke with extra cherries. I'll be back in a minute."

A waitress brought menus for all of them. Jay asked Adri, "What do you recommend?"

She said, "I'd say the *Chile Rellenos* for Dev. The chiles are fresh and this is the perfect season for them. Paloma likes *Enchiladas Suizas*, chicken with green sauce and sour cream, I guess that's what makes them Swiss. Ray, are you ordering your *tio's* tacos as usual today?"

Ray said, "Of course, three kinds of tacos, *carne asada, carnitas* and *barbacoa*." He turned to Jay and said, "When I was little, I loved my *tio's* tacos so much, I kept trying to get Uncle Vic to rename his restaurant *Tio's Tacos*!"

Vic came back to the table with the drinks tray. He gave Ray the cherry coke.

Ray said, "Thanks, *Tio*. I can hardly wait until I'm old enough to have a Margarita."

Vic passed out the Margaritas to the adults and said to Ray, "Hey man, when you're sixteen I'll make you one on the sly when your mom isn't around." Paloma pulled a face at her brother. He laughed and said, "What? It's not as if you and I weren't polishing off the leftovers in the kitchen when Pop wasn't looking!"

Paloma laughed, "Wow I forgot we used to do that. No wonder I like these so much; they're a childhood memory!"

Jay said, "Vic, this drink is delicious. Is the tequila *Cazadores* or maybe *Milagro*?"

"Good call, *Milagro*! Wow, a tequila man; my sister

apparently has good taste in men as well as tequila."

She said, "You know I haven't had *any* taste in men in the last ten years. Tequila yes, good taste in men is new for me." Paloma raised her glass and said, "A toast to good men!"

They all raised their glasses and Vic said, "You guys all ready to order?" They nodded and Vic looked at Adri and asked, "The usual for little sis?"

She hesitated for a second and thought a while. She usually got the cheese *enchiladas* with extra onions. She thought about Dev and how she dreamed of having the proverbial 'whole *enchilada*' with him, but since he still hadn't even kissed her, she thought that dream was becoming more and more unlikely. She nodded to her brother and said, "Yes please—and extra onions as usual."

Powdered Sugar Donuts and Broccoli Trees

Little Michael had strung three powdered sugar donuts on a chopstick and supported the length of the chopstick between two open kitchen drawers. Peg figured he must have had to do some climbing to gather together the chopstick and donuts to manufacture this device. His skinny little legs were crossed as he sat on the floor attempting to spin the donuts along the length of the chopstick. The result after a spin or two was a pile of largish donut chunks and a flurry of powdered sugar on the floor. He was humming his spinning song. The singsong unintelligible chant haunted her and repeated itself over and over in her head. But now, she was determined to be compassionate about his need to spin things.

She went over to him and put her hand on his shoulders, and like awakening a sleeper, said, "Michael, dear. Michael, it's Grandma. I need you to be here with me We need to clean up the donuts. They are to eat, honey, not to spin. Okay?"

He was still humming. She put her arms around his little chest and lifted him up on to a kitchen chair. He was beginning to get heavy even though he was very skinny. He was almost four now and the doctors said he was at 99 percentile of height for his age, but only at 37 percentile for weight. She and her daughter-in-law had carefully charted his progress, but since Mary had disappeared, Peg had been too sad to bother with such things. Peg looked at the powdered sugar on the little boy's fingers and thought he should be eating the donuts, not spinning them. She grabbed a paper towel and wet it and began to wipe the sugar from his slender fingers. She wiped each finger separately and then kissed that fingertip. Just as she completed the last finger the boy seemed to end his reverie and she said, "Hi honey, it's me, Grandma. You've been spinning again. The doctor says we should talk together more. Okay? Can you try to remember to talk to me?" His eyes met hers for a tiny instant and she stroked the hair off his forehead and gave it a little kiss. "How about we make us some lunch and then after your nap we can take a walk on the beach? Would you like that?"

She pulled out a step stool and stood the boy at the edge of the counter and went to the refrigerator. She brought out some leftover broccoli and Kraft Macaroni and Cheese. She stood next to him and began to arrange a plate. He liked the macaroni cold and the broccoli that way too. She said, "Okay, remember how the broccoli looks like trees? You make a picture of them on your plate. Do you want to make the macaroni the sand today, or maybe rocks? I'll get you a Sand Tart cookie, the ones you like so much."

The boy placed the spears of broccoli on either side of the plate and then with his fingers pushed the macaroni along the bottom of the plate. He took the cookie and put it at the top of the plate. Peg went to the fridge to get him a glass of milk. She came back to admire his handiwork. He pointed at the cookie and said, "Sun." It was the first real word he had said in a year. Peg felt the incipient growth of hope welling up like the tears in her eyes. Afraid the sound was a random anomaly, she tried to hold back her feelings as well as the tears.

After lunch she held his hand and said, "Let's go find Mr. Kitty before our nap." They walked around the house and found the cat in the living room asleep on the windowsill. Peg took the boy's hand and pulled it across the cat's fur which was warm from the afternoon sun.

She lifted her hand and the boy continued to stroke the cat and then said, "Keey."

Peg remembered that 'kitty' was the first word he had said when as a one-year old he first began to toddle around the house following the cat. Hundreds of words had quickly followed as the joyful child began to name his environment. These words were followed by short sentences and then by more and more complex ones. Then almost two years ago the sentences and words that had so exuberantly tumbled out of him stopped and the spinning began. She was swallowing back sobs as the boy turned to her and looked in her eyes. She said, "Mr. Kitty is so happy you remembered his name. He has waited a long time for you to say it. He thought maybe you had forgotten him. Now today let's take our nap on the couch together and maybe Mr. Kitty will want to come over and cuddle up with us. He's such a good boy just like you are, don't you think?"

Michael looked right at her and shook his head up and down and said, "Yes."

Peg lifted the boy up on the couch and put an afghan over him and smiled at him. She ran her fingertips across his forehead and lightly across his face and lips until he drifted off. She sat on the opposite side of the couch, stretched her legs up along his under the cover, slipped on her reading glasses and tried to concentrate on her book. Failing at that, she stared at the sleeping boy while her mind insisted on reliving the last couple of years.

When Mary and Michael had come back from Harvard things were blissful for Peg. She was in love with her grandson and she loved Mary like the daughter she never had. In many ways it was the most satisfying time of her life. Her son came home for the summer which sped by before he had to leave for India in October to complete his field work. He was documenting a nearly extinct tribal language in the Indian state of *Arunachal Pradesh* near *Bhutan*. Mary was anxious to visit India and had begun to study its history and culture motivated by the knowledge that her Gypsy people had originated there. But conditions in the area were primitive and Mary was completing the naturalization process to gain U.S. citizenship. So it was decided that as difficult as it might be for the young family to be apart from one another, that Mary and Michael should spend the year at home with Peg and go to India when he was older and her citizenship was settled.

In early spring, Peg realized Mary must be going stir crazy with just her mother-in-law for company. So she called Tom, who she had known since he and her son were in junior high together, and asked him to include Mary in some activities with people closer to her own age. He was glad to help and discovered Mary was interested in learning about mushrooms, his area of academic expertise. Mary was shy and felt self conscious about her lack of education, but Tom invited her to sit in on his seminars and made her feel that her information about folk uses of herbs and fungi were invaluable to him. Peg was excited for Mary to go on a mushroom hunting weekend with Tom and his students. She thought it would build Mary's confidence and be fun for her. She remembered that she had asked them to bring home mushrooms. If she was lucky, chanterelles, or even truffles. While they were away, she and Michael talked about the Easter Bunny and went shopping for little tablets of Easter egg dye. They picked out a Peter Rabbit dressed in a little vest with tiny buttons holding a carrot. Michael carried it around trying to introduce it to Mr. Kitty. Mr. Kitty was of course unimpressed. They both were excited for Mommy's return and the idea of dyeing eggs for next Sunday.

But it wasn't sweet Mary who returned, it was the goddess Tara. This wasn't some New Age huckster channeling an imaginary being who had lived in Atlantis or the continent of Mu. It wasn't a pitiful person who said they had been abducted by aliens and medically tortured. It was the girl she loved as a daughter, the mother of her grandchild and her son's wife, and Mary was barely there. On Saturday when they dyed Easter eggs, 'Tara' painted her eggs with red nail polish then put on white dots with white paint.

Tara wanted Peg to experience the glory of the mushrooms. Peg declined. She took her to a psychiatrist who specialized in 'bad trips' and described Mary as having experienced a schizophrenic break from reality brought on by the *Amanita muscaria*. He explained that this was the florid or active phase of what might be a first psychosis and that often with drug therapy, as well as cognitive therapy, patients had a chance of not suffering another such break. He told them that Mary had a better chance of success because she was female, had a sudden onset of the schizophrenia, had no history of drug abuse, and had a good support system. Peg contacted the university and was able to get a message to her son to call her ASAP. He reached her within the week and offered to cut short his research and come home, but Peg insisted he stay as he only had a few months left to finish. He gave his mother *carte blanche* as far as Mary's treatment. Tom, whose feeling of remorse, guilt and responsibility were enormous, became Peg's touchstone. Mary however was non-compliant, refusing to go to appointments and take the Haldol the doctor prescribed. Peg tried to disguise it in various ways to get Mary to take it, but 'Tara' could always tell and then she would accuse Peg of trying to destroy her.

A month into the nightmare, Michael had started retreating into his own world. He spoke less and less. He stayed in a state of stillness sometimes for hours. Then he began to hum and chant in a kind of gibberish that sounded vaguely like language. Next, the spinning of objects began. Before Mary's transformation into Tara, he would often stand on the deck of Peg's little house overlooking the ocean and pretend to be the captain of a boat. He turned the decorative ship's wheel and would guide his mother and grandmother through rough waters always avoiding pirates. The women would say 'Ahoy Matey,' and 'Aye Aye Captain' and 'Captain Michael is at the helm.' Now he stood at the ship's wheel, and spun it always in one direction, while singing his spinning song.

One day when his Grandmother and he were going down to the beach, he filled a sand pail with all his little wheeled toys. Peg thought this might be a good sign. When they reached the smooth hard packed sand near the water, Michael took out his little shovel and began to dig. He took out a little truck and then a car and then another and placed each on end, half burying them in the damp sand with only the back wheels sticking out. When he lined up half a dozen or so, each abutted close to the next one, he began to spin their wheels with one hand in one direction. It reminded her of people in National Geographic television specials, spinning prayer wheels in the high Himalayas. Peg watched him until the water rose around his crossed legs and the tide encircled his line of toys. He made no effort to get out of the steadily rising water. Finally Peg took his hand, leaving trucks, pail and shovel for the sea.

That night Peg confronted Mary and accused her of feeding the boy mushrooms. Tara came out in all her horrifying glory and a rage ensued of epic proportions. Peg called the police and Mary was taken to Metropolitan Psychiatric Hospital in Norwalk on a three day hold. Three days became three months. After her son's return from India they brought Mary home and carefully monitored her behavior and administered medication. They also took Michael to Children's Hospital as well as U.C.L.A., both of which concurred on a diagnosis of autism. They ran toxicology screens and there was no evidence of the alkaloids present in *Amanita Muscaria* or of any other drugs in his bloodstream. They were told that it was possible Michael had been dosed with mushrooms previously and that the alkaloids had left his system by the time they took the tests. On Christmas morning, when they were ready to see what Santa had brought Michael, they couldn't find Mary. They never saw her again.

For two years Michael had been the same and they had not heard from his mother. Peg had ruminated over these past events a thousand times. As the afternoon sun warmed her, she could feel her grandson's sleeping legs next to hers and she drifted off to sleep. The next thing she knew Michael was shaking her shoulder and clearly said, "Grandma, wake up it's getting dark." But she didn't know how dark things could be. Two weeks later, Michael would disappear just as his mother had.

Bag of Fish Tacos

The west side of the Seal Beach Pier on weekend mornings was a happy mix of little boys on belly boards, elementary surfers, and way out where the swells began to rise, serious old long boarders. All of them were there to enjoy the ride. Dev and Ray sat patiently astride surfboards like cowboys keeping watch over their charges. In surfing, the spoils come to the patient, and like the cowboy who keeps a careful eye on his herd watching for a break, surfers have to watch and wait. When the swell rises just so, only then must they paddle deep and fast rising to join the wave. But in between sets, there is a floating quiet. It's those waiting quiet times when surfers, like cowboys, can talk.

"Hey Ray, how come your mom and Jay aren't here today? They usually like to hang out with us on Saturday mornings."

"Yeah, I know. My mom has been dragging Jay around to all her usual haunts. I think they went to watch those crazy roller derby ladies brutalize one another."

"What is roller derby?"

"Wow Dude, you know so much, but you don't know anything about ordinary weird American shit!"

Dev smiled. He loved this kid. "Yeah so bring me up to speed!"

"Well, it's a team sport and I really don't know the object of it. But the skaters grab on to somebody by the arm and catapult themselves forward super fast and then they jam each other hard in the ribs and boobs and stuff with their elbows."

"That sounds awful!"

"No shit! I don't get it either. You'd think it's all dykes on bikes or S&M types, but there are some normal type people there too. But listen to this, Man. My mom has been taking Jay to every blues bar where the bands she produces play, but also rockabilly bars, stinky old biker dives, and even some punk concerts where everybody is bashing it out in the mosh pit. Next thing you know she'll be dragging the poor guy to some tattoo parlor down by the Pike and making him get 'Paloma' inked across his butt! I can just see the poor guy's ass – 'PAL' on one butt cheek, 'OMA' on the other."

Dev started cracking up, visualizing Jay's derriere tattooed in Old English script in all its gothic glory. Laughing hard he said, "That is a really weird image Ray, especially since *oma* means 'grandma' in Dutch and German!"

Ray looked at Dev, his left eye half shut and his mouth squiggled up like he just tasted something terrible. He giggled and said, "Yuck! I may never be able to walk behind Jay again."

Still laughing, Dev looked over his shoulder and saw a swell rising behind them, and said, "Hey let's go for it. I think we can take off on this one."

They pushed down hard with their hands on the edges of their boards, then straightening their arms, rose up on the boards to a kneeling position. Then quickly they bent down so they could reach down and paddle as fast and deep as possible. The wave propelled Ray slightly ahead of Dev, its momentum developing. Dev yelled, "Okay Ray, pop up!"

Dev caught the wave and stood watching the skinny boy wobble in front of him his arms akimbo at his sides as he struggled to keep his balance. He rode maybe fifteen feet before he fell off.

Dev rode the wave nearly to shore and saw Adri, a small sketchbook in her lap, applauding their success. Dev waved to her and smiled, turned his board around, lay on his stomach and paddled out again.

Adri had been sketching the shafts of light slicing through the pilings of the pier interspersed with the cool shadows cast in the sand and water, but as noon approached the low slanting light had disappeared. She decided she would walk up the street and buy them all a pile of fish tacos. Ray loved any kind of tacos and she would have them make Dev's with just slices of avocado and all the delicious cabbage oozing with seasoned Mexican sour cream.

Ray and Dev were out beyond the little waves again, waiting for an outside swell. They were relaxed and happy from Ray's successful ride, the sunshine and shared laughter. As they rose and fell with the swells, Ray said, "I like Jay, he seems solid to me, and I feel safe around him because he's been your good friend for such a long time."

The kid looked so sincere and vulnerable that it gave Dev pause. "Well, Jay is a very good man. I don't think you've anything to worry about with Jay liking your mom."

Ray said, "I want her to be happy, but I think she's trying to scare the shit out of Jay so he'll give up on her. She hasn't been with anybody since my dad split."

Dev looked at the boy and asked him, "Do you think your mom still loves your dad?"

"I know she loved him once but he betrayed her and my *tia's* dad too. Maybe I'm the only one still really screwed up about my dad. Do you know I still talk to him mostly every day? He calls me from Mazatlan. I want to go visit him when I'm eighteen. Until then, my mom won't let me go."

Dev asked the boy, "When did you last see him?"

"I haven't seen him since I was little, like when I was just starting school. My mom took me twice to Mexico back then. But then she got scared he'd snatch me away from her or something. She thinks he's probably a big time drug lord or gangster. I think he was in a gang when he was young, but was good at music and got a scholarship to college. He's super smart and brilliant at math. That's how he was able to defraud

Adri's dad. I think he took a bunch of their money into Mexico with him. You know, it's so weird and sad. I talk to him about school, sports, music, and he tells me to be good to my mom and obey her, but I never can get the courage to ask him why he did that terrible thing to all of us and then just ran away. I'm such a hopeless chicken shit, maybe I'm just like him." Ray was surprised he admitted that out loud.

"Sometimes it hurts so bad to approach a truth about yourself, you just can't do it," Dev said. "I have those struggles too. It seems I have trouble untangling the truth of who I am and what I'm afraid of knowing."

Ray looked very solemnly at Dev across the water and paddled a little with one hand so he could turn and see his eyes more clearly. "Yeah, like you're so scared of knowing something it becomes invisible to you!"

Dev smiled at the boy. "Yeah, you've got it exactly, like you've this big revealing truth within your grasp and then 'poof' it disappears." He continued to smile and said, "You know, Ray, you may be surprised at how much alike you and I are. I don't have any idea who my father is, or where I was born. I'm pretty sure I was kidnapped from my family when I was maybe four or five. That is part of the reason I came here. To find out who I am."

Ray's jaw dropped, "Wow man, I'm sorry! Who took you and raised you?"

Dev laughed, "Sometimes I think I was stolen by Gypsies and raised by Yeti."

"Abominable Snowmen? You're kidding, right?" The boy looked so shocked and confused that Dev quit laughing.

"Well no, not at all abominable at all, just unusual and different, I guess. Anyway," Dev continued, "the first thing I remember is a beach, much deeper and flatter than this one, you know one where the sand goes a very long time before you get to the water. I remember the feel of the warmth of the sun on my back and the surface of the sand and digging my hands deeper in the sand into the coolness . . ."

Just then they heard Adri yell down at them from up on the

pier, "TACOS!" She held the bag up high and waved it back and forth for them to see. She looked down at the two of them, her little nephew now on the verge of manhood and the enigmatic man who was the source of the lovesickness that bedeviled her. She could see Dev's strong tanned back as he turned toward the beach to paddle in. She wished he wasn't so beautiful to her. She was growing weary of being in love. She imagined that if her heart just broke it might be a great relief.

As they paddled into shore Dev said, "Listen, call me anytime you want to talk or need anything. Seriously, okay? My phone number is easy to remember; it spells n-i-r-v-a-n-a, you know, like the band."

Testarossas with a Twist

Jimmy Dracos' head bobbed in time to the *Beachboys* cranked up loud on his Camaro's sound system, his hand beating out the rhythm on the steering wheel—'good, good, good, good vibrations.' He was feeling jazzed because he'd discovered that Dev Tagore was dating the younger sister of an old high school buddy of his. Vic Cruz and he'd both been CIF wrestling champs in high school, but in different weight classes. He was meeting Vic at his new restaurant, *Cruz,* near the marina off Pacific Coast Highway.

Jimmy had been following Dev Tagore all over town. At first he had followed him in his Camaro, or borrowed his wife's beige Camry, but that was a pain in the butt. Then he went to Tagore's house in Seal Beach and attached a tracking GPS unit to the inside of the back bumper of the guy's old blue Volvo. It made life much easier. He discovered that one of the houses Tagore visited belonged to the sister and half-sister of Victor Cruz. Jimmy knew Little Vic pretty well. They had been tight in high school and Jimmy's family, like most of his neighborhood, used to eat at Big Victor's Mexican Restaurant. When Big Victor died, Little Vic—who was 6'4" and weighed maybe 220—opened a couple more restaurants. Victor's #3 and #4, and more recently a themed place called *Cruz*. Jimmy remembered Vic's older sister Paloma. Even as a freshman she was incredibly hot. She had been Miss Artesia or Miss Someplace or other. Then after that she was a singer in a band that had a hit. So Paloma was a kind of local Latina celebrity in Artesia, Hawaiian Gardens and Long Beach.

Dracos had never seen the younger half sister. He remembered the rumors about Vic's mom leaving his old man for some rich Dutch dairy owner. It was a big scandal when he was in grade school. He remembered his mom saying Mrs. Cruz had dishonored her family and that she should never darken the door of *Holy Family* again and deserved excommunication. Jimmy guessed back then it was unheard of for a mother from a traditional Catholic family to leave her children and husband for another man. The younger sister, Adrianna with the funny Dutch last name full of vowels, must be that guy's kid.

He knew Tagore was meeting with that towel-head, Mansour, down in Anaheim once a week. Jimmy had seen Dev give Mansour that envelope and the diamond at the restaurant. Mansour worked in construction for a company that built freeways and runways. He lived in a nice apartment in Buena Park, around the corner from Knott's Berry Farm. It worried Jimmy because he'd heard the two conspirators mention Disneyland and the Queen Mary. Mansour lived right by Knott's. He could case out the amusement park every night if he wanted to. Jimmy figured he had probably bought himself a yearly pass! Mansour's access to freeways, runways, amusement parks, and the Queen Mary had Jimmy losing sleep at night. That guy had access and opportunity to many places where terrorists could cause havoc and where countless people could get hurt. It looked like Tagore could fund all Mansour's activities. He guessed that Tagore was probably in charge.

Mansour had been born in the United States and had no record at all. He didn't show up on any of the watch lists that Jimmy had access to; but now after that whole Arab Spring fiasco, the bombing of *Charlie Hebdo* in Paris, the growth of ISIS and home-grown terrorists like the Boston Marathon bombers, the West Coast was overdue for an attack. Long Beach was repeatedly mentioned as a prime target for terror. Its harbor had a huge volume of ships since it was the primary commercial port in California. Everybody knew it was just a matter of time and that another big attack was inevitable. Jimmy Dracos wanted more than anything to stop it and save innocent lives.

Vic agreed to meet at 3:00 at his new restaurant. It was July and it was hot with that smoggy overcast reflected glare that L.A. gets. Usually it was cool right by the water, but not today. The pavement undulated waves of visible heat under a dead looking sky. Jimmy was relieved to get in the cool restaurant. He was met by a long haired girl in a paisley hot-pant suit, her long legs balanced on clunky platform shoes. She led him into the darkness and sweet whiskey smells of the bar. The room was circular, and perched in the center on what looked like a hydraulic garage lift shone a rotating brilliant blue 1968 L88 Corvette. Dull black heavy fabric accented with chrome and blue neon created the walls. Talk about a man-cave, this place looked like a billionaire's garage. The whole place was an homage to American muscle cars of the 60's and 70's. Jimmy had been in restaurants that had fifties rock and roll drive-in motifs, but this was a glammed up version for the next generation of car nuts. In the background Rod Stewart's rough voice asked, 'Do you think I'm sexy?'

Jimmy thought Rod Stewart was proof that a homely nobody could get all the models and actresses a guy could want if he had fame and money. He was wondering how much this set up had cost Vic when he saw him come into the bar. Vic was wearing tailored jeans and an expensive Hawaiian shirt, you know the kind with real coconut buttons, the kind Jimmy could never afford. He was a huge guy, but in great shape. He looked like he could crush a man in each arm without being even slightly out of breath.

Vic, a head taller than Jimmy, grabbed him in a half hug and shook his hand. "Good to see you man! Whaddya think of my new place?"

Jimmy said, "It's something else – is that your Vette?"

"Yup, isn't she just about the prettiest thing you ever seen, except maybe for Cheri here?" Vic winked and smiled at the redhead behind the bar.

"A couple of Testarrosas, Babe."

He turned to Jimmy saying, "I named all our fancy drinks after cars – Testarossa is a Ferrari of course, but it means 'red head' in Italian. So the clever little redhead behind the bar invented a little signature something with cranberry juice, white rum, lemon and orange juice and a float of grenadine on top."

Cheri handed them both tall glasses of ruby liquid with a twist of orange crimped over the edge. "Come on Dude, let me show you my office and you can tell me what I can do you for."

As they walked out of the bar, Jimmy asked, "You got something going on with Cheri?"

Vic said, "Nah, just having some fun. I need to watch my horny ass cause divorce is a bitch to pay for. I hired a decorator to design this place and I guess what she really had was designs on me, cause I married her. She's a stone cold fox and likes the finer things."

Jimmy could tell that Vic's wife had expensive taste when he went in the office. The place looked like something out of a magazine. Vic sat on a leather couch and Jimmy followed suit.

"So what's up Dude, you sounded pretty concerned on the phone."

Jimmy turned himself toward Vic and said, "Your half-sister, Adrianna."

"Yeah," Vic said, "what about her?"

"Well I think she is dating a guy who might be up to no good."

"You mean like take her for all her cash or what?"

"Well," Jimmy said, "That's possible, but I'm worried that he might be somehow involved with a terrorist organization or be just an independent wild card."

"No shit!"

"Yeah, no shit. I wondered if you knew anything about him."

"Is he a tall nice looking dude with a ponytail, light eyes and a kinda olive complexion?"

"Yeah, that sounds like him."

Vic said, "Well my sister Paloma and this Indian lawyer guy and Adri and the guy you're talking about came in at Vic's #2, you know the one in North Long Beach? They had my nephew Ray with them and they seemed pretty cozy. My sisters come to my restaurants every couple of months and I always sit down and have a Margarita with them. They both like the way I make a Cadillac, you know, the one with a sidecar of Grand Marnier?" Vic laughed, "Another drink with a car name – you just can't beat it!" Vic looked directly at Jimmy, "Shit Man, does Paloma or Adri know about this?"

"No, I was hoping that one of them could help me. Give me some information—provide some surveillance—you know, help me find out some stuff about the guy to see if we're on the right track."

Vic said, "Well, I remember that they asked me about my new restaurant. The Indian lawyer guy said something about the Long Beach Grand Prix. He thought that it would be a perfect fit with our muscle car theme if we served food there. I thought it was a pretty good suggestion, it would be great publicity. The guy with the ponytail wanted to know all about the event. I told him it was the biggest thing for tourism in Long Beach. That over 200,000 people went to the Grand Prix. He was really fascinated because he didn't know anything about it."

Dracos said, "Shit! If he bombs the Grand Prix, it could be way worse than the Boston Marathon. Oh my God. I gotta get something on this guy—and soon!"

Vic said, "The Grand Prix is in like April, so you don't have to worry about that right away."

Jimmy said, "Oh yeah, I forgot. I'm just extremely nervous about what this guy is up to."

"If Paloma thinks anybody is fucking with our little sister, you can count on her killing him before he performs any act of terrorism. He'll be one dead Arab! The guy doesn't look Middle Eastern to me though, more like maybe, I don't know, Yugoslav, or Greek."

Jimmy said, "You mean like me?"

Vic laughed. "You know I didn't mean anything by it Dracos!"

"No, I'm just pulling your chain Man. You're right; he's hard to get a bead on. His passport is Canadian and his last name is Indian—not like Tonto, but the other kind. But his paperwork looks super shady. He's some kinda genius linguist translator working here with a green card, but he hangs with some suspicious dudes. I think he's hinky as hell and I have a really bad feeling about the sonofabitch. And he's messing with your family!"

"You know my half-sister is rich, maybe he wants to tap that in more ways than one."

"Like how rich man – like what could he get his hands on?"

"She's like super corporate rich. They had all this dairy land in what is now Cerritos and that was subdivided and sold in the 70's. The dairies have moved twice and now I think they're a number of them out of state. The whole thing is a huge conglomerate. You heard of *Holland Foods*?

"Yeah, I've seen commercials on T.V.—happy goats and cows smiling and dancing in a field of tulips. Right? Jesus, she must be loaded!"

"Yeah. You remember Ray Vargas? He was Paloma's husband, a couple of years ahead of us? He and Paloma had that *Vatos Tacos* band that had that hit song that Paloma sang?"

Jimmy nodded. He remembered Ray had been the cool older guy walking the luscious Paloma around the quad. They were like the gods of the high school. Funny how stuff changes.

"Well," Vic continued, "after he and Paloma got married, Adrianna's father Phil gave him a job helping run the company and Ray was bleeding it dry. Paloma didn't know. Then before he got arrested Ray got his ass outta town and went to Mazatlan."

"So you inherited money from this Dutch guy and got money for this place?"

"No, I got bupkiss, *nada*, and a whole pile of no shit. Paloma got like seventy-five grand a year. That's why she quit teaching and started to produce some records. Adri let's her live in the old house and put her on the board of directors of some cheese company they both thought up. Neither of them has to do a goddamn thing. I inherited my dad's restaurants and worked every day mashing *frijoles* and sweating over a tub of hot oil frying tortillas since I was eight years old. I worked my butt off to get everything I have. Phil Reukema took my mom away from us and left me with nothing." Vic's forehead was sweaty and he wiped it down with both hands. He rubbed his hands across the bridge of his nose and eyes. When he took them down his eyes were still closed.

Jimmy was surprised to see this big guy so disturbed. "Jesus man, ain't life a bitch?"

Vic opened his eyes, looked hard at Jimmy and said, "Let's talk about this more over another drink or two. Then we'll have a steak and share a bottle of my best Cabernet. I want to help you any way I can." He lifted his glass and said, "To old friends."

Bad Egg

The painting was smaller than her usual canvases. In it she placed Dev on the small retaining wall in his yard with the ocean and sky behind him. He was dead center on the wall, his feet tucked under him lotus style stroking Pabu, the blue eyed cat. She had under-painted the sky an inky blue. The far horizon, a mixture of thalo blue and alizarin crimson, was wine dark. The clouds were the finest she had ever accomplished, ominous, mysterious, but with little remnants of light breaking through. The sky was darker than she had first intended, far more portentous then she had envisioned. But she knew that paintings often discovered a life of their own. Not wanting it to be so bleak and foreboding, she added the evening star Venus, glowing where its light broke through the clouds. The ocean was dark and leaden with little reflection of the ominous sky. She planned for Dev's figure to be the most well lit part of the painting. His lithe body was easy to capture, his folded legs in jeans and a plain white tee shirt. The cat was smoky brown against Dev's faded blue Levis. Its blue eyes were the same value as the pants and it gazed directly at the viewer. The painting was perhaps the best she had ever done. But it had a problem, Dev had no face. She had intended to have him looking forward just like the cat, his gray eyes the color of the sea. At first she had imagined him as very solid and realistic, but somehow the notion of his face in shadow with the cat more solid than he, was appealing too. Right now there was only a flat empty egg shape of flesh tone where his face should be. She squinted at the picture. Humpty Dumpty sat on a wall. She was at that sticking point artists hate.

She was stuck in more ways than how to paint Dev's face. Really stuck. Stuck on him. Stuck in a relationship seeming to go nowhere. Stuck in her head, which thought about him incessantly. Stuck in her body, which longed so much to have him inside her. Stuck in fear, that he didn't care about her. Stuck, feeling like a stupid child. Stuck like an idiot lovesick woman. Stuck.

She decided to take a break and take care of her usual morning chores. Her studio was open and loft-like. Because she created complex and layered paintings, and lived above her ornately decorated shop, she wanted this upstairs area to be very plain and well lit. She had all of the walls of the old rooms, except the bathroom, broken out and skylights added for additional natural light. Her bedroom was in one corner, sitting area in another, a tiny kitchen in the third corner. The remainder of the large space was her art studio, fitted with both flat and vertical shelving for canvases, frames, mat boards and paint. She had a drafting table, a long flat work table, a couple of easels and all the other paraphernalia of the artist's trade. Since she lived where she worked, it was important to her that she keep things relatively neat, so she always made her bed. She went over to the bed; its covers were askew.

She sat on the edge and began to cry as she smoothed the sheet. The bed was all loneliness. She had spent the previous night pretending he was in it with her. She reddened a little, feeling ashamed, but mostly furious with herself. She tore off the sheets and wadded them in a ball and threw them over by the door. She would take them downstairs with her and put them in the washer in the back room of her shop.

The little frying pan was left out on her tiny white enamel

stove and she decided to make herself an egg. She put on the coffee and stuck a slice of sourdough in the toaster as the pan heated. She sizzled a little butter and picked up an egg. As she held it in her palm, its plain oval smoothness reminded her of Dev's unfinished face in her painting. She carefully cracked his little head open, laughing at the analogy. She wished she could crack him open. She gently opened the egg and carefully dropped it in the browning butter. She hated it when she broke the yolk.

Her cell phone rang.

"Hello."

"Hello, am I speaking to Adrianna Reukema?"

"Yes. May I ask who is calling?"

"Yes, Miss Reukema, my name is James Dracos with the Long Beach Office of Homeland Security."

"Really?"

"Yes, Ma'am. You can call the Long Beach Office and ask for me if you are uncomfortable; your call will be transferred to my desk. It is wise of you to be vigilant. Would you like that number?"

"No, it's okay. I just can't imagine why you would call me."

"I understand, Miss Reukema. I believe you are acquainted with a man who calls himself Dev Tagore."

"Yes."

"Well, we have a few questions we would like to ask you."

After agreeing to meet Mr. Dracos, she looked at the frying pan, her egg sunny side up and faceless. It stared blankly up at her. She took a fork and stabbed it, watching the yolk slowly run out.

Butter Tea

Dev was trying to think about the problem of Adri. He was the creator of the problem and perhaps because of that, his sharp powers of concentration would not follow his thoughts down the Adri problem path. He was sitting *zazen* on a pillow made by the monks he knew in the mountains, gazing at his bare wooden floor. Pabu strolled across the floor and delicately settled on Dev's lap between his crossed legs. The cat looked up at Dev and met his eyes. Dev leaned over to stroke under the cat's chin when it reached its paw up and touched Dev delicately on his lips. Pabu made him feel like he did when he was with Jay's Great Uncle Rakesh. The man who had made him feel safe and had taken such good care of him then; and even now provided Dev the inheritance that allowed him great freedom. He wished Pabu was the reincarnation of Rakesh so he could express his love and gratitude. Then he thought to himself that such desire was irrational mumbo jumbo.

He remembered that the Dalai Lama had said he might choose to reincarnate next time as an animal or an insect. Dev smiled at the absurdity of stepping on the incarnation of the Dalai Lama or spraying him with Raid. It seemed a most ridiculous notion that a flea on his cat could hold the soul of a spiritual master. As he stroked the cat he began to clearly visualize the house in Antwerp. He remembered the coach house where Rakesh parked his Pugeot and above which the kind housekeeper Elsie lived. There was a courtyard with a long reflecting pond with golden fish in it between the house and coach house. In the summer when Jay was there, they played under the pergola near the pond until twilight when Uncle Rakesh called them in. Then up in their shared room they chatted until they fell asleep.

In those days, the days before he was sent away, he spent his time with Rakesh or talking to Elsie and helping her in the kitchen. She spoke French, Flemish and Dutch, so it was fun for him to learn words and phrases as they made meringues called *merveilleux* that they filled with whipped cream. He would sprinkle Uncle's with crumbled ginger cookies and take a plate to his library while Elsie carried the tea tray. Uncle Rakesh would always say after tasting the treat, "It is indeed *merveilleux,* and you, my boy, are a marvel too." He would clasp Dev's hands between his gentle old veined ones, and smiling, say, "Isn't life wondrous?"

Dev absent mindedly stroked the cat, and remembered the pleasure of being in the library with Rakesh sitting in his easy chair while Dev lay on the rug before the fire. Dev remembered the illustrations in the books coming alive in the fire's flickering light.

His thoughts shifted to his mother but there seemed little to remember. Was she away most of the time? Then he could see her as she was when the monks came to visit, exquisite in a green silk sari with ornate gold and emerald earrings. Did she imagine that the monks would be enchanted by her beauty and she would turn their heads?

He remembered their robes; the color reminded him of things Elsie mixed up in the kitchen —mustard, ginger, paprika and other spices. The taller unsmiling one wore white socks with his sandals. The little one had wire rimmed glasses and as sweet a smile as Dev had ever seen. They brought a European man with them who wore a vest and hat. His mother smiled and took the man's hat and cast down her eyes and then opened them to gaze at the man, his hat in her hand. Even now Dev felt a little sick with what he perceived as her pretense at flirting coyly. He wondered why his mother acted this way with the man. She usually did not try to appear obsequious in any way. The solemn monk didn't scare Dev, but this other man unsettled him, probably because he kept looking at his mother. They called him 'Herr Doktor Professor Something' or other. Dev realized the adults thought the man very important.

Then the man showed him some writing and asked him if he could read it. Dev recognized the writing immediately and said it aloud from memory. The important man said, "His pronunciation is flawless. You realize how very ancient this Sanskrit writing is?"

Next, the monks placed some objects on the table, a pair of glasses, a cup, a watch and several objects that were completely foreign to him, then asked if he recognized them. Dev told the monks he didn't recognize them. Next they opened three scrolls and Dev said he recognized one. He remembered the writing which looked different from all the others; it seemed to be something he knew very well.

The monk in the white socks asked Dev, "Can you read this?"

Dev said, "I remember it. It speaks of a profound *bodhichitta* focused on compassion and the skill required of a *tulku* to control rebirth. It has instructions on how to control the subtle body in the death *Bardo* and generate the grosser body at birth." The smaller monk was weeping. Everyone was quiet for a moment.

Then the important man said, "There are cases of xenoglossia in which a patient presents with the ability to speak foreign languages with no rationale to account for that ability. *Xenoglossia* is from the Greek and simply means 'foreign speech.' There are many cases detailed from India where this would be accepted as evidence of reincarnation. For example, a child may speak *Marathi*, in a family whose language is *Bengali* or *Hindi*. In the West these cases occur very rarely and often seem to be fraudulent. There is the famous case of Rosemary from Blackpool, a patient who presented herself as the incarnation of the wife of Pharaoh Amenhotep III. The case was proved fraudulent. As I recall one of the evidences being that she described camels as a method of transportation, a purpose for which they were not used in Eighteenth Dynasty Egypt. There were also misgivings about her sponsor, who may have manipulated the translations of her speech. There is one interesting European case from the 1930's, where a Hungarian teenage girl, who dabbled around with mediumship, spoke perfect Spanish and claimed to be a working class Spanish woman of twice her age. As far as I know this woman lived her life convinced that she was indeed that Spanish woman. However, I have never heard of a case of such a young child exhibiting knowledge of the most ancient *Sanskrit* texts as well as an understanding of the *Tibetan Book of the Dead*."

The important man turned toward Uncle Rakesh and said, "I surmise you are from India. Am I correct?"

"Yes, I was born Rakesh Mehta, a *Hindu* of the *Pulinpari* Caste. I am a businessman, a diamond broker. I know little of Buddhism. I only know English and the European languages used here in Belgium and those not as well as I would like. I am not a practicing *Hindu*, and own no ancient texts, just a modern version of the *Bhagavad Gita*. The boy has enjoyed the illustrations in the *Gita* as they are very pretty. Neither his mother nor I have any idea of the source of his abilities. I have attended various lectures on philosophy, metaphysics and Jungian psychology, which is how I met his mother; however, I have no specific belief system. I suppose I am open to all possibilities but adhere to none."

Uncle and Mother showed the learned man to the door. His mother, still smiling, gave the professor his hat. Dev could hear them discussing the possibility of studying him at the University. But before he could hear more, the monks asked him to show them to the kitchen so they could have some tea. Elsie put on the kettle, but they shooed her out, giggling that she wouldn't like their kind of tea. They had a little bag of tea and a jar of something and they mixed all of it up and filled the teapot with boiling water.

"We must wait while the tea steeps, but we should like to get to know you better," said the smaller monk. "We wonder, is your mother good to you and do you love her?"

Dev said, "Of course, she is my mother."

To each other the monks began to speak as if Dev wasn't there. The one in the socks said, "Why would such a noble one choose to be incarnated in such a woman? I feel she is difficult and I have very bad feelings about her. She claims she does not know the father."

The sweet monk asked Dev, "Little one, do you have a father?"

Dev replied, "I asked my mother once about a father. She said Rakesh is better than a father. I know I was with others before I was here. They loved me. I miss the lady with hair like clouds so much. My mother tells me I must have dreamed all that."

"Mr. Mehta said you didn't always live here. Wasn't your mother with you before you lived here?"

"I don't remember her there. "

"Where was this place?"

"By the waves and in the sky." Said the boy.

The monk with the white socks poured tea in each of their cups and said, "It is still too hot to drink. You must wait until we tell you it is safe to drink."

Dev watched clouds of golden globules first spin, then migrate slowly around the top of the tea cup. While he waited and watched his tea, the monks continued to speak as if he could not hear them. The one with the white socks said, "He was not misled by the false ritual objects we put before him and he identified the scroll from the *Sidpa Bardo* correctly, while ignoring the others. "

The little monk looked at his companion, his eyes once again brimming with tears, and said, "He understood the most profound heartdrops of the *Bardo*. I believe he must be a very great *tulku* to be able to explain the transmigration from the luminal state to rebirth. I don't know whose incarnation he may be, only that his seems to be from the most ancient of lineages. He knew the ancient Sanskrit text the professor showed him as well as the Tibetan, from the *Book of the Dead*. It will be for our masters to answer this mystery."

Dev never moved his eyes away from the cup until the smaller monk said, "You are very patient, little master. It is all right for you to drink now."

Dev lifted his cup and took a small sip. It tasted smooth and salty.

"Do you like the tea, boy?" Dev smiled. "Does it remind you of something?"

"It reminds me of my home."

"Where is that?" asked the sweet monk.

"It reminds me of the ocean."

The monks knew that only the highest were associated with the ocean of compassion and wisdom. Was this child indeed one of the beloved masters here again on earth to help mortals? The one in the socks said, "Do you remember anything else about that place, boy?"

"I remember a wheel."

"Can you draw it?"

They gave him a pencil and paper and Dev drew a small circle within a larger circle with eight spokes radiating out from the center. The sweetest monk wept again and said, "Boy, this is the *dharmachakra*, the wheel of the law or of the dharma. Did your mother or Rakesh teach you this, or have you seen it in a book?"

"No, it is from the place I come from. It is from my beginning, the place I started."

That night, Dev heard Rakesh argue with his mother. Rakesh said, "I don't deny that he possesses what appear to be supernatural abilities. But he is a boy, happy and cherished in this home. Even if he is the reincarnation of some great master, he needs protection, guidance and love. You needn't remind me again that I have no legal rights to him. However, if you take him away I will no longer support you or your interests. If you allow him to at least spend summers here with Jay and myself, I will provide for both you and your son."

Dev, his mother and the sweet monk left the following day.

Cold Espresso

Dracos met Adri for coffee at *The Library*, a coffee shop on East Broadway in Belmont Heights. She said she'd be sitting on a couch near the windows. The place was dim after the bright August glare. He looked around, his eyes adjusting to the dimness. It was an old building with a brick arched front window. The brick look was uncommon in the area and he liked the funky vibe. One hundred and twenty people died in the Long Beach earthquake of 1933, many from falling bricks and debris. As a result, building codes changed and bricks were definitely on the out in this neighborhood. As his eyes adjusted he scanned the room, dark and homey with old oak tables, bookcases piled with books and comfy couches under the windows. She said she would be by the window. Since there were only a couple of gay guys chatting and holding hands and one young Asian woman studying what looked like some kind of medical text, she was easy to spot.

She sat on a couch reading a book, her figure in silhouette backlit by the sun. He expected her to resemble her sister Paloma, a statuesque beauty queen. He was surprised to see a slender girl with long nut brown hair, dressed in Levis and an embroidered shirt. She wore no makeup and seemed rather plain until he got closer when he could see the perfect symmetry of her face and blue eyes against tanned skin. Most men would rate her older sister right up with Angelina Jolie at her sexiest. But Dracos could envision this sweet-faced girl as the governess in a Jane Austen story. She was simply old-fashioned pretty.

He extended his hand and said, "I am sorry to meet you under these circumstances."

Her hand trembled slightly as he held it." That sounds like somebody died. I'm afraid I don't know what the circumstances are."

"Sorry, we'll get to that, but first I want you to know that I've known your brother Vic since we wrestled together in high school. We were buddies back then and are still in touch on occasions. I spoke to him before I contacted you. Feel free to speak to him if it makes you feel more comfortable." Dracos pulled out a badge and his I.D. to let Adri examine it. "Can I get you something to drink?"

"Sure, I'd like an espresso please."

She looked at his credentials which seemed real enough to her and watched Dracos as he walked up to the counter to order her drink. He was on the short side, well built with broad shoulders and dark brown hair. He wore a navy blue suit with light brown calf oxfords. The brown shoes with the navy suit bothered her aesthetically. She might have found deep oxblood or black acceptable, but those shoes should be paired with khaki. She chastised herself for thinking like the snobby fashion police and realized that she was terrified of what this guy might have to say about Dev. Dracos turned, carefully carrying two *demitasse* cups of espresso. He met her eyes and flashed her a winning smile.

"Good book?" He asked as he set down their coffees. She was reading Sue Grafton's, *'S' is for Silence*.

"Yeah. My nephew is a precocious fourteen-year-old and he likes detective novels. You know, Raymond Chandler, all that stuff. He turned me on to Elmore Leonard who is wonderful. I really like these too. I guess I identify with the young woman detective. I don't have the whole alphabet, but I've accumulated quite a few. I don't have "N" or "R" and I'm missing a whole bunch of the early ones. Sorry, I'm chattering on, which I do when I'm nervous. I guess you want to tell me something or ask me some questions that I'm afraid I don't want to hear."

"Are you sure you don't want something to go with your coffee, a croissant or a muffin or something?"

"No, thanks, this is fine. I didn't eat breakfast, but I'm not very hungry, just nervous. I guess espresso was a stupid choice huh?"

Dracos reached over and patted her hand, and said, "It's okay; everything is gonna be just fine."

Adri slipped her hand from under his and, placing both elbows on the table, supported her face in her hands and looked directly at his small light brown eyes. "Please let's get this over with," she said.

"How long have you known Dev Tagore?"

"I met him in May when he sat next to me at the counter of Lupe's restaurant— now it's August so that makes it four months. It seems longer," she said, her eyes downcast.

"Is the nature of this relationship romantic?"

She closed her eyes for a second and exhaled. "Well, we have dated, but I guess it has become more of a friendship. His best friend is dating my sister and that seems to be kind of serious. We all do stuff together including my nephew Ray. We go places and hang out at the beach at Dev's house. He's teaching Ray to surf. We all went to a Long Beach State baseball game. We all root for their team, 'The Dirtbags'; anyway we do stuff like that."

Dracos looked at her and smiled, "So you're a 49-er too?"

"No, Paloma went to school there. That's where she got her teaching credential, but she doesn't teach any more. She has started some other businesses. I went to UCLA, so a Bruin fan."

"And what do you do for a living?" Dracos smiled again.

"I paint and own a gift shop in Belmont Shores."

"Is that it?" Dracos knew the answer.

"I inherited some dairies from my dad and Paloma and I just started a little cheese business. So I keep busy." She looked down at her espresso. She hadn't touched it. "I'd like to know why you're interested in Dev?"

"I am just beginning a little research on Mr. Tagore, but I need to speak to you in complete confidence if I proceed any further. I would not ask for this if it wasn't of possible importance to the security of our nation."

"The security of the nation? Really? I think that unlikely. Listen, Dev is my friend. I don't like going behind his back. It is not something I am comfortable with unless there is some very compelling reason. So please explain or get a court order or something." Now she was more pissed than scared.

He said, "I know it must seem weird coming out of the blue like this, but your brother is concerned as well. He asked me to avoid speaking to Paloma as he was afraid she could be a bit, let's say, *unpredictable*, when it came to you. You know, very protective."

"Why would she need to protect me? I think maybe I need to get a lawyer." She began to stand up to leave.

"No, no, you don't understand. I just want you to reassure me that Mr. Tagore is not the man we are looking for. You can help rule him out as a person of interest and then you can go back to your regular life. No harm, no foul."

She sat back down and said, "I still can't imagine what this is about. I can think of nothing that would make me think that Dev is a bad guy. It just seems impossible to me. He is a kind, generous, calm, and very private guy. He's a scholar, a linguist and that is his disposition. He's a vegetarian for heaven's sake – I don't think he even swats flies. You have to give me an incredibly good reason to answer any questions about him. The fact is I hardly know anything at all about him anyway."

Dracos said very quietly, "Don't you think it's strange to have dated someone for, what did you say, four months and not know much about him?"

She did think it was peculiar, but everything about her relationship with Dev was different and confusing to her. But that didn't mean he was some kind of criminal. She had never looked at his odd behavior as problematic except in the light of her enormous infatuation and desire to be loved by him. This befuddlement was compounded by the fact that unlike other men, he did not seem to reciprocate her affection in a romantic or sexual way. She always thought of his diffidence in terms of what was wrong with *her*. She even wondered if maybe he was gay and she was just some kind of experiment. She kept her eyes down, looking at the espresso, and didn't answer Dracos.

"Did you know he attends a mosque a few times a week and speaks Arabic?"

That surprised her. It seemed unlikely; but he did seem to acquire languages and he'd apparently spent a good deal of time in India – maybe Pakistan too. She said defensively, "No, but there is nothing wrong with going to a mosque."

Jimmy put his lips together in a tight little smile and said, "No, of course there isn't. But Mr. Tagore seems to have false documents, including a birth certificate that is suspect as well as a Canadian Passport that looks fishy. We wonder if he is really the man that he's portraying. He also seems to have access to a great deal of money without the income to document its source."

Adri looked at him, and said, "Dev's best friend is Jay Mehta, and they lived together much of their childhood. Jay's uncle left them both a bunch of money I think. Jay inherited his old house in Bixby Knolls and they both speak of him fondly. The fact that he has money made me feel more comfortable about him. Sometimes when guys find out I have money I feel like they're interested in me for the wrong reason."

Dracos replied, "Any man would be nuts to want you for your money. You're lovely, sweet and obviously very loyal. I can understand your mistrust, but you underestimate your attractiveness."

She didn't want the compliment to feel good, but it did. She asked, "What did you tell my brother?"

"Exactly what I told you, really nothing more. We had a drink, a steak and rehashed old times. There isn't much more to tell. Mostly we want to rule out anything that might jeopardize our nation's security. By the way, the great uncle you mentioned was born in Peshawar in what is now Pakistan, a place very friendly to the Taliban. We think you're in the best position to assist us. How about I let you think it over and maybe talk to your brother. I could pick you up tomorrow and we could get some lunch. You can let me know how you're feeling about it at that time."

Adri stared at her cold espresso. A little film formed a sludge in the middle of her cup like a tiny little oil slick. She felt nauseous. "Dev is going out of town for a few weeks on some personal business. He asked me to take care of his cat and pick up the mail." She was on the verge of tears. She wondered why in the world she let that slip out. She picked up the small espresso cup and downed its cold, bitter contents.

Coffee with Curdled Cream

When Dev first arrived in America he was astonished that there were churches of no recognizable denomination on nearly every corner. In front of these non-descript buildings there were often large marquees with clever, if perhaps tasteless, sayings. This morning driving to the mosque in Orange County, Dev had seen one that said, *'Read the Bible, it will scare the hell out of you.'* He turned the Volvo east on Chapman to avoid the traffic near Disneyland. He could see the Matterhorn in the distance on his left and it wasn't long before he saw the spires of the Crystal Cathedral on his right. Robert Schuller had started his ministry in an abandoned drive- in theatre and then parlayed his charisma into a televangelist empire. Not so different from Disney, except that Schuller's empire had ended in bankruptcy.

Dev thought about American's religiosity, recalling that geneticists had identified a 'religious' gene which was present in nearly half of Americans and Europeans. Their study hypothesized that feelings of innate optimism in human beings and a sense of positive connectedness to the greater universe could convey physiological as well as psychological benefits. Thus the gene could provide an evolutionary benefit, even encouraging those carrying it to have larger families. Perhaps that accounted for the contrast between people who felt absolutely no necessity to seek a rationale for existence itself, or even for a creator God, to those who felt an aching separation and deep longing to be reunited with godhead. Absolute atheism must allow an individual greater freedom. Not, he thought, so much a moral freedom, but rather a freedom from that unfilled emptiness.

The harsh late August light flattened the landscape making it look almost two dimensional. He passed another church. Dirt streaks ran from its flat roof down the side of a faded pink stucco façade. Along its length, in darker dusky pink stucco, were a series of appliquéd arches leading nowhere. The sign out front read, '*Get off the phone and go to the throne.*' Dev sighed. Better advice for cell phone users with diarrhea than those with an unquenchable spiritual thirst. He thought about the 'taking up of serpents' in the South, and the 'sky burial' he had witnessed in the Himalayas, where corpses were fed to vultures on the charnel fields. After the large carrion birds had done their thing, the remaining bones were bashed up with mallets and the workers added tea and yak butter so the crows and hawks would enjoy all the tasty tidbits left by the vultures. This practice was intended to benefit the soul of the once human carcass by giving sustenance to the birds. And Dev thought, maybe life really was for the birds. He turned the corner onto the street where the mosque was located and passed a sign on a storefront advertising palmistry and fortunetelling. It made him think of his very own Tara, whose disciples thirsted so greatly for religious experience they were eager to drink her piss.

He spotted Mansour standing on the sidewalk outside the drab little storefront mosque. Dev wondered what percent of the population might have the 'God' gene in Muslim nations. He pulled the Volvo up to the curb, put it in park and looked over at a few bearded men entering for morning prayers. It was a good thing that local mosques didn't feel the need to put cute sayings about Mohammed on a marquee. Better to keep a low profile as Muslims in America. He got out of the car and walked across to greet his friend. Mansour was dressed, as usual, in denim work clothes, boots and a knit watch cap. As he approached the mosque, Dev pulled a folded white *kufi* out of his pocket and put it on his own head. He didn't know how Mansour could stand a knit cap in the summer. Dev greeted his friend, "*As-salamu alaykum*."

Mansour grabbed his hand, hugged him, and gave the polite response, "*Wa alaykumu s-salam,*" and continued excitedly, "Before we go to prayers, I want to present you with these *misbaha*. These are the prayer beads of my father, may peace be upon him, and these stones must remember at least 10,000 of his prayers."

Dev, touched and surprised by his gesture, said, "I am honored, but surely you should keep these in the family."

Mansour placed the amber beads in Dev's hand and closed his fingers around them and said, "I believe that I just have, because you are more a brother to me than a friend. Here, let me tell you about the beads and what they signify. *Misbaha* come with thirty-three or ninety-nine beads. They are used for reciting the greatest and most beautiful names of *Allah*. The larger handle-like bead is called the *Imam*, and just as in our prayers in the mosque, the *Imam* leads us. As you say your recitations, you click each bead and release onto the next counting bead." Mansour took the beads from Dev's hands to demonstrate. "Let me show you." Mansour shifted the beads in his hand, selecting the largest bead. "So beginning from the *Imam*, you would say *Al-Badi,* meaning the Incomparable, the Unattainable and the Beautiful." Mansour pushed that bead away and clicked the next in place, saying, "*Al-Arwal*, meaning, the First and the Beginningless, *A-ahir*, the Last, the Endless, and on to the other of the 99 beautiful names of Allah. For me, the most elevating of the names is the one which means that God is the Self-Existing by Whom all Subsist. Reciting these beautiful names of Allah has truly deepened my relationship with the sublime. And it will be my humble honor if you accept this *misbaha* as my brother in spirit."

Dev said, "I thank you for such a great gift, my brother."

Mansour once again placed the *misbaha* in Dev's hands

and kissed him on both cheeks. Then he said, "I'm sorry I'll be unable to share a meal with you today, as I must leave right after prayers. I am finally beginning the supervision of the concrete crew which will be constructing the new runway at Long Beach Airport. As you know, I have waited for this opportunity for a long while. So this gift to you marks a very auspicious occasion."

The men performed their ritual ablutions, stacked their shoes in the rack and entered the prayer hall. The mosque, packed with believers, was small and stuffy. While the *Imam* led the prayers, Dev's mind could not concentrate on the Arabic. His monkey brain was playing and would not rest. He thought about Adri and what a ridiculous job he'd made at pretending to be a normal American guy dating a normal American girl. He really sucked at it. Jay was right; he was still just poor old Pinocchio trying to be a real boy. Perhaps if he bothered to look in the mirror he'd see that his nose was steadily growing.

He moved the beads through his fingers aimlessly. Last night he'd been reading various translations of *Rumi* poems. He thought it interesting that a medieval Persian *Sufi* mystic would be the best selling poet in what was pretty much an anti-Islamic America. Maybe the readers didn't know that *Sufis* were Muslims and that their mysticism was born of the Koran. Five years ago Dev would have been motivated to learn to read the poet's work in the original Persian as spoken in the area in what is now Afghanistan where *Rumi* was born in 1207. But he realized that Arabic was the last new language he would learn. It seemed to be enough. He continued the circling of the beads through his fingers. He thought more about the bizarre fact of *Rumi's* success in America. Was it possible he actually beat out Maya Angelou, Robert Frost, Allen Ginsberg and Tupac to the top of the poetry Top Ten? He snickered to himself and the man next to him glared at his rudeness. Glad when prayers were finished, he said goodbye to Mansour and decided to go get breakfast. There were probably a few cafes on the way back to Seal Beach.

The first place he saw that looked promising was an old

renovated bungalow painted green with flowers and vines. The gravel parking lot was pretty full, so he figured they must be doing something right. He took a seat in the back corner and asked for coffee, a couple of scrambled eggs and rye toast. He was gazing out the window, still thinking a little about Rumi. The waitress filled his cup and he poured a little cream in. It was slightly curdled and a couple of small bits of white solids lingered at the top.

He began to stir it quickly and watch the little curds spin. He chuckled because the white specks wheeling like planets around the sun reminded him of whirling dervishes. Rumi's son founded the *Mevlevi* order, known as the 'whirling dervishes.' *Dancers for God*. He continued to watch the curdles as their spinning slowed and thought more about the *Sufi* dancers. Dressed in tall white hats, which represented the tombstones of their egos, they began by walking counter clockwise just as worshippers circle the *Kaaba* in Mecca. On the third circle they began their turning with arms crossed across their chests so that they resembled the number one, God's unity. As they spun, their wide skirts circled whirling outward and, though anchored on the ground, they flew the heavens in their cosmic circling in the remembrance of God.

As he visualized the Sufi's dance, Dev became transfixed by the images that spun through his mind. He could see prayer wheels spinning and spinning, dogs chasing their tails faster and faster, second hands of clocks sweeping and then he remembered tiny marshmallows spinning in cups of hot cocoa. Next, he saw his own fingers spinning toy truck wheels, and then his hands on a large ship's wheel turning and turning, always in the same direction. Then as if from a great height, he saw the top of a single dervish's white hat spinning in tighter circles, a little off center but like a top spinning faster and righting itself until it was centered. Then humming, spinning, smaller and faster it became a pearl, then just a fragile opalescent bubble, shrinking, smaller into a single point of light and then dissolving his consciousness into the sea of unending bliss.

As the waitress set down his eggs, he returned to himself. He knew the time had come for him to make his formal and final goodbyes.

Grilled Salmon Feast

Jimmy Dracos had called Adri four times. Finally, under what seemed to Adri like duress, she promised that she would call her half-brother to hear about all the reasons she should trust Dracos and betray Dev. She hadn't. Dev had been gone ten days or so, and she was at his house doing her cat-feeding, pick-up-the-mail duties. The blazing late August heat in the L.A. basin had sucked in the Marine layer like water color paper wicks up color, so that here at the edge of the Pacific it was cool and overcast. The previous Monday had been Labor Day and even though most kids were back in school now, there were a few chilly families lying on their towels or building sand castles, their only forays into the surf to refill sand buckets for moistening the moats and crenellations of the castles they built.

It was nearly noon and she knew soon the haze would burn off and the late afternoon would bring plenty of beachgoers to cool off from the inland heat. She had watered the few succulents that survived in the salty air, picked up Dev's mail and paper, and was now on the small patio calling the cat. He didn't appear, so she decided to pick up his dish and water bowl and take them back in the kitchen and give them a good scrubbing. As she ran the water, waiting for it to heat up, she gazed out the porthole window at the little patio. The surfboards had been put away in the garage along with the wetsuits. There was a little table, a couple of chairs and a small hibachi. She was wondering what a vegetarian cooked on the hibachi, maybe eggplants and peppers, when a high-pitched terrible screeching startled her. A tawny striped cat barreled down off the wall from the next yard followed at breakneck speed by Pabu. They tangled in the yard, and as she ran out the back door they knocked over a pot and kicked over the little hibachi.

"Scat!" She ran out to shoo away Pabu's nemesis, but they were both long gone. The pot was broken, soil and succulents strewn out next to the hibachi which was also tipped on its side, spreading a puddle of ashes and pieces of charcoal on the bricks. She wondered if Paloma might have an extra pot in the Artesia house that she could repot the succulents in. The succulents were interesting ones with stripes of pale yellow, green and a light rosy color. She thought it would be a shame to lose them. As for the ashes, that was going to be a messy cleanup.

She reached under the sink and grabbed a couple of plastic bags, a whisk broom, dust pan, and some rags which she dampened in the sink and squeezed out. She went outside and picked up the succulents and as much of the soil as she could manage and put them in the plastic bag. Then she took the whisk broom and began brushing up the ashes and remaining dirt. In the ashes she saw a glint of red glass and some green and clear glass too. She brushed her hands against one another to get off some of the ash and soil and then very carefully tried to pick out the glass without cutting herself. She wondered why in the world there was glass in the hibachi. She picked out a big red piece and saw it wasn't broken glass, but glass cut to resemble a gem stone. She continued picking out the bits of colored glass, each faceted, some green, others blue, more red and finally some clear ones. She took the handful of stones into the kitchen and carefully rinsed them off. She held a big green one up to the light at the funny little porthole window. The rich jungle green stone was full of little striations, inclusions that glass would not have. The red stones were a darker pinky maroon, and two of those were not faceted, but rather large oval smoothly polished cabochons. She put one of them in the flat of her palm and gently tilted it back and forth. She could see the light diffract into a star formation. It didn't take a gemologist to realize that these didn't come from the Walmart craft department.

She gathered the stones up and went back outside to stick them back in the bottom of the small barbeque. As she gathered up ashes and half burned briquettes and replaced them over the loose gemstones, she wondered why Dev would keep them there. She realized that Jay's uncle was a gem merchant and that would possibly give him access to stones. But it was weird to hide them there. Old ladies hid their money in sagging sofas only to forget and unwittingly donate them to Goodwill, but Dev wasn't an old lady. Jimmy Dracos' insinuations had put a worm in her brain and it was drilling away at her curiosity.

She decided she should do a little snooping on her own just to put her mind at ease. She finished cleaning the patio, closed the door and began to wonder where to begin. She walked to the oak table in front of the picture window where Dev did his work. His laptop wasn't there, but there were some piles of papers and documents, so she decided to take a peek. She leafed through various things written in *Hindi*, or some other strange alphabet. There were copies of documents with signatures by Jay and affixed with various official looking stamps as well as California notary seals. There was a stack of magazines, mostly *National Geographic* and *Surfers*.

As she went to put them back, the cover of the top *Surfer* caught her eye. It showed a surfer inside a crystalline green wave with an ancient temple on the shore behind him. The caption read, *Surf India*. She began to thumb through the magazine to see more photos, when an envelope slid partially from its pages. She pulled out an oversized manila envelope addressed to Dev Tagore at the Seal Beach address in foreign looking handwriting. The postmark was from Vancouver B.C.

Something stirred in her the memory of the myth of Cupid and Psyche. Her dad used to read it to her from her *Child's Book of Greek Mythology* when she was little. It was her favorite and she made him read it to her again and again. In the story, Cupid pierced by his own arrow, fell in love with the beautiful, but alas mortal, Psyche. The gods allowed him to have her as his wife on the condition that he only visit her in darkness and that she never lay eyes upon his godly beauty. She was content with her lot until her stepsisters, jealous of the palace in which she was ensconced, hinted that her husband was most likely a hideous monster, too ugly to behold. Of course Psyche, apparently soul sister to Pandora, couldn't contain her curiosity and had to take a peek. She lit a candle and gazed at her husband while he slept. His beauty was awesome, his white wings folded over him like a blanket. As she gazed on his face transfixed, a drop of hot wax fell from her candle on to his perfect cheek, waking him. That is when the all out Greek tragic shit hit the proverbial epic fan.

Adri hesitated for an instant, but then thought perhaps the contents would reveal some more about Dev's background, or his previous life. Inside the larger envelope was another white envelope addressed to Mr. Dev Tagore, c/o Ven. Ani Pema Drub at the same Vancouver address on the upper left hand corner of the outside manila envelope. The smaller envelope had an Indian postmark from March of this year. She opened the interior envelope, its top previously slit by a paper opener, unfolded it and read the letter.

My Darling Dev,

I miss you so much and need you back in my life. I love you more than you can ever know. Any injuries I may have caused you, I pray for your forgiveness. Please don't give up the life you were meant for and please don't forsake me. I beseech you to contact me directly and cease this foolish hiding out away from me. You know it is wrong. It is unbearable. I beg you.

Love, Tara

Adri felt cold seep from the center of her chest down through all her extremities as if she had been injected with some lethal substance that would suck all the joy out of her, forever turning her heart into a lump of ice. She put the letter back in the envelopes and stuck them back in the *Surfer* magazine. She went to the bathroom and retched. She ran the cold water, splashed it on her face and then, determined to sound normal, dialed her sister Paloma's cell phone and waited for her to pick up.

"Hi, Baby! What's shakin? Jay and I are at Joe Jost's and I just creamed his ass at pool."

Adri could hear Jay in the background say, "She's a hustler Adri. No man can ever trust her!"

Adri said, "Did you bet him something?"

"Yeah and I'm gonna collect on Friday night!!"

"God, don't tell me, I can't bear to even imagine."

"Well," said Paloma, " It's something I've always had an unrealized fantasy about." Adri could hear Jay laughing in the background.

Adri asked, "What are you guys doing at a bar at lunchtime?"

"Oh, Jay wanted to meet me for a romantic luncheon, so I had him bring me here."

"Paloma, you're so nuts, that place still smells of beer from the Great Depression. How very romantic!" Adri exhaled and said softly, "Listen Pal, I really need to talk to you."

"Well, Jay's about to leave. He has to go back to work. Why don't you come down here and have a beer and we can chat. I don't have to get home right away. Ray will probably go to the library after school. I'm just gonna reheat yesterday's leftovers for dinner tonight."

"Okay, I have to finish up here and I'll be there as soon as I can. Bye." She hit *end call* on her phone and shuddered. In her joy, Paloma didn't pick up that Adri felt as if her world was collapsing in on her. She returned to the kitchen and saw the smoky colored cat at the door. She opened it and he came in and swirled around her legs meowing his hunger and loneliness. She picked him up and he purred as she clasped him to her chest. Tears fell onto his fur. She put him down and picked up a can of *Fancy Feast* Grilled Salmon, pulled the tab of the can up and plated the pink, gooey gourmet gorp, trying not to gag.

Joe Jost's Pickled Eggs

Adri put Pabu outside and locked Dev's door. She got in her car and drove up to PCH, turned left and followed it past the VA Hospital, then turned left on Anaheim. She passed the park and drove west through a treeless old business district. All flat topped roofs and simple facades, the stucco buildings had probably been built in the twenties and had not become gentrified or improved much since then. The sun was harsh and the street looked bleached and colorless. The bar shared a building with what had been a bait and tackle shop. There was plenty of parking and she saw her sister's van in the lot. She pulled up next to it and went in the bar. The dark old tavern was a visual relief after the barren sunlight outside. Adri supposed it hadn't changed much since the twenties. Old timey taverns like this were probably commonplace in Boston and Chicago, but Joe's was unique in Southern California.

Paloma was sitting at the end of the bar, chatting with the bartender as he polished a glass. She spotted Adri in the mirror behind the bar and turned to greet her. The older sister's long dark hair was caught up by a red ribbon in a high ponytail. She was wearing white pedal pushers dotted with rosebuds, red ballet flats and a white eyelet short-sleeved blouse tied up under her chest exposing her midriff. Her face looked fresh and radiant. Adri thought that only Paloma could pull off that Calypso midriff without looking like she fell off the banana boat. Pal got up and hugged her sister and asked, “What’ll it be? You want to eat first or shoot some pool?”

“I think I’ll let you give me some exercise at the pool table before I eat. I’m thirsty though, you want another beer?”

“Sure. I’m drinking the Busch Bavarian. I’ll go back and get us a table.”

Adri leaned over the bar, ordered two draft Busch Bavarians and gave the bartender a ten. Joe Jost’s was famous for many things, among them delicious pickled eggs and the coldest beer in town. She carefully carried the two schooners back through an opening beyond the bar into the pool hall. She passed the little old-fashioned glassed-in office and then the peculiar antique peanut roaster on her left. The dingy walls were covered with photos of friends, patrons and luminaries, interspersed with old oil landscapes painted on canvas yellowed by nicotine and time. The wall near the pool table had a lot of pin-up calendars which she didn’t remember from before.

Adri had never beaten her sister at pool. Oh yeah, when she was little her dad or Pal would line up her shots for her and let her win; after she was about ten that never happened again. She just really never could see the table tactically. It simply didn’t interest her. Funny, she could imagine the composition of a painting fully in her head, but game playing was a different kind of thinking she just didn’t have.

“I’ll spot you if you want,” Paloma said as she chalked up her cue. “Your break.”

“Don’t bother. Whatever handicap you give me won’t help. I like to play just so I can watch you clear the table. It’s a beautiful thing. Did you impress the hell out of Jay?”

Adri filled the rack alternating solids and stripes with the 8-ball in the center, then rolling the entire triangular rack and the balls within, she positioned it exactly. She removed the rack and Paloma handed her a cue. She had a lucky break and the three ball went in the right corner pocket. She then was able to get the six ball in the same pocket. She missed her next shot and knew that her sister would clear the table.

Paloma picked up her cue and started picking off balls like lint off her blouse. She said, "Well, I beat him. Of course every time I bent over to shoot I would try to make my ass look as perky and cute as possible. I'm sure that didn't hurt the outcome. But he's no novice. Apparently when he was in law school he shot a lot of pool. Then he let it slip that when he spent summers with his uncle in Belgium they played billiards—you know the kind of pool table with no pockets and just a few balls. I've never played that. Jay said that he and Dev also played *caroms* all the time when they were little. When you go in the shops over in Little India there are *carom* boards everywhere."

"Is that the game with a pretty square board with net pockets in the corners?"

"Yeah, you flick these checkers looking thingies across the board. Jay says he and Dev will teach us how to play. He also said the Indians invented *caroms*, but pretty much he believes the Indians invented everything, from decimals and zero to Fibonacci number sequences. I, on the other hand, argue in favor of the Mayans who were the greatest mathematicians of the ancient world. I tell him that's why my son is so good at math and I'm good at music, while he has trouble figuring out how much to leave for a tip. It proves the superiority of our Mayan gene pool!"

Adri was conscious of her sister's ebullience. Her color was high and she looked wonderful. She could never remember seeing her smiling with such ease and constancy. Adri hesitated to bring up what would surely sound like a one girl pity party she was throwing for herself when she talked about Dev. But she needed to tell her sister about the letter. She probably wouldn't tell her about all the jewels in the *hibachi* or mention Jimmy Dracos. Before she did that, she needed to talk to her brother to check the guy out and see if he was for real. The whole deal was just too unlikely for her to countenance. All she could wrap her head around right now was that Dev had another woman and it was killing her.

Paloma said, "Do you remember your dad bringing us here when you were little and he was teaching me to shoot pool?"

"Yeah, it was in the daytime, right? I guess you could bring kids because they have food and pool. Was mom still alive then?"

"Yep. It was here shooting pool when I began to love your dad. After Mom left home, my father had us convinced that Phil was the devil incarnate and that he was a vile home wrecker. Thank God your dad had enough money to get a lawyer who made sure that we could visit our mom and Phil every other weekend. Your dad was so sweet and easy. I remember how much she smiled and laughed when she was with him. He'd tease her in cute ways and be silly with her. His eyes would sparkle and crinkle up and she just melted around him. He was patient with me and teaching me pool was a good way to get to know me. I was pretty good at it right from the start. But it was watching Mom be so happy that nurtured my love for him. He would always make the same stupid joke when we were here just before we left. It would be late on Sunday afternoon and the court order said I had to be returned to my dad by 5:00 p.m. Phil knew how hard it was for mom and me to part. Just before we'd leave he'd say, 'Paloma honey, it's a good thing you're going to your dad's tonight. That's because your mom says that after I eat pickled eggs, if I break wind, it smells like Satan's armpit.'"

Adri smiled. "I don't remember that one but I remember he could be really silly to relax you if things were tense. He knew if he said something goofy and funny and you laughed at him you'd feel less anxious."

Paloma lifted the back of her cue high behind her and jacked the cue ball right over the eight ball to put her last ball into the pocket. After Paloma sank the eight ball Adri said, "Let's get a booth. I need something to eat."

They moved up to a booth in the front. All of the booths were high backed varnished plywood with the world's flattest seats. Unfortunately, Adri had worn shorts and she knew that her thighs would end up sticking to the plywood. The booths were difficult enough to get in and out of without having to release the suction formed on your thighs. She ordered a 'Joe's Special' (sausage, Swiss cheese, pickle and mustard on rye), a pickled egg and another beer. Paloma had eaten lunch earlier with Jay and just ordered a pickled egg and a coffee so she could start to sober up. The sandwich and eggs arrived and Adri was quiet while she wolfed down the first half of her sandwich. The pickled eggs were yellowish since the recipe used turmeric and the spicy vinegar from jarred jalapenos. She took a bite, and with her mouth still a little full, Adri asked her sister, "Did Jay like the pickled eggs, since they have that little bit of bite?"

"He thought they'd be better with even more chiles and turmeric. I told him I liked them just the way they are, but I'd try making some spicier ones if he wanted."

Adri said, "Maybe Dev would enjoy them since he doesn't eat meat." She gulped down some more beer, gathering the courage to tell her sister what she had come to talk about. She was ashamed, but she knew Paloma would understand. "Speaking of Dev, I did something I feel terribly guilty about."

"Really? Well good for you; do tell!"

"I looked through Dev's stuff to find out more about him."

Paloma shook her head and laughed at her little sister. "Well, of course you did! First chance I got I looked through Jay's nightstand drawer which had a giant tube of lube, condoms, a package of Benson and Hedges cigarettes, a gold—real gold—like 20 carat Dunhill lighter and a little ashtray. His medicine chest had some tampons in it too. This evidence led me to believe that I wasn't the first one to hit the sack with him. But it's my intention to be the only one from now on. I checked again recently and the lighter and cigarettes had magically disappeared. I didn't check for the tampons, but who knows, they might be useful in a pinch."

Adri put her elbow on the table and leaned her forehead in her hand and began to rub it.

"Shit! Did you find something really creepy?"

"I found a letter from someone named Tara who said how much she loved him and how she couldn't live without him and how he should come back to her."

Paloma said, "Well, that settles the question of whether he's gay or not. That's good for you I guess. So maybe he's just biding his time after ending a relationship. You know, maybe he's just now coming up for air and afraid to start something new, not wanting to hook up on the rebound." Paloma looked at Adri, whose head was still in her hand. "Jay has made my prying questions about Dev off limits. He says I need to respect you both enough to not butt in. He figures you're smart and old enough to take care of yourself and that you need to talk to Dev directly. That's the only argument we ever had. You know, other than who is better, Mexicans or Indians. I asked him about Dev's responsibility for leading you on. He finally agreed to say something to him. I don't know if he did, because this was just before Dev took off and left you to clean up after his damn cat."

"I like the cat."

"Ah, screw the cat." Paloma exhaled, blowing out through her lips making a less than lady-like raspberry. "Speaking of screwing, I think that's what you need to do. You need to find a guy and get all the attention you're missing; maybe it will help you get your confidence back."

Adri looked sideways at her sister and said, "Oh, good advice coming from someone who didn't even go out on a date for almost ten years after you divorced Ray's dad."

Paloma, tight lipped, said, "It was different, he was my husband and he betrayed our whole family, stole money from your father, fled and left me jobless and alone with a four-year-old son."

Adri suddenly realized how significantly different it was. She wasn't married, engaged, going steady or even intimate with Dev. "I'm sorry, you're right, there is no comparison. I'm just so fixated, looney tunes, and now jealous over the guy that I can't think straight. I don't have any confidence anymore and probably you're right and I should date someone else. I'm such a wimp I can't even confront Dev and ask him what the hell's up."

Little beads of sweat had appeared on Paloma's forehead.

She brought her hand up to her mouth covering a small belch. She said, "Sorry, gotta hit the head. I fear the effect of those diabolical pickled eggs is sneaking up on me."

Whiskey Sours

Dev had been gone for more than four weeks and she was beginning to wonder if he was a figment of her imagination. She thought that even if she was no more than a cat sitter to him, he should have gotten in touch by now. Jimmy had been courting and cajoling her, encouraging her to tell all. She told him repeatedly that she had absolutely nothing to tell. Recently she had become aware that he was courting her as a woman, not just as a prospective lead in a case he was trying to crack. She let him. Maybe Paloma was right and a little romance was the antidote to Dev.

Jimmy had never been in Adri's store. He found a parking place, no easy task on Second Street on a Saturday night in Belmont Shores. He walked down the block past people dining outside with their well-behaved dogs on leash while sipping craft beers. He was always a little intimidated when he walked through places he thought of as kind of hip. He wished he fit in, but his discomfort let him know that this wasn't his lifestyle even if he wanted it to be. At the next corner he spotted *El Corazon en Fuego* in an old stucco Spanish Revival style building. He looked in the shop window and saw that it was what his wife would call an upscale boutique. Instead of the usual mannequins, there were what looked like real Greek or Roman statues, only partially clad in embroidered blouses and velvet shawls. One wore a hat like a giant fruit bowl that reminded him of that lady with the maracas in old black and white movies. Twinkling lights were twined throughout the display, reflecting the gleam of silver pendants, rings and bibelots. Usually with one look he'd think, "too rich for my blood," and go to Sears to hunt for a piece of jewelry on sale for his wife's birthday. It was surprising to him that in spite of her advantages, Adri seemed very down to earth. He liked her as well as wanted her.

He walked in and a bell rang. He saw her standing behind an ornate antique cash register. She called out, "Just let me lock up and set the alarms and I'll be right with you."

"Your store is beautiful. I'm impressed!"

"Thanks, it's kind of fun to shop for it, but the day to day stuff is kind of a pain. Now I leave that mostly to my manager. It was so hot today. Do you think I need a wrap?"

Jimmy had never heard anyone actually use the word 'wrap,' just in books and to describe things that looked like cold burritos in funny colored tortillas. "Probably a good idea. Maybe we'll take a walk on the beach after dinner."

She grabbed a red shawl and threw it over her shoulder. She was wearing slim fitting black pants, some kind of white lacey top and red pumps that matched her 'wrap.'

"You look delicious. I've never seen you dressed up. I take it as a personal complement that you'd get even prettier than usual to go out with me." She walked toward him and he noticed her hair was up. She was wearing red lipstick and gave him a welcoming smile, so different from the mistrusting looks she gave him a couple of weeks before.

"Where are we going?"

"I thought Walt's Wharf in Seal Beach, okay? Then maybe a walk on the pier."

"Sure, that's fine." But Adri was thinking about her walk with Dev on that pier. She grimaced to herself and decided she'd better buck up and quit thinking about the past and move on. "I love getting that salad there. You know the one with the candied nuts and a piece of grilled salmon on top. And I think I'm ready for a martini or a whiskey sour before, and maybe wine with dinner too."

He ordered clam chowder and then the seared Ahi. They both had whiskey sours and the waiter suggested a light rose with the meaty tuna. Jimmy agreed and Adri noticed that the wine was the same color as her salmon. She also noticed she was pretty squiffed. She looked down at her black pants and they were covered with crumbs from the crusty French bread. She brushed them off and then reached for some more of the wine.

Making conversation, she said, "Did you get to see your son today? It must be awfully tough for him dealing with the divorce."

"I took him to the batting cages in Signal Hill. We had a great time, and he's still at home in his same room with the same routine, so things haven't changed that much for him." Jimmy had taken his son to the batting cages, but he knew that a divorce would only happen if Adri wanted to marry him. He thought that if that happened it would make a better life for everyone. He truly believed that with a woman like her he could become the kind of father and husband that people would look up to. Debbi would get a great settlement and he suspected she might be glad to get rid of him. He hadn't been the world's best husband. But with this girl in his life, he knew he could be his best self. "Would you like some dessert, maybe more wine?"

"No thanks, I'm really full and half drunk. So I'll just use the ladies room." When Adri stood up, she realized she was drunker than she thought. She toddled off to the restroom unsteadily while he took care of the bill. She brushed off any remaining crumbs, reapplied her lipstick and tried not to think of what would happen next. But when they stepped outside the air was balmy and she could smell the ocean. She was surprisingly relaxed and happy.

They walked to the pier where she had walked with Dev. She said, "Let's go down to the playground instead. I'd like to swing on the swings."

She took off her shoes when they reached the sand. It was still warm on top, but if she dug her feet down she could feel its coolness. She sat down in the canvas swing and he began to push her. She hadn't swung in years and the combination of whiskey sours, wine and the summer night made it all feel very special. He pushed her higher until the chains of the swing began to chink and shudder. She yelled, "Uncle! I can't take anymore." Then as the swing began to slow, she jumped out and landed in the sand on both feet, at least for a few seconds before she tumbled over.

He said, "Well, I was going to give you a 9.3 when I thought you'd stuck the landing, but it looks like you need more practice!" He began to chase her towards the water. When he caught her he put his arms around her from behind and held her tight. She could see the breaking edge of the waves slicing the darkness like a silver knife. He'd grown hard as he held her and began to kiss the side of her neck. Still holding her tight with his left arm, he began to remove the pins from her hair and as he did, he put his chin on the top of her head. She felt the strength of him even with only one arm around her and the insistence of his body against hers. He kissed the nape of her neck and she could hear his arousal in each of his breaths. He threw the bobby pins in the sand and gathered her hair up in his right hand and murmured, "I think I'm falling in love with you."

She twisted a little to face him, but her hair was wound round his hand. She could see the twinkle of the lights on the oil drilling platforms on the dark horizon and hear the pounding of the waves. The news on the radio had announced there was a large hurricane forming off Baja and that in a few days there would be record heat and huge surf. Seal Beach was south facing and she knew it always took a beating in storms, but right now it was beautiful. He unwound her hair from his hand and turned her towards him. Putting his arms around her waist, he lifted her up a little and kissed her. She knew that all first kisses were a surprise, and his was hard and insistent like his body. She reciprocated, and wondered how her mouth felt to him. He lowered her to the ground and she put her face in the crook of his neck. Only then did he relax his hold on her.

She turned herself within his embrace to look at the ocean, his arms still encircling her. Suddenly she stiffened and said, "Oh shit! The cat!"

He tightened his grip around her. "What cat?"

"Dev's cat. I forgot to feed him. I need to go and feed him."

"Screw the cat!"

She remembered her sister said the same thing, both of them with the same motive in mind. "I adore the cat and he's probably really hungry." Relieved that her responsibility to the cat would postpone her deciding what to do next, she said, "Oh come on, it won't take more than ten minutes."

"So you adore the cat. What about me?"

She grabbed his hand and pulled on his arm and said, "Come on silly, it's just up the ramp and a couple of blocks down Ocean."

This time Jimmy got to enter Tagore's house through the front door and with a key. He wondered if this was her way of letting him snoop around some more while pretending she had no responsibility for betraying Dev. She hurried into the kitchen, turned on the light, unlocked the back door and began calling the cat. He busied himself at the bookshelf, once more perusing the titles. He thumbed through a couple of the comic books and pushed aside the little book titled, The *Diamond Sutra,* and took a Kleenex out of his pocket to pick up the beautiful little jeweled silver box he'd seen on his first visit. He could hear Adri talking to the cat with sweet endearments in the other room. He heard her say, "Do you want some tea or coffee or something? He doesn't have much in the cupboard but that. No cream or milk for the coffee, but if you like it black it would be okay."

He thought a second and said, "Is the coffee instant? I hate instant." If she had to brew the coffee it would give him more time to look through Dev's papers and potential hiding places.

She peeked around from the little kitchen and said, "Not instant? Okay, then I'll brew some. I'll put on the kettle and have it done in a jiffy."

Jimmy said, "That would be great. Thanks. I'm going to use the head, okay?"

"Yeah sure, it's the middle door in the hallway."

Dracos looked at the ceiling in the hallway and spotted the trap door to the attic. He grabbed the straight backed chair from the bedroom and placed it under the trap door. He climbed up, pulled his smart phone from his pocket and turned on the flashlight app and pushed the wood up to look into the attic. It was little more than a crawl space, but he could see a line of white banker's boxes at the far end under the eaves. He was dying to get up there to investigate, but knew he couldn't do it now. He quietly lowered the opening in the ceiling, put the chair back in the bedroom and went in the bathroom to check it out.

Adri called out, "The coffee is ready."

She heard a loud scratchy noise followed by a substantial clink and then the toilet flush.

Jimmy came out and said, "The toilet was running. I had to get in the tank and readjust the seal."

"Oh, thanks. Here's the coffee. We can sit here at the table." She set down two mugs. "There is sugar if you want. Sorry there isn't anything much else but cat food in the house."

He smiled, "I'm pretty full, so no cat food for me. The coffee will do."

They drank their coffee quietly while Adri held the cat in her lap. Jimmy didn't like the idea of the cat, let alone the cat at the table, but didn't say anything. They finished their coffees and she headed to the kitchen and began to wash the mugs and the cat's dish. He put his arms around her waist again and nuzzled her neck breathing into her hair. After she had finished, he turned her face towards him to kiss her.

She put her hand to her mouth and said, "Sorry, my breath tastes awful. They're not kidding when they call them whiskey sours."

Jimmy pulled a stick of gum in a yellow wrapper from his pocket and offered it to her.

She said, "No thanks, I hate Juicy Fruit."

Flaming Hot Cheetos

Ray was worried because he hadn't heard from his dad. He left sixth period World History class and sat in the quad and tried to call him down in Mexico. They usually talked right after school every day. He hadn't been able to reach him yesterday and it worried him today, when his call didn't go through again. It was overcast and so was he. He sat on the brick planter and his butt just got sore and a little damp. Probably it was some problem with the satellites or towers or some stuff like that. The last time he'd talked to him, his father had been excited and said that he had some big news he was going to share with him pretty soon, but he needed to make more arrangements before he could tell Ray about it. He said it was something that he thought Ray would be happy about.

Ray began to stroll under the gnarled and twisty trunks of the California Pepper trees that lined the street by Cerritos High School; their weeping branches occasionally released a drip of moisture on the sidewalk or his head. He looked down at the new Carl Perkins style shoes that his aunt had given him for his birthday. They weren't blue suede like in the song, but had black splotches on white, or maybe the other way around; kinda like pinto pony or Dalmatian hide. He hoped to God they weren't really made of either of those, but they were the coolest kicks he'd ever seen. He pulled his hoodie over his pompadour, stuck his Ipod in his ear, and the shuffle played, *Down Where the Drunkards Roll* by Los Lobos. It was sad and pretty and full of such longing that it squeezed his heart. He had no idea what the words meant, but like Dylan's *Tangled up in Blue*, it made him feel loss and love and a whole bunch of feelings he couldn't put a name to. He felt so sad and lonesome for his dad. He hoped he could see him soon. But his mom said he couldn't go to Mexico until he was eighteen. He knew a lot of his hurt was because he couldn't understand why his dad had done that bad thing of stealing money from his *tia*. The question lived in his chest—hard, cold and always hurting. But he never could get himself to ask his father—*how could you've done this awful thing to us*?

He opened up a package of Flaming Hot Cheetos like he did every day after school. He loved their crunchy, citrusy, hot bite. He licked the maroon powder off his fingers, knowing they would be stained almost purple by the time he finished the package. He crossed the street to the Cerritos Public Library. He walked past a large silvery donut shaped sculpture and looked at the sliced swirling top hat upper story of the building. He was interested in buildings and thought he might want to be an architect. He was good at math like his dad and was artistic like his Aunt Adri. He didn't *really* want to be the big cheese at one of her factories like he kidded her when he called her *Tia Queso*. That sounded like a drag. He'd rather eat cheese than make it. She sure made some good cheese at her factory though. *Tia* Adri and his mom were on the board of directors of the new company. They had named it after his grandma, *Beatriz*. It was what they called a 'boutique' cheese company; that sounded kinda cutesy like a little fancy dress store, but they said it just meant that it was small and specialized. His aunt had designed a very cool logo and now they were selling cheese at all the fancy gourmet markets. They made these tasty goat cheeses, like with all kinds of nuts and herbs and stuff on them. He didn't know exactly what the stuff was, but they were delicious and in fact, he thought, would go really good with his Flaming Hots right now.

He entered the Cerritos Library and walked past an enormous aquarium which created a wall separating the children's section from the rest of the building. Today, two scuba divers were cleaning it. Now that was a pretty cool job. He watched the rays and small sharks and marveled at them like he had when he was a kid. He used to love to come to the children's section and watch the fish and wait to see the elusive moray eel. Then he'd walk past the aquarium and through the magic portal into the children's library inhabited by a full size T. Rex. But nowadays he liked to hang out in a different area of the library. Most of his friends went upstairs to the study carrels and plugged in their laptops, but he liked to sit alone. He walked past a Tudor style fireplace and high backed wing chairs in the reading room and went down the central hall under the Dale Chihuly hanging glass installation, its tendrils seemingly caught in a shaft of sunshine like anemones and seaweed waving gently in a calm sea. It reminded him of when they took a fake submarine ride in Catalina Island and saw a forest of swaying golden seaweed and orange Garibaldi fish darting in and out of sunlight and shadow.

This central hall led him down to the Craftsman-style periodical room. It was like a trip back in time to an earlier California. It seemed as if he could walk out of history class, cross the street, and suddenly be in the 1930's. The architect had created a Mission-Style pavilion within the library. Heavy oak timbers were joined with pegs and lit by bronze lamps with mica shades. He could imagine he might see Phillip Marlowe walk by, or Sam Spade hiding out behind a newspaper. He loved those L.A. Noir detective stories and the way things looked in those old movies. Students didn't often come to this section so he felt like it belonged to him alone.

He sat in a Stickley-style Morris chair, got out his history book and began to review for the test. He tried to think about World War I and the Archduke Franz Ferdinand, but his mind drifted. He doodled an 'archduck' with a sash and a crazy plumed hat on his book cover. Then he began picturing the back of Amy Kim's neck at the desk in front of him last period. She had these soft fuzzy hairs that kind of crept down her neck a little. No wonder he couldn't concentrate on the reasons why the Serbians and Austrians led the world to war, when all he wanted to do was nuzzle Amy Kim's neck. He gave up and decided maybe he'd go see if he could find a photograph of Dashiell Hammet.

He looked up to see a man in his late twenties come into the room. He had on long tight white socks, Levis that reached only to his shins and a glowing white tee shirt. His head was shaved and Ray could see the tops of a tattoo in old English script peeking out above the neck of his tee shirt. The guy looked like he'd just got out of prison and was totally out of place in a library. Ray wondered which gang he was in, *Chivas* or *Arta* from Artesia or *H.G.* in Hawaiian Gardens. He began to worry that the *vato* was going to ask him where he was from. He always said, 'Nowhere.' He didn't want anything to do with gangsters. He had heard a rumor that his dad and his mom's brother Victor might have been in H.G. when they were younger, but that was a long time ago. Ray started to pretend to concentrate on his reading, but the guy came right up to him.

"Hey man, you Ray?"

Ray looked up at him, and said, "Yeah who's asking?"

"Sorry Man, I'm Gerardo. I've got a message for you."

"Huh? From who?"

"Your Pops Man. He's here down in the Gardens. He wants me to bring you to where he's staying at. He doesn't want the cops to see him. He knows where you go after school. I'm supposed to bring you to him."

"No shit! Why didn't he tell me? Is that why he hasn't called me?"

"I don't know nothing about that *Ese*. All I know is you're supposed to come with me. Come on, he's waiting on you!"

Ray's heart was pounding and he couldn't think clearly. He was shocked, but couldn't believe his good luck. He was going to see his dad.

Ray gathered up his books, threw them in his book bag and

followed Gerardo to his car. He got in the passenger side of an older model brown Camry. It had a little statuette of the Virgin of Guadalupe on the dashboard. It smelled like weed.

Gerardo said, "You want a couple of hits on our way? You seem kinda nervous Homes."

Ray said, "Yeah okay I guess."

Gerardo handed him a joint and said, "You light it dude. Go ahead and take a couple of tokes. I'll catch up with you later, *eh*? I need to concentrate on my driving. *Tu sabes*?"

Ray lit the joint. He'd only gotten high a couple of times before and didn't really like it, but this was a strange situation. He felt awkward with this guy and didn't want to seem ungrateful. He wanted to be cool with him and also with his dad. He hadn't seen his father in so long he wasn't sure that he would even remember what he looked like. So he inhaled a couple of hits. He noticed the pepper trees he'd walked under earlier as they headed south past the high school. They looked weepy and far away to him. He felt sleepy and sick; then he saw no more.

Flaming Hot Cheetos Redux

His eyes wouldn't open. His body was shivering wildly, almost bouncing with the shudders that wracked his small frame. He was awake, but he was no one, alive but with no awareness of self or memory, only a drive to survive. Gradually his identity began to emerge from this amnesia. He wanted to cry but it hurt really bad like a stone was in his throat and tears wouldn't come. He reached up to his eyes and noticed his hands were bound. He felt something slick over his eyes. 'Oh Jesus God where are my eyes? Somebody took my eyes.' His nose was backing up with unshed tears and his throat seemed to grow larger and more painful. He couldn't catch enough breath.

Desperate to breathe, he felt for his mouth, touching a smooth tightness. He began to realize it was duct tape and someone had bound and taped him. He worked his hands up toward his lips to work the tape away from his mouth so he could get some air. He picked at an edge of the tape, worrying it away from his cheek. His nose was so clogged with snot that he needed desperately to get air through his mouth. With cold dead fingers he rolled and fiddled and finally got a grip on the edge of the tape. He put both sides of that edge between his numb fingers. It slipped out of his grasp. He pushed his fingers together on either side of the corner of tape until they hurt and he could feel the pressure in his knuckles, and then brought both hands down with a jerk. This released a tiny corner of the tape from his mouth. He stuck his index finger in the tiny gap and started working an opening. He was able to insert the top of his finger into his mouth between the sides of his lips. He pushed it in hard up to the first joint and quickly pulled it out so he could get some air. His tongue was flooded with sour, salt, hot. In his darkness he could remember maroon fingers stained by Flaming Hot Cheetos, and then as he inhaled through the opening in the tape, he remembered everything.

He just breathed for a while. In deeply, out in short bursts. He was relieved and a little less scared. Where the hell was he? He decided he'd take half the tape from his mouth and be able to re-stick it down if they came to check on him. He began to gradually work the tape from his eye. It hurt a lot more than from his lips and the remnants of spicy salty powder from his fingers stung his eye. Who the fuck was the guy who told him he was taking him to his Dad and why had he been so stupid to just go with that prick in his stinky pot infused old piece of shit car? I must be the dumbest dumb shit in the whole world. He was both ashamed of his neediness to see his father and angry that he'd been so easy to fool. He didn't want his old man to be the one responsible for this miserable bullshit. He kept old photos of him in his desk drawer. Ray realized he had begun to look just like him, dark and very skinny. Maybe this was some kind of initiation, like being jumped into a gang. Then he tried to get a grip and hissed to himself, "Shut up *tonto*, don't be such a fucking baby!"

Suddenly pale light met his eye. There wasn't much light where he was being kept, but compared with the utter darkness of his taped eyes, it seemed easy to see. His face was close to a wall that appeared slightly curved. He blew his nose and salty watery mucous covered his lips and the back of his hand, but he could breathe better. He inhaled deeply through his nose and it smelled musty and dank, but not unfamiliar. He thought whoever tied him up wasn't a very sophisticated criminal. He read all those mysteries and any idiot bad guy should know not to tie his victim's hands in front of his body.

He had never been so cold and the circulation was cut off pretty badly from his hands and feet. He twisted his skinny little body and tried to bounce onto his back from his side so he could get a look at something other than the weird curved wall that he was staring at. He managed to get on his back and raise his head a little. He could see that the room came to a point towards his feet. He was in some kind of bunk, the mattress was covered with rough orange fabric with piping, and the wall he'd been facing had a piece of newspaper taped over a small oval window. That's when he realized he was in a compartment in the bow of a boat. Thoughts of being dumped at sea, never seeing his mom, never ever getting to go home again and dying in the ocean overwhelmed him. He began to sob and he choked a little and then retched. He threw up the mucousy maroon remnants of his Cheetos; they dribbled down the side of his face mingling with his tears.

Hamburger Happy Meal

He dreamed he was swimming through the library. The sharks were all around and the water was very cold. He kept wondering why he didn't have a wetsuit like the frogmen. He could breathe but it was very hard and it hurt to breathe in the icy water. The T-Rex with his tiny arms couldn't swim so he just stayed on the bottom of the library. Ray swam past the pretty fireplace and down the hallway past the library checkout counter and then he and the water rose until he was swimming among the glass Dale Chihuly sculptures. They had sprung to life as real undulating golden seaweed. Brilliant orange Garibaldi fish peeked out of the crevices and scary narrow silver barracuda darted towards him. He could see his mother and aunt further down near the periodical room, their long hair floating with the seaweed. They looked so pretty and he thought he could hear them singing mermaid songs. Then he looked up toward where the roof should be and he could see the bottom of an aqua surfboard with two silvery legs and feet dangling through the liquid distortion above him. He needed to swim up to the surfboard and warn Dev about the moray eel and something else important that he couldn't quite remember. But the harder he swam the farther the board was from him. He was kicking hard but realized he had on his black and white Carl Perkins shoes, not swim fins. He was sinking faster and faster until the blue surfboard was very tiny above him. Then from the bottom of the pool, the T Rex was saying, "Hey Kid—hey Kid—hey Homie*!*" He could feel the creature's little reptile arms pushing on his shoulder. It said, "Wake up *pendejo,* I got something for you to eat."

He sat up so fast he hit his head on the roof above his bunk. He felt his hands and they were still bound, but he remembered he'd neglected to re-tape the corner of his mouth. Gerardo grabbed the tape from the corner of his mouth and pulled it off quickly. He said, "It hurts less if you do it fast." Ray was surprised Gerado hadn't bothered to notice that it was already partially un-taped.

Ray sucked in great gulps of air. His lungs hurt bad and his head was pounding. He didn't know if it was from the drugs or from smacking it on the roof of his bunk.

Gerardo said, "I got you a Hamburger Happy Meal and a bottle of water."

"Thanks man, I'm really thirsty." Ray had decided to be as calm as possible and to try and find out what was going on. He didn't want to keep being a crybaby. He wanted off this boat, and though he wasn't strong, he knew he was smart. Gerardo opened the bottle of water and placed it in Ray's taped hands. He guzzled it down so fast the plastic bottle popped and crackled as it caved in. He could hear Gerardo unwrap the hamburger and he replaced the empty water bottle in Ray's hands with the burger.

Gerardo said, "Oh Man, I hate it when the fries are cold." Ray tried to chew on the hamburger but despite drinking all the water he had too little saliva to chew it. He kept on trying and did a little better but it hurt like a bitch to swallow.

Ray said, "Hey dude, didn't the meal come with a coke? I'm still thirsty." Gerardo held the coke and Ray finally got the straw into his mouth and guzzled some down.

"I liked Happy Meals when I was a kid like you. So I thought you would too. This one has a super hero toy. Look at it

Bro, it's really cool." Only then did Gerardo apparently realize that Ray's eyes were still taped. He grabbed the loosened corner from below Ray's left eye and tore the duct tape up halfway. Ray could make out in the dim light Gerardo holding a little toy. As his eyes adjusted he recognized the shiny silver figurine on its flying board as the Silver Surfer. Gerardo held the toy and zoomed it through the air making whooshing noises. It was then that Ray realized that not only were Gerardo's fries cold, he was at least a few fries short of a Happy Meal. He wondered if this might make Gerado even more unpredictable. Ray knew about being bullied and understood what it was like to be different. He also had read about the 'Stockholm Effect.' So Ray decided he'd try to befriend Gerardo and play on his feelings that he was just a little kid. So he said, "Oh man, I love the Silver Surfer, he's so cool! I heard there is an old series with him called *Galactus the Devourer* that has kick ass art. I'd like to read those."

"When I was locked up I had a nice teacher that let us look at comics. I like the Hulk the best, him and Wolverine."

"Thanks man, you really did me a solid cause I love Silver Surfer. I mostly like Marvel, but I like the Green Lantern too, even though he's D.C. But Silver Surfer is so righteous! Have you read any with both the Hulk and Silver Surfer? I know there are some but I don't have them. Maybe you could come over to my house some time and borrow some of my comics. You'd like my mom. She used to be a music teacher. She also sang in some bands you might know. She was the singer in the *Vatos Tacos*. My old man played lead guitar."

"Yeah, I think I heard of them. What kinda music?"

"Rockabilly or maybe sorta psychobilly; sometimes she calls it beanerbilly. She was in a bunch of weird bands, *Paloma and the Greasers*, *Quiff and the Dickies*, and a girl band called the *Fluffy Tacos*. Those all sound kinda nasty huh? But the *Vatos Tacos* had some local hits, and a lot of people liked them."

"Is she in a band now?"

"No, not after my dad ditched us and went to Mazatlan."

"Yeah I heard." Gerardo looked down and said, "Listen, Kid, I lied to you about your dad. Your pops didn't have nothing to do with this. The big man who hired me told me to say that bullshit to you, so you'd come with me. I feel bad about that. *Lo siento*."

Ray wasn't sure if he was relieved or even more frightened. He was pretty sure his father wouldn't hurt him, but that meant that somebody else had kidnapped him. He said to Gerardo, "Thanks for telling me that. I was feeling pretty sad, cause I love my pops."

"Yeah, I get it. My dad split after we came up from Mexico. We came up when I was seven and stayed with my *tio* in Cudahy. He worked at Farmer John; you know, where they make the bacon, sausage and shit. Then my *mami* moved in with her boyfriend and we went to live in the Gardens. I went to school at Hawaiian Elementary. It was cool there. Is that where your mom was a *maestra*?"

"No, she taught music at Wilson High in Long Beach."

"I got kicked outta regular high school right away and went to CYA in Norwalk. Then I went to Tracy in Cerritos. The teachers were really nice there, but I got arrested again. So then I got sent to camp at the CMC West and then I ended up in CMC East for nine years. The camp was cool; we got to work on putting out fires and stuff. But California Men's Colony East sucked."

Ray had heard of CYA, that was the California Youth Authority and that is probably where the teacher that let Gerardo read comic books was. Apparently he had spent a bunch of his life in prison. Ray guessed that he had done something pretty bad to get locked up for nine years – probably sentenced to stay twice that. He wasn't going to ask him about that. Instead he said, "I gotta piss bad man. I'm about to wet my *chones*. Can you take me to the bathroom?"

"Yeah, maybe, I guess so. Couldn't you just go in a cup?"

"No Dude, I gotta take a dump too."

"Okay but don't take the tape off your eyes." He stuck the loosened tape down over Ray's eye. Gerardo helped Ray off the bunk, putting his hand gently on his head like a cop guiding a prisoner into the cop car.

He led him across the corridor to the head, then directed him to the toilet. He said, "You gotta sorta pump the thing on the floor to flush. I'm thirsty, I'm gonna get me a beer. Call when you're done." He closed the door behind him.

Ray pulled the tape up where it was loosened over his eye. He was in the bathroom of a boat, but there was no porthole to see out of. There were pretty aqua hand towels with embroidered seahorses, sea shell soaps in an abalone shell and a blow dryer on the counter. He quietly opened the medicine chest. There were a bunch of lipsticks, eye pencils, mascara and a tweezers on the lowest shelf. The next shelf had toothpaste, two toothbrushes, dental floss, a razor, shaving cream and a couple of condoms. The top shelf had Tums, Aspirin and a prescription bottle. Ray stuffed a toothbrush, tweezers and the dental floss in his pocket. He figured it would be hard to use the disposable razor to do any kind of MacGyver weapon thing with, but even though it would not be great to get caught with it, he stuck it in his pocket anyway. As for the floss and toothbrush, he could always tell Gerardo that he always brushed after every meal. He reached up and got four aspirin out of the bottle and grabbed three Tums. He threw the aspirins in his mouth, ran the faucet into his cupped hand and drank as much water as he could hold, then chewed up the Tums.

Gerardo yelled, "You about done in there, Kid?"

He glanced at the prescription bottle and pulled it out. It was for Oxycodone. He had a feeling that was something Gerardo might enjoy. He filled his pocket with a dozen or so, leaving the bottle on the counter in his rush.

He yelled back, "Yeah, I just gotta get this pump thingie to work!"

He grabbed the condoms and stuck them in his jacket pocket and wondered what McGyver would do with them, then realized he'd probably use them when he got laid which was probably after every episode. He loved watching those old re-runs on T.V. He thought the only way he'd ever get lucky, is if he got his pitiful ass off this boat and didn't die doing it. Ray knew for sure that he was way over his head, sinking in some very deep shit. He turned and pumped hard with his oversized black and white Carl Perkins shoes until the toilet flushed. As he stuck the tape back over his eye, he yelled, “I’m done!”

Mountain Dew and Dos Equis Dark

Ray woke to very loud shuddering sounds. His mattress seemed to convulse. Beneath him the engines of the boat roared. Then doors, cabinets and other mysterious boat parts began to vibrate rapidly and crazily near him. Just when he thought the boat might explode, the resonating pulses stopped and the engine noises evened out. He was still groggy from the drugs he'd been given last night when Gerardo, apologizing repeatedly, gently injected him. He didn't stay conscious for long.

He woke again later, not knowing how long the boat had been moving. He could feel it hitting swells and thought they may have traveled farther out to sea. He decided to try to get out of his bindings and hide somewhere else, maybe get a life jacket and jump overboard, anything that would give him a chance to survive. Gerardo had neglected to re-tape the duct tape over his mouth and Ray tore it off easily, then ripped the tape from his eyes as fast as he could. He brought his taped wrists up to his mouth and began to try to chew and rip them off. The tape didn't yield to his biting, only ripping slightly along its silvery length. He tried instead to figure out which was the outside end of the tape so he could grab it with his teeth and unwind it by holding its edge in his teeth while pulling his wrists in the opposite direction. He'd sometimes get a good grip pulling it up a fraction of an inch. As he tired, his jaw and teeth ached, so he rolled his head back on the cot to rest a little. His mouth tasted like a sewer, and when he exhaled, he could smell the foulness of his own breath. Dim light shone through the newspaper taped over the porthole.

He looked up at the newspaper and wondered if it was the Long Beach *Press Telegram* or the L.A. *Times*. He knew it was stupid to let his mind wander away from escaping, but then he saw the brass flange for opening the porthole. He kneeled on the bunk and worked his wrists against the flange trying to saw off the tape. That wasn't working so he hung his wrists over the flange using his entire weight trying to stretch the tape out. He hated the sticky shit! He stretched and pulled, but the tape would only stretch a little and was cutting painfully into his wrists.

Exhausted and hopeless, he stopped for a while and suddenly remembered he had stuck all the stuff from the bathroom in his pocket. He lifted his bound wrists from the porthole flange and shimmied on to his side. Using his bound hands, he tried to fish the plastic razor out of his pocket. He could feel the toothbrush, then the foil edge of the condom package, and then he slid his finger along the sharp edge of the razor. Feeling like a fool, he realized he'd stuck it in handle side down. He fiddled and fished feeling the sharp blade against his fingertips and finally got the razor out and manipulated the handle between his teeth. Now, he began to saw the tape in earnest. The disposable razor cut slowly through the silver layer, his hands moving back and forth against the razor held tight in his teeth. He bit down on the razor hard and heard the plastic begin to crack. He kept sawing, his eyes focused on the four square inches of duct tape in front of his face. More of the silver coating gave way and he could see the razor was making inroads into the tape's fibrous interior. Within a minute or two the tape gave way and he freed his hands. He shook them, the tape still flapping around them, and rubbed them hard. He saw that his finger and palms were covered in a light film of blood.

He looked at his hands and saw that he'd cut his fingertips getting the razor out of his pocket. He brought his fingers closer to his face to look at the cuts and the warm iron smell of his own blood overwhelmed and frightened him.

He reached up to the porthole and tore the newspaper away. It *was* the Long Beach *Press Telegram*. He looked down at the paper in his hand and recognized Tim Grobaty's face. His mom and *tia* always read his column. He sighed and looked out the porthole. The sun was low over what looked to him like an endless sea. The emptiness filled him and he was sure he would never see his family again. He rested a little and thought. The boat must be pretty far out because he had been to Catalina before and you usually didn't have to wait long to see a boat on its way to or from Avalon. He was very thirsty again. He didn't know if it was tomorrow or the day after tomorrow. His anxiety and confusion seemed insurmountable, but he knew he must keep trying to get away. He decided to creep around and find a weapon and a hiding place.

Just then he heard footsteps coming down the ladder and someone slam the door to the head across the hall. He quickly got up. His foot was asleep but he jumped and dragged himself out into the hall and shut his cabin door as quietly as he could. He climbed up the wooden steps to the main cabin and looked around. The tiny galley was neatly fitted out with wood, with a kind of booth-like table and benches. He could see out the larger side windows and saw a tanker or some other big ship very far away to his left. Then looking up to his right he saw another ladder and at its top a view of more sky. He climbed up the wooden rungs, his foot now tingling but working, and peeked around the corner. He could see what must be the bridge of the boat with a big wooden helm and lots of dials, but nobody was there. Then he heard the loud sucking noise of the toilet being pumped and flushed. He quickly climbed the rest of the way up on to the bridge. He noticed a red fire extinguisher in the corner, grabbed it and went out the side door, which was hooked open onto the outside deck. He looked forward and Gerardo was sitting next to the railing near the very front of the boat. He heard him retch and realized the dude was seasick. He moved to the left trying to balance himself because the boat was pitching a lot. The fire extinguisher was heavy and the railing was slick with dew. He slid on the wet deck, but managed to move farther toward the back of the boat, while hanging onto both the railing and the fire extinguisher. Still groggy from the drugs, his heart began to pound and he remembered there was someone else on the boat and he needed to hide. For a second he hoped it was his dad, but remembered what Gerardo had said about lying to him. This kidnapping had to be about something else. Maybe they wanted his aunt's money. He held tight to the fire extinguisher and continued working his way toward the back of the boat.

He heard a man come out of the door to the bridge and walk out to the front deck of the boat. He was speaking Spanish to Gerardo, but Ray couldn't make out what he was saying. The wind was blowing his words away. Then he heard in English, "You stupid dumb fuck!"

He couldn't hear Gerardo at all. The man came fast down the side of the boat toward Ray but turned and went into the bridge and down the ladder to the cabin. Ray could see him by looking in through the big portholes on the side. He was a big man with huge shoulders. Ray couldn't see his face because at that angle it was concealed by the hood of his sweatshirt. The man began to turn and Ray wanted to look at his face but realized that then the kidnapper would see him too. He ducked down low and looked around. He saw another ladder, but this one was vertical steep metal. He wasn't sure he could get up it with the fire extinguisher in his hand. He unbuttoned the top button of his pants and unzipped and then stuck the fire extinguisher down the waistband of his jockey shorts. It was cold, hard and cumbersome, but Ray was skinny and he squeezed the zipper back partway. He started climbing and just after he got to the top he heard the man yelling.

"Where the fuck is the kid? What the hell did you do, you stupid son of a bitch." The sound was still spotty but carried on the wind better up there.

He heard Gerardo say, "I didn't do nothing, the kid is here."

Ray heard the man shout again. "No, he must have got loose." The wind changed and he heard the words, "Oxy, bottle and my name." Then the wind rested a little and Ray heard the screaming man saying, "Shit! Shit! We have to find the little prick, he knows who I am!"

Ray now looked around the topmost deck. There was a winch in the center, a dinghy and a couple of weird yellow plastic paddle boards or kayaks. He crept up closer to the front to look over the edge to see the men below him on the prow of the boat. The yelling man was broad backed, not built like he remembered his father.

Gerardo yelled, "He's a nice little kid, you better not hurt him!"

"Don't you tell me what to do—*Tonto*, fuckin' retard!"

"Take that back *puto*! I don't want you to hurt the kid."

The broad shouldered hooded man slapped Gerardo across the face. Gerardo struck back, and the bigger man started to hit Gerardo again and again, banging his head against the railing. Ray thought that he was going to kill him. With the fire extinguisher still stuffed down his pants he climbed down the steep aluminum ladder and made his way along the narrow deck alongside the larger portholes toward the bow. The boat was lurching in unexpected ways. Ray pulled the fire extinguisher out from his pants, grabbed it in both hands, and stumbled across the wooden deck, hitting the back of the bigger man's head as hard as he could. He bashed him twice, and the man lay on top of Gerardo whose head was hanging back over the deck, his face and mouth bloodied. Ray could see blood was seeping out from the edge of the big man's hood onto the deck. Both of them lay still. Ray dropped the bloodied fire extinguisher on the wooden deck and it began to roll back and forth in an arc in time with the pitch of the boat leaving a small bloody crescent in its wake. Ray felt woozy and cold. He was shaking all over. He had killed a man. He needed to get help somehow.

He lurched back onto the bridge. There was a large ship's wheel, lots of shiny dials and cords, and above them what looked like radio equipment. There were three different things that looked like phones. Then he heard the radio, "This is warship 713, be aware of my presence near Coronado Bridge." Ray thought that was the bridge that went to Coronado Island down by San Diego. We must be really far south, maybe in Mexico off the coast near T.J. or Ensenada. Then he heard a different voice, "Coast Guard warning, watch carefully for individuals on paddleboards for the annual Manhattan Beach to Catalina paddleboard race, now approaching Rocky Point in light fog." Now Ray was totally confused about where the boat might be.

He thought if he could find his cell phone, at least he might be able to turn it on or make an emergency call and they could locate the boat. He knew that by now his mom and aunt would be going nuts trying to find him. He was pretty sure Gerardo wouldn't have thrown away the brand new iphone his *tia* had given him. It was too valuable. He wondered if Gerardo was smart enough to turn it off so it wouldn't be tracked and then hide it to get later.

So he decided to go below and see if he could find where Gerardo had put his cell phone. He went into the main room and started to look on every shelf. Then in the galley he pulled open all the kitchen drawers and found the knives. He put a sharp short paring knife in his pocket. He could feel the toothbrush and dental floss. He stuck a second knife in his other pocket. He began climbing the wooden steps down to the back of the boat to see if there was another cabin. Moving back past his little cabin and the head, there was a door at the end of the hallway. He opened it and saw a mussed up bed in the center of the cabin pushed up against a wall that must be the stern of the boat. He started looking on the nightstand, bookshelves, and then noticed another door. He opened it. It was a second tiny bathroom. He looked on the little counter. No phone.

He ran back up to the ladder steps, climbed up to the main area and started looking on surfaces there. There were dirty dishes in the sink, the wrappers from his Happy Meal, an open green can of Mountain Dew and a half drunk bottle of *Dos Equis Amber*, but no phone. He was so thirsty that he picked up the Mountain Dew and gulped it down. The drink of nerds and hillbillies. Still thirsty he grabbed the *Dos Equis* and gulped down its warm bitterness. He wondered what happens when you combine hillbilly nerd with the *Dos Equis* Guy. Do you become the most interesting redneck in the world? He realized his mind was wandering again. He shook his head and focused on the phone. It must be in Gerardo's pocket. His head was suddenly clearer and he realized he'd have to roll the dead man off of Gerardo to be able to get into his pockets. He climbed up to the bridge again and went to the side door to go out on the bow where the two men lay. He started out the door onto the deck when he heard something far above him on the topmost deck. He looked out on the wooden slats of the bow and Gerardo lay alone. The fire extinguisher was gone too. All that remained was the little bloody tracery of its rolling arc. He looked up at the dials above the ship's wheel on the bridge and saw that all the cords to the phones had been cut. They swung back and forth like pendulums to the rhythm of the boat as it rolled to and fro in the swells.

A Few Swallows of Water

Ray watched the swinging of the cut spiraling black microphone cords above him for a moment, then looked out through the glass windshield of the bridge and saw only water. All around him only water. He was so incredibly thirsty his throat hurt and his lips were cracked and sticking to his teeth. He knew he needed to hide from the big guy who was apparently still alive. Ray couldn't go out and look for his cell phone in Gerardo's pockets because the guy would see him if he was still up on the top of the boat. He figured it would be better to look for some place to hide.

He moved through his thirst and exhaustion. Doing anything seemed better than staying still. He crept as quietly as he could down the wooden steps into the main cabin. He looked around, trying to see if there was someplace he could get inside of to hide. There was just that table with the curved padded bench, the couch and some bookcases. He walked around the counter into the galley, and opened the lower cabinets, but they were full of pots and pans.

He went down the next set of steps and into the short hallway. There was a small washer and dryer tucked behind the steps. He was skinny, but didn't think he'd fit in them. That left the two bedrooms and bathrooms. There was nothing in his little cabin but the bed and he didn't ever want to go in there again. He figured he might be safest if he locked himself in the little bathroom by the larger cabin at the rear. So he went in and sat down on the toilet, locked the door and listened for the man. Sitting on the toilet with the boat swaying back and forth he thought he was gonna hurl. He gagged a little but nothing came up. He remembered he had knives, but if the guy broke down the door it would be good to have something longer or heavier or somehow more dangerous than the paring knives.

He stood up and realized that this tiny bathroom didn't have a shower like the other one. People probably used it mostly to take a pee during the night. Ray realized he hadn't peed in a long time. So he stood and faced the wall, rocking back from one foot to the other with the pitch of the boat, and tried to go. The urine wouldn't come and it hurt a little. Finally some pee came out but it was really dark. It looked like the *Dos Equis* dark amber beer. He didn't flush. He was too afraid to run the water to get a drink because he might be heard.

He heard heavy steps coming down the hall. And then after a minute or so, he heard three little 'tinking' sounds like a cell phone being turned on. Then the man's voice high pitched and strange began to speak. Ray realized he was disguising his voice.

". . . a million in unmarked bills for the safe return of the boy and security that I won't blow a bunch of people up in the biggest terrorist attack since 9/11. If you contact the cops and I don't get the money by tomorrow, I'll cut the boy's head off and film his beheading for you and the rest of the world to see! Then I'll blow up hundreds, maybe thousands of people, and that responsibility will be on your head too—just like your boy's head—which you'll see rolling around on the ground!"

Ray was so far past terrified that he felt numb. He heard a snapping noise as the man shut the phone. He realized it must be a flip phone, maybe a cheap one that the guy would throw away. Ray thought he might have more than one phone then. He heard the guy curse again. "Fuck! I gotta find the little *pendejo*."

Ray heard the man's footsteps as he walked back down the hall and up the steps. He waited a second and looked for a weapon. All he could find was a plastic toilet brush, which he figured would hurt pretty bad if you poked it in somebody's eyes. He unlocked the bathroom door and opened it as quietly as he could. Now on the bed where there had been nothing before, lay two phones, neither of which were Ray's. One was a flip phone, the other a smart phone. He figured the smart phone would have some kind of tracking ability, so he picked it up. He called his mother's number and heard her voice, "Hi this is Paloma. I'm not available right now. Please leave your name and number and I'll get back to you as soon as possible."

"Ma, Pick up it's me!" Ray whispered urgently. "I'm kidnapped on a . . ." Before he could say 'boat' he heard the recording time out with a buzzing tone.

Ray couldn't think of anybody's phone number because he was so used to using the contact features of his iphone to call his aunt and friends. Then he remembered that the last time Dev had taken him surfing he told Ray he could call him anytime. They were out in the water and since he couldn't write it down, he had memorized his number, no, not a number, a word. N-i-r-v-a-n-a, like the band. He punched it in and hoped he had it right.

Ray heard, "Hello."

Ray whispered, "Dev it's me Ray. I'm kidnapped on a boat. There are two guys, one is maybe dead the other is trying to hurt me. I've gotta find a place to hide. My mom isn't picking up her phone."

Dev heard that the boy was sobbing a little. "You're not kidding are you?"

"No, Man. For real!"

"Okay, on a boat, kidnapped?"

"Yeah, way far out in the ocean. I'm so fuckin' scared man. Help me please."

"Is this your phone?"

"No, the kidnap guy's."

Dev said, "Does he know you have it?"

"No, I need to hide right away."

Dev could hear the fear in the boy's voice and what must be the humming of engines in the background. He said, "Listen, there has to be a way down to where the engines are. Maybe a trap door in the floor, probably in the main area. It might be under a rug or something. Find it and hide down there. Put the phone back where you found it and try to go down to the engine room and pull the trap door hatch back down. I'm calling your mom and the police right now."

"He said no police when he made a phone call. He said if he didn't get money, he would cut off my head. Oh, Jesus, please help me."

"Leave the phone on so they can find the coordinates of the signal. And listen Ray, I've got your back I won't let you down. I promise you that. Go now and stay put."

"Okay, but I'm so scared."

"Yeah, me too. But Ray, all of us love you so much. Think of that while you hide okay?"

"Bye. Tell Mom and Tia I love them."

"Done! Go now!"

Ray could hear the big man turning over the kayak or dinghy or something big on the top deck hunting for him. He put the phone back where he found it on the bed. He ran up the short steps to the main area, saw a small rug on the floor, grabbed it and shoved it as far under the couch as he could reach. There was an inset ring in the hatch. He lifted it up and sure enough there was a ladder down to the engine compartment. He felt around for a light switch and found it. He crept down the steps into the engine room.

The area was surprisingly clean. The engines were shiny like ones you would see under the hood at a car show. He saw some tools and a bottle of what was labeled distilled water. Still holding his toilet brush, he closed the hatch above him. He grabbed the plastic water bottle, found the light switch and turned it off, then settled in to wait to be found or rescued. The bottle of water was light. He unscrewed the cap and glugged the few swallows of stale water left in it. He felt above him for the handle of the hatch and held it down tight.

Double-Double, No Meat

It had been cool a few weeks ago when Dev parked the Volvo in Lot C, the long term parking at LAX. This afternoon when he opened the door, the waves of heat that hit him were dog and baby killers. He rolled down the window on the driver's side and got in. The fabric seats were tolerable, but when he touched the steering wheel his hands jerked off its sizzling surface. He reached for his jacket in the back seat and threw it over the steering wheel. He hoped the car battery wasn't dead from sitting so long. He pressed the accelerator to the floor, put the key in the ignition and it turned over on the first try. As he merged east onto the 105, the mountain tops weren't visible, the horizon instead filled by towering anvil shaped thunder clouds. He had accomplished what he hoped to do and felt a sense of relief. He looked at the ominous clouds building over the mountains. He had spent too much of his life in mountains. He was glad to be done with them.

He threw his jacket in the back seat since the heat of the steering wheel had dissipated, leaned over and unrolled the passenger window to let in more air. He was covered in sweat but as he increased his speed, the hot air began to evaporate the moisture on his face and the hair at the nape of his neck became increasingly cool.

He realized he was very thirsty or hungry or both. He got off the freeway and drove a little bit, then spotted the yellow and red arrow sign of an In-N-Out Burger. There was a line of cars at the drive-thru window and he joined the queue. Jay always ordered a double-double, fries and a shake. Dev looked at the menu and couldn't figure out what to get. A girl's voice asked for his order, and he said, "I'd like a double-double, fries and a vanilla shake and no meat on the double-double please."

"What?"

He repeated himself.

"That's no meat, right? Would you like your onions grilled?"

"I don't know. Sure, I guess."

"Okay, Sir, that is one double-double everything on it but the patties, with grilled onions, fries and a vanilla shake. Will that complete your order?"

"Yes thanks."

"Please pull up to the window."

Dev watched as the girl sidled her way around the crowded preparation room and worked her way over to the window to hand him his milkshake. He pulled the paper off the straw and took a giant swallow. His forehead singed with the hit of cold ice cream. The girl handed him a bag and he drove through, hunting for a place in the shade to park. He noticed his phone attached to the charger in the Volvo's lighter and he thought he better switch it on. It had been off the whole time he had been gone.

The fries were hot and salty and he was hungry for something savory. Hot salty greasy fries were just the ticket. The ice cream headache subsided as quickly as it had appeared. He hadn't eaten much but rice, millet and vegetables for weeks, and the fries tasted great. He unwrapped the paper from his burgerless burger and tucked into it. It was fabulous. Thousand Island dripped into the wrapper and coated the tomatoes, onion and lettuce. The cheese was American and he didn't even care if it tasted and felt like plastic. It was delicious. After he'd wolfed it down, he wiped his hands on a wad of napkins, and sucked hard on his straw to get every last bit of the now melted vanilla shake. His phone rang and he jumped a little. He looked at the number. It was from the 562 area code, but he didn't recognize it. Probably somebody trying to sell him solar heating or clean his carpets.

"Hello."

He heard a boy whispering, his voice strained and high. It was Ray. He told Dev that he was kidnapped, on a boat, and guys were trying to hurt him. He said the phone he was calling from was the kidnapper's and that his mother wasn't answering his calls. Dev believed him immediately and told him to hide in the engine compartment. Adrenaline swam through Dev's limbs and he became conscious of his own heart swollen and pounding. He wasn't sure what to do. He sat still a moment. He dialed Adri.

"Hello?"

"Yeah listen, I just got a call from your nephew saying he was kidnapped on a boat. He can't get through to his mom. Do you know about this?"

"Wait. Let me step outside, cell reception sucks in here."

He had heard hesitancy in her voice and asked, "Are you okay? Can you talk?"

"Yes. I'm outside. The kidnappers say no police, but there is a cop with us, a guy from Homeland Security. I'm not sure I should talk to you. Is Ray okay?"

"He was a couple of minutes ago. He sounds terrified. He says he's on a boat with two guys. I told him to hide in the engine compartment. But I have the kidnapper's phone number. Ray called from his phone. He said that Paloma didn't pick up when he called."

"Jesus." She began to weep. "Thank God he's still alive. I don't know what to do. I shouldn't be talking to you."

"Why is there only one cop—and from Homeland Security? You need to contact the FBI, the Coast Guard, all of that."

"They said they would kill him. The cop is an old friend of the family."

"Well Ray's in deep shit, so you may hate me for this but I'm calling the cops."

She sighed and began to sob.

Dev said, "I'll call back as soon as I can. I'm back in L.A. on my way home. I'll get on the 605 in a minute. I'm going to make the call now."

Dev called 911. He told them about the call from Ray and the number the call had come from. He told the operator he was in the car driving home. She asked where the residence of the child was. He didn't know the exact address, but said his name was Ray Vargas, his mother's name Paloma, and they lived on Belshire in Artesia. The operator said she was connecting him to the Cerritos Sheriff's station.

First he spoke to a sheriff's officer, who said he would call him right back. But instead, when the phone rang, it was Petty Officer Leslie who identified himself as the watch stander at the Coast Guard Station in San Pedro. Dev explained the phone call from Ray. Officer Leslie said they were going to try to track the cell number from the phone call and send a helicopter out to those coordinates. He told Dev that there were no alerts for a kidnapped juvenile currently. Dev told him that he had received the call from the boy, but that the mother and sister were working with a single officer from Homeland Security. The family should be at the residence on Belshire. Officer Leslie said he was on the other line with the Cerritos Sheriff's station. Dev should hang up so the sheriff could contact him. Dev hung up.

The traffic slowed to a trickle as the 105 freeway merged with the 605. He banged his hands against the steering wheel and yelled, "Come on, come on!" Just when he thought the phone would never ring, it did. It was a different voice who identified himself as Sergeant MacLean. Dev told him the whole story again. MacLean said they would send a car out to the Vargas house on Belshire.

Dev said, "I'm coming into the station. I'm at Alondra now. I should be there soon." He hung up and dialed Adri.

"Meet me at the Cerritos Sherriff's Station. That's by the library and the high school, right?"

Adri said, "Yes."

"I'll be there in 10 minutes tops. I just got off the 605 and onto the 91. I go down Bloomfield, right?" There was no response from her. "Are you there? Did you hear me?"

"Yes. I heard you. You go down Bloomfield, it's right by the library. You're a suspect, Dev."

"What?"

"They think you did this."

"Bullshit. The Coast Guard says there is no report of a juvenile being kidnapped."

"Yeah, but Jimmy says Ray is in less danger if we just comply. I'm supposed to pick up the money at 2:00, it's 12:30 now. I'll just give you the money, Dev, I just want Ray back."

"What are you talking about? This is nuts, I want him safe too."

"Dev, the police have been following you for a while. Please, don't do this to us. I just want Ray back."

"Does this cop chew Juicy Fruit gum?" There was silence on the other end of the line. "Oh! I thought they'd sent a private detective after me to find out where I was. Adri, leave now and meet me at the sheriff's station."

She was standing in the front yard. She went to her car and as she put the key in the ignition, three black and white police cars, lights flashing, came careening around the corner.

Dos Equis Darker

Ray's arm grew tired of holding the hatch down. He fiddled with the toilet brush and stuck the long plastic handle through the pull on the trapdoor and felt until it seemed to stick out beyond the hatch opening. At least it would slow the guy down if he looked for him down here. The engines were thunderous. He patted along the side feeling for the tools he had seen, but couldn't find them. For now, he figured he should just lie low. He felt around some more and determined there was room to stretch out. He was so tired. He tried to pray some, but only knew to say that he wanted to live to be a good man and help his mom. He promised himself and God, if there was one, he would always be the best person he could be. He also prayed for Gerardo and that he should be forgiven for being a hood because he'd been dealt such a crappy hand in life. Ray also promised God and himself he would help Gerardo by being his friend. The monotonous droning of the loud engines, the praying, and his utter exhaustion caused him to drift off to sleep and to dream.

The water was gleaming like living translucent jade and as he wiggled his fingers alongside his surfboard it sparkled and shimmered. Looking down through the water he could see his Carl Perkins black and white shoes magnified and wavy looking. Dev was next to him sitting on his surfboard waiting for an outside set to come in. On the other side of Dev was the *Dos Equis* Man. He and Dev were chatting. Ray continued to watch the water scintillate as he strummed his fingers through it.

Dev said to the *Dos Equis* Man. "Do you remember Ray from before?"

The older bearded man looked at Dev and, smiling, said, "Of course, how could I forget our good friend Ray? Don't you think he's a lot like we were when we were boys?"

"Oh yes." Dev said, "He is just like we were."

The *Dos Equis* Man looked at Ray and then turned toward Dev and said, "I remember how we were all together once. Can you remember that far back?"

Dev responded to the man with a nod. "Yes, I have an inkling of that time."

Just then, the *Dos Equis* Man, looking back at the lineup of waves, shouted, "Outside!"

Ray saw a towering wave coming from their left, glowing with spindrift flying off its crest. The *Dos Equis* Man started paddling and then popped up with one foot forward on the board and rose on the glassy green wall. Ray noticed he was wearing Speedos that had the same splotchy black and white pattern as his Carl Perkins shoes. As he dropped down into the tube, sprinkles of water flashed and glimmered in his beard. He passed by Ray and yelled, "Stay thirsty, my friend!"

Ray began to paddle as deep and fast as he could to catch a wave. He couldn't see Dev, but felt the wave take him. He entered a perfect pure tube of green, glassy and hollow, and he sped through it with the energy of the sea propelling him. Harmony with the sea filled his being in the timeless green chamber. Ray looked down at his black and white Carl Perkins shoes again and realized this might be a dream. He squatted down as the wave's tube narrowed and became tighter, and then hurtling through it, he heard loud grinding sounds. He tried to wake himself but still was rappelling through the narrowing wave now at uncontrollable speeds, the pulverizing sounds becoming almost unbearable as the wave squeezed itself around him.

He woke drenched in cold sweat, the boat's engines making tortured grinding sounds. Ray smelled the strange ozone smell of hot electricity. Suddenly there was deafening silence. The engines had ground to a halt. He listened and could hear the whining and pinging of hot metal. He was afraid now of fire and reached above him to turn on the light. His hand bumped into the toilet brush jamming the trapdoor. He reached around and felt for the switch, but when he flipped it nothing happened. He reached up again and started to slide the toilet brush out from the latch. He carefully pushed the hatch up a little and saw it was dark above him. He drew the hatch down and listened for noise and movement. His ears were ringing and he could feel the boat rolling to and fro more than it had while it was moving. Then he realized that if the guy wanted to restart the engines, he'd probably come below to see what was wrong.

Inch by inch he opened the hatch. He had been in total darkness so long that what little ambient light there was from the night sky allowed him to see most of the main room. He saw no one. All he could hear was the surge of the swells and a few creaking sounds. He decided to climb up to the main room. His body was stiff and suddenly he got a terrible cramp in his calf, the muscle knotting into an excruciating ball. Trying not to moan he rubbed hard on the muscle to get it to unknot. Cautiously he moved up the ladder and quietly closed the hatch. Then the fingers of his right hand began to seize and draw up in cramps too, his fingers pulling at tortured angles. He thought about the *Dos Equis* Man who told him to stay thirsty, so he went behind the little kitchen counter because he figured he needed to drink some water. He found the sink and quietly turned on the faucet, but nothing came out. He knew he had to drink so he turned around to where the small refrigerator was behind him. He opened it. No light. He felt inside and there were a bunch of cool bottles. Grabbing one he tried to twist off the cap, but it was the kind that needed an opener. He wondered what the *Dos Equis* Man would do. Open it with his smile? Ray put the bottle in his mouth and tried to open it with his teeth. It didn't work. He needed to snoop around so he took out two of the icy bottles and put one in either pocket. Quietly he began to case the boat for the big man.

He wondered if Gerardo was alive and remembered his promise to God and himself. The boat was lurching back and forth. The futon couch thing had slid a few feet across the floor as the swells rocked the boat. He clung tightly to the wooden handles on each side of the ladder and crept up to the bridge. No one was there and the radios were silent, their cut cords twitching back and forth like angry cat tails. The side door to the bow of the boat was still latched in an open position. Ray looked to his left and right and saw no one, but could make out a dark shape where he had last seen Gerardo. The boat was pitching wildly. He stayed in a low crouch for balance and crept up to Gerardo who still lay in the same position as he had after the big man beat him. He touched his leg, then his cheek. Gerardo was very cold. He put his ear down near his face and listened for breath. Ray thought he heard something, but if he was breathing, it was really shallow. He got up again and headed along the decking. A wave came over the railings and washed over the deck soaking the unconscious man. Ray thought Gerardo shouldn't get any colder; he wanted to cover him with something.

He stayed very low and semi-crawled back to the place right below the windows of the bridge where there was a bench that looked like it might open into a deck box. He could see in the darkness much better now. He opened the bench lid and saw some sun hats and some blankets in there. He took the blankets and crouching low, walked back to Gerardo. He took one of the blankets and stuffed it up under Gerardo's legs because in first aid class they said you should elevate the legs to avoid shock. Then he covered him with the other blanket. He went back to the deck box to see what else he could find inside. He was hoping for a flashlight. He felt around beneath the hats and felt sunglasses, bottles of what were probably sunscreen and a jacket. Trying to keep his legs steadied despite the rolling of the boat, he grabbed the jacket and struggled to put his right arm in the sleeve. Instantaneously light filled the area in front of him. He could see his skinny startled face surrounded by a halo of brilliant white light reflected in the windshield glass. In the glare of the powerful flashlight he noticed that the boat had giant windshield wipers.

"Well aren't you the good little fucking Samaritan? Covering up that idiot. Very considerate. Where the hell have you been?"

Ray said nothing. The voice seemed familiar somehow.

"Stand up and don't turn around, you meddlesome little prick!"

Ray stood up, keeping his hands at his side. He could still see his reflection in the windshield, the light contracting as the big man moved closer. Ray got ready to duck.

Another big swell came and the boat pitched violently. The reflection of the light swung to the right. Ray grabbed a beer bottle from his pocket and swung it around. He held the bottle high above his head and came down on the huge man's head with a lucky strike. The bottle broke and the man crumpled, the flashlight crashing to the deck. Ray was surprised that he went down with a single blow. He wondered if he had hit him in the same spot as before. He could smell the beer and feel its cold trickle running down the sleeve of the jacket. He jumped on the man's back, ready to hit him with the other bottle, but the guy lay still. Ray wondered what to do and felt in his non-beer pocket. Still no use for the condoms, but as for the dental floss, 'Yes!'

Still sitting on the guy's back, Ray scooted down onto the guy's butt and grabbed his feet. Ray took the dental floss and started wrapping the big man's ankles round and round with the floss. It was the minty kind and he could smell it. He was so grateful that he made another promise to himself that he would always floss daily. Another wave came onto the deck, but Ray kept wrapping. He wrapped around and then up between the man's ankles nice and tight. Right now he hated this guy. Then he realized he had to tie up the kidnapper's hands and do a better job than Gerardo had done with his. He grabbed one arm and the man moaned. He thought he didn't have much more time. He had used up all the dental floss. He grabbed the guy's one hand and pulled it onto the small of his back, then the other hand next to it, and Ray moved up and sat on both of the man's hands. The guy moaned some more. Ray looked at his Carl Perkins shoes. They had leather laces. Now he loved his shoes even more. He pulled one off using the side of his foot against the top of the heel. He grabbed the shoe, untied the bow and unlaced the shoe. He moved his body up further on the guy's back and heard him exhale loudly and begin to stir. He wrapped the lace securely around his wrists and tied it with as many weird granny knots as he could get out of the now short lace. He thought the guy was pretty well bound, but he'd look for more things to tie him up within a minute. He thought of hitting him over the head with the other bottle of beer and christening him 'cocksucker,' but realized that went against the promises he made when he tried to pray.

The deck was wet and still pitching. Ray spotted the big rectangular flashlight. He picked it up and held on tight as he rounded the corner onto the bridge. He didn't look at the radio, the helm or any of the gauges, just hurried down the next set of steps and into the galley. He knew the *Dos Equis* Guy was right. 'Stay thirsty.' He opened up the fridge, shone the flashlight in and saw nothing but beer, vodka, a jar of mayonnaise, cheese and some green olives. He took the light and looked around on the counter and spotted the bottle opener. He grabbed a beer, popped off the cap and glugged down as much as he could, then said aloud, "I don't always drink beer, but when I do, I prefer *Dos Equis*."

Little Carrots

Dev got off the 91 at Bloomfield and barreled the Volvo down the few blocks to the Cerritos Library. He turned in and wound around the parking area behind the library looking for the Sheriff's Station. He spotted it, parked and ran up the wide shallow stone steps past three fountains bubbling away in the heat. He entered a high-roofed atrium filled with tropical plants. It didn't look like any police station he'd ever seen. Then he realized he'd never been in a police station. On the left were three glass windows with slots on the bottom like you see in banks. He went to the window and told the woman that Sergeant MacLean was expecting him.

A tall uniformed man gave him a wave through the bank of windows and motioned him to the door on the left. He opened it and extended his hand. Dev shook it, and said, "Is the boy's aunt, Adri Reukema, here? She said she'd meet me here. She was getting ready to go pick up the ransom."

MacLean walked Dev behind a partial wall and motioned for him to sit in the chair by his desk. "No. The officers have just arrived at the house on Belshire. Probably she is answering questions there."

Dev handed the sergeant his phone. "The last number is the

one the boy called me from. I gave the number to the coastguard too. But, maybe the phone itself will be useful. The boy was terrified. I told him to hide down in the engine compartment."

"Did he say how long he'd been on the boat, or give any description of it?"

"No. He said he called his mother, but she didn't pick up. I think he said he left a message. Your guys should look at her phone too, it will have the same number. I just told Ray where I thought he could hide from the guys who kidnapped him. So we weren't on the phone too long."

Sergeant MacLean was jotting down notes and asked Dev, "Why would the boy call you? What is your relationship to him?"

"Oh, I'm friends with his aunt, the one who is supposed to meet me here. My best friend is dating Paloma, that's the boy's mother. I've been teaching Ray to surf and told him he could call me anytime if he wanted."

The sergeant pushed back his chair and asked, "Would you like some coffee? We have a fresh pot."

"No thanks. I'm too nervous. Do you know if the Coast Guard is looking for the boat?"

The officer poured some coffee into a white Styrofoam cup and tore open a yellow packet of sweetener, stirred the contents around the cup with a stir stick and said, "Yeah I'm sure they are and probably the L.A. County Sheriff's helicopters are too." He turned toward Dev and said, "My kids don't know anybody's number by heart, they just push the contact on their cell phone. How is it that the boy would know your number by heart?"

"My number just happens to spell out the word 'nirvana,' you know, like the band. I told him that."

A light was flashing on the phone on MacLean's desk. He picked it up and said, "What have you got? Is there a message on the mother's phone? Yeah, that's good. You need to bag it. We need to get it to the Coast Guard and our people ASAP. If it's a new phone and has the E911 GPS Aware characteristics they can *ping* it. If not, hopefully they can triangulate the cell phone network's towers to get the coordinates of the boy's last location. I have Mr. Tagore's phone here. Is the sister still there, or did she go to get the money? That's good."

MacLean acknowledged Dev by meeting his eyes as he continued his conversation. "Who is it that wants to talk to me? Homeland Security? Okay, put him on the line."

The sheriff sat down and took a sip of his coffee, and said to Dev, "There's tea if you'd prefer. The sister is still at the house. This kind of stuff always takes a long time and is pretty agonizing I know."

Dev said, "Okay. I guess I will. Thanks." He went to the counter and picked up a teabag. As he tore it open and poured hot water over it, he heard MacLean identifying himself to the man from Homeland Security, and then listening without speaking for quite a while. Finally the sergeant said, "Okay, right. What is the name and number of your superior?" He picked up his pencil and jotted something down and said, "And your I.D. number? Yes I will, right away. Thanks." MacLean returned the phone to its cradle and said, "Mr. Tagore, enjoy your tea, I'll be back in a second."

The sergeant got up and went around the partial wall and began a conversation with the lady who had been at the window. Dev could barely make out her voice as they spoke. The sergeant returned to his desk and said, "Sorry, I need to have some things checked out. I want to call the Coast Guard. They need the cell phones to generate a *ping* to track the boy's whereabouts. Oh, by the way Mr. Tagore, you said you were driving back from LAX this afternoon when you first called me. Could you tell me where your flight originated?"

"Well, I flew out of *Srinagar,* which is in *Kashmir,* then to *Delhi*. I stayed overnight there and then flew to London, then from Heathrow to L.A. non-stop. It's a very long journey."

The officer wrote down more notes, apparently about the flights, and said, "I bet. I hate long flights. I flew to Scotland once. It wiped me out. Excuse me. I need to make that call."

As MacLean dialed the phone, Dev got up to add more hot water to his cup. He hadn't noticed before, but he saw that they had a can of the same tea Adri had in the back of her little shop. The label pictured a little monk, mug in hand, sitting in full lotus in front of a snowy mountain peak. He was lifting a cup of chai up towards his sweet smile, steam curling up and encircling his head like a halo. In vaguely oriental lettering over the mountain top the label read *Instant Mystic Chai*. Dev opened the can and smelled the sweet spicy concoction and was transported back to that night with Adri and remembered how amused he had been at the idea of an 'instant' mystic. A physical wave of shame and regret engulfed him. It was a sensation that was foreign to him. He was guilty of causing her suffering and that made him ashamed. Not concentrating on pouring the hot water, he overfilled his cup. He lifted it to his lips and carefully took a sip. The stainless steel elevator doors at the end of the room opened and two officers came out toward the desk and nodded to the sergeant. MacLean said, "Mr. Tagore, could you put the tea down."

Dev turned back to the counter and placed his cup down. Sergeant MacLean said, "You are a suspect in a kidnapping. We are going to take you downstairs for questioning and put you in custody. Please put your hands flat on the counter." The two officers came up to him and grabbed his arms and put them behind his back and cuffed him with plastic cuffs and then patted him down. They read his Miranda Rights off a little card, escorted him to the elevator and took him down to the floor below street level.

One of the officers pressed a code into an electronic lock and they entered the jail. There were no bars, just doors with heavy stainless steel handles and narrow vertical windows. It was very cool and empty down here. They walked Dev over to some kind of computer, placed his hands on a plate and a set of fingerprints was generated. Then they had him stand with his feet in yellow footprints on the floor and took his photo.

Dev said, "This is not at all like on T.V. It's much nicer. May I call my lawyer?"

"Yes, there is a phone in the cell. You can make a few phone calls."

"Really? I thought I just had the one."

"Yeah, that's on T.V too. We will bring you dinner in a little bit, and then you'll be transported to the Lakewood Sheriff's Station for the night. You'll go before a judge tomorrow. You may have access to the phone immediately. Any questions?"

"No, I'm fine. Thanks."

MacLean opened the cell door. It had two narrow bunks, a tiny stainless steel sink in the corner, and a stainless steel toilet without a seat. He entered and they shut the door. The phone was on the wall between the bunks and the toilet. It was stainless steel too. Dev called Jay and got him on the first try. He asked him to come down to the jail and he would explain everything when he got there. He hung up and sat on the floor crossing his legs and emptying his mind for a moment to try to detach from the chaos of the situation.

He thought about the ancient *Paali* texts in which the various meanings of the notion of 'detachment' were enumerated. In English the word might refer to a military group dispatched to some other place, but more commonly it meant a person who lacked interest in others, somebody who was indifferent—who just didn't care. The Eastern meanings were different, without those negative connotations. There were four kinds of non-attachments. He was thinking about the one called *viraaga* which within itself had four additional strands of attachment. He thought of them as 'graspings,' and one of them was the attachment to human relationships. This one was supposed to bring you a shit-load of trouble, and since here he was, locked in a cell, he supposed it had. But grasping sounded great to him. He wanted nothing more than to hold on to the boy and know he was safe. He wanted to be free to love and be loved. He wanted attachment with all the messiness, heartache, and devastation it might bring.

Sergeant MacLean knocked on his door and opened it, handing him a boxed meal. He said, "Your lawyer is on his way down."

Dev said, "Thanks, you've been very kind. I am so worried about the child. Is there any way I can find out what is going on?"

The officer looked at him for a few seconds and said, "I'm sorry. I'm going off duty soon and they will be transporting you to the Lakewood jail. Listen, I'll get your attorney's card and give him a call if I hear anything."

"Thank you so much." Dev opened the box. Inside was peanut butter and jelly on wheat, an apple, a juice, milk and a bag of tiny carrots. He opened the carrots and looked at them. Carrots that small should have a tiny root and the little green top; he must have pulled little carrots up at some time in *some* life. For a minute he wondered just how they got the short little carrots that way. He threw one in his mouth and started chewing. A little like sawdust, but pretty carroty. Indeed, life was full of mysteries.

Gypsy Schnitzel

Dharamsala was snowy and cold in November but her kitchen was warm and homey with the large cooking fireplace filled with the last of the logs. The house, built during the period of the British Raj, was rebuilt and expanded after the *Kangra* earthquake of 1905. This kitchen, intended to be staffed by many servants, had worked well when she had many devotees. She had sent them all away a few weeks before and now she was alone in this huge place. She was accustomed to her followers taking care of everything from wood chopping to cooking and that was why she was low on wood. She would have to hire someone from the lower village to take care of the wood and help with some chores. He could help her pack her belongings, most of which she intended to sell. If she ran out of wood before then, she would simply turn on the oven and leave the door open to stay warm. She was living full time in the kitchen and had even made herself a bed on the floor. It was the perfect size for her. She realized she was content and peaceful for the first time in many years.

The windows over her sink were steamy and she could barely see through the diffused wavering curtain of moisture. Drips of moisture trickled down the window revealing low winter light striking the snow on her rhododendrons. She reached her index finger up, touching the steamy window. A rivulet ran down to meet it. When it reached her finger she wrote her name in large naïve script. *Mary*. She was Mary again, free of Tara. She felt as if she had been an invalid for years and the last few weeks were a kind of strange, silent vacuum of recovery from her long illness. Her mind was free and her own. The goddess Tara had departed her silently and without the fuss and fanfare that had accompanied her arrival. No phantasmagoric polka dot mushrooms or magnificent elephants, no thunder claps, in fact, not even a whisper of goodbye. She departed without so much as a 'by your leave,' and was gone. It had a finality and certitude that Mary had never experienced before. Tara had taken up so much space in her that now she felt empty and clean.

She was hungry, in fact famished. Perhaps she had been forgetting to eat. She looked in her cupboards. There wasn't much left. There was a can of whole peeled tomatoes and a jar of Hungarian peppers that she had shipped over with other European goods. She had both sweet and hot paprika and lots of onions. She would make *Zigeunerschnitzel*—Gypsy Schnitzel. Her grandmother had learned the recipe from an old German woman who sometimes stayed in Kent in the gypsy encampment where her grandparents kept their caravan. The schnitzel was made with pounded breaded pork or beef. No pork up here in the hill station, little beef, but lots of lamb. She thought there was lamb in the freezer, or she could just make it without the schnitzel part, just with vegetables over rice. It sounded delicious, Gypsy comfort food.

She sliced off the whiskered end of an onion and began to peel off its papery brown husk. The pungent aromatic oils filled her nose and her eyes began to stream. She wiped her eye with her sleeve and kept on chopping. The tears kept running and she squeezed her eyes tight shut for relief. She realized that Tara had never felt much. Loss mixed with regret and sadness began to fill the empty cavern carved out by Tara's departure. All of Tara's drive and brilliant energy had left her. For a moment,

Mary was back in Hermosa Beach in that little boat-like house on the Strand. They had put Michael down for the night and she could see Peg, her face tanned and lined, glasses low on the tip of her nose. She was cross stitching little Christmas designs to be put in tiny frames to hang on the tree. They were for friends and relatives, and she let Mary pick out her favorite, a Christmas tree with each bough tipped with tiny glowing candles. Mary felt the overwhelming loss of Peg filling the vacuum inside her. She would give all of her treasures for that little ornament and to have Peg love her again.

The jar of peppers was hard to open. There was no man around to ask for help. She banged the sides of the jar lid with a heavy knife handle and tried again. Her hands looked old as she grasped the lid and they hurt when she tried as hard as she could to open it. So much time had been lost with Tara. She laid the jar on its side in the sink and ran the hot water over the place where the lid and jar came together. She tried again and there was finally a pop and release of air as the seal broke apart. She thought Tara had been the seal that kept all of her feelings out. She pulled out peppers and decided to use the whole jar. She wasn't going to be staying in *Dharamsala* much longer, not long enough to use up many leftovers. She drained the jar through her fingers catching the slightly soft and slimy peppers. There would be fresh peppers in California. She laid them on a cloth to drain and picked up the big can of San Marzano tomatoes. There were tinned tomatoes available in India but these had been shipped over without regard for cost because Tara liked them. Only the best for Tara.

She opened the large can of whole peeled tomatoes. Skeptically she looked down at the membranous orbs. These tomatoes were always a challenge. If you squished them in your hands the inside would sometimes spurt out under the pressure of your grip and splotch not just your clothing, but the walls. She gave the tomatoes some thought—and the potential of their misbehaving innards made her remember the 'great tomato trick.' The *Rom* name for the trick was *hokkani boro*, or just *hakkni*. To Mary's mind it was an evil scam. She could understand why its victims would hate Gypsies and call them 'Black Bloods.' She would never do the trick and her family never did it either. She was good at *pen dukkerin* and believed she had a true gift for fortune telling. When she read the Tarot cards or people's palms, she felt a connectedness to them and a sense that she was helping them move forward in their lives. She never thought of these people as suckers or marks. She was sharing her gift, not perpetrating a fraud. Of course she had done little cons, but mostly just using men to get a place to stay or some money, just like so many other women did. She never thought this was any more of a confidence game than what other young women she knew did to survive. She had used her beauty, youth, and mystery to lead men on, all the while trying to avoid having to sleep with them as long as possible. She was aware that it wasn't very nice but it wasn't the kind of fraud that the 'great tomato trick' was.

The *hakkni* was evil. She slid her fingers under one of the tomatoes in the can and stuck it in the stem side loosening the core and thinking about the trick. What the grift consisted of was telling some suffering and miserable mark who came to have his fortune told, that they should bring a tomato from their home on the next day. The tomato was rubbed all over their body while reciting mysterious sounding malarkey incantations. Then the switch would be done by sleight of hand and the tomato would be replaced with the one that had been previously prepared by inserting unpleasant things into its core. The practitioner would then cut the tomato open and whatever lurked inside would represent the evil that beset the poor cursed mark. Usually there would be horrible bits of matted dark hair, dead bugs, and perhaps peeled grapes to represent the evil eye. Of course then the trickster told the horrified mark that all the curses could be removed but it would take a lot of money to do so. Her husband had told her that this was the origin of the phrase 'hanky panky,' from the Romany *hakk'ni'panki*, referring to the 'great tomato trick'. His knowledge of language was astonishing. She smiled thinking about him and realized she still loved him, even so many years later.

Since the Goddess had made her hasty exit from Mary's psyche, she realized she had much atoning to do. Her husband, of course, needed to be apologized to, and 'apologize' was a meager word for what was required. There were grievances that could not be redressed, but only acknowledged. Heavy on her soul was the hurt she had caused her mother-in-law, Peg. She would be a very old lady now if she was still alive, so Mary needed to book a flight to Los Angeles right away. She suddenly found herself praying to the God of her childhood, the one she had said the 'Now I lay me down to sleep' prayer to as a little girl. She asked Him please to let Peg be okay so she could tell her that she was sorry and how much she loved her.

She took her finger out of the tomato and placed it in the large stockpot. Just as she was going to squish it, she recognized that she had indeed performed the 'great tomato trick.' She had set in motion a huge complicated twenty-five year confidence game. Not just by becoming Tara, but far worse, she had performed the 'great tomato trick' on her son Michael. Manipulating and subtly inserting misleading clues and hints into his very core which had certainly changed the course of his existence. The sweet Buddhist monks had been her unknowing shills. She didn't even know where her boy was. She only knew that, with good cause, he hated his mother.

Toilet Water

He had fallen asleep for a little while on the migrating couch. When he woke it was shoved against the wall and was sliding rapidly back toward the other side of the boat. It hit the table on the other side of the cabin and he jumped off and tried to get his bearings. It was still dark. He didn't know if he'd slept for minutes or days. He made his way toward the little steps down to the head. The boat now began to pitch back and forth in a different way, bow to stern and back again. He grabbed every possible surface to make his way to the ladder. Now the couch was sliding toward him. He grabbed the wooden handholds as its corner slammed toward the doorway. He lowered himself down the steps and went in the bathroom. He'd secured the door with the hook at the bottom previously so it wasn't slamming. He went in and looked at the toilet. He unzipped and tried to pee and nothing came out. His head was killing him and he could feel his lips had cracked into big fissures. He turned toward the sink and there was enough ambient light that he could see a darkened image of himself.

His eyes were sunken and he looked haunted and already dead. There was a short tumbler on the counter; he remembered it was turquoise glass with little fishies swimming across its surface. In the sink was the pill bottle that he had emptied into his pockets for Gerardo. It must have rolled into the sink from the rocking of the boat. It was still rolling back and forth wildly with the movement of the boat. He grabbed it and then remembered the big man yelling furiously at Gerardo about the pill bottle. He had said, "Oxy bottle my name." Ray tried to read the bottle to see the name but it was too dark. He had a very bad feeling about the bottle. He threw it back in the sink and tried to think through his headache how he could get some water to drink.

He remembered that Ghandi drank his own pee. But he thought maybe that was just a story like George Washington's wooden teeth. He'd have to ask Dev or Jay if it was true. The thought of his friends made his throat tighten up and hurt. He wanted to see them too, not just his mom and his *tia*. He could feel tears form in his eyes and thought it wasn't a good idea to waste the water crying since he couldn't even pee. He turned toward the toilet and tried again, but to no avail. Out of habit he felt the need to flush so he pressed down on the little flusher foot press on the side of the toilet. It made a sucking noise and to his amazement, water came out! He realized the tank was full and must be gravity-fed.

Just then, the boat slid down a swell and slammed him against the wall. As the boat slid down the other side of the swell, he grabbed the tumbler from the sink and sat on the floor. He scooted himself across the floor to the toilet and put the glass in the toilet. He began to pump the flusher and the toilet filled to above the tumbler's top and then the water flooded in and filled it. He guzzled down the toilet water as fast as he could, counting the swallows. He got up to seven. He depressed the flusher again with his left hand and filled the tumbler again and drank, then once again.

He knew he needed to go up and check on Gerardo, but didn't want to because there was that huge lump of a man laying on the deck up there. He wondered if the guy was dead. He could barely stand to think of that lump and what it might mean. But Gerardo might be dying too and he was afraid the younger man might get washed off the deck if he didn't move him someplace safer.

He scooted his butt out of the bathroom into the hallway. The boat was rocking so wildly that he figured the swells must be enormous. It felt as if it might capsize. He made it to the wooden ladder steps and grabbed a hold of the third one to pull himself up. Once upright he could reach the mahogany handhold on the wall. He thought whoever designed boats must be very clever. Maybe he'd like to design boats when he grew up. He was always thinking about what he'd like to do with his life when he grew up. Then he realized he probably wouldn't survive to grow up, but if he did, he would never ever want to get on a boat again.

The couch had slid kitty-corner across the room. He held onto its top and walked himself toward the ladder leading up to the deck. He grabbed the rungs and hesitated, thinking about the goddamn big lump of man that had been near the door. He decided if the lump was still there he wouldn't look at him. He went through the door onto the slick deck and against his better judgment he looked at the lump. It had moved and was currently against the railing to his left. He wondered if it had been rolling to and fro across the deck with the swells.

It must be close to daylight because he could clearly see Gerardo's form up right at the bow of the boat and the sky seemed lighter. Maybe Gerardo had gotten stuck there somehow, because it looked like he hadn't moved much. He could see that the swells were splashing over the railings of the boat, and before it pitched wildly again, Ray sat down. The scooting seemed an effective way to not fall over and so he continued forward. As he moved himself toward Gerardo, his torso wobbled to and fro like one of those toys with a weight in the bottom. He remembered a shiny red clown from when he was little that you could push over and it would pop right up. This memory made him want to cry again, but he shoved himself forward.

When he reached Gerardo the man was soaked in a puddle of sea water that was rolling back and forth around his body.

He touched the man's arm and it was very cold, but Ray could see his chest rise and fall. If more swells came up, Gerardo might drown in the puddle. He decided he needed to drag him somewhere safer. He scooched back a little and tried to pull on Gerardo's feet to drag him away from the edge of the boat, but he was too heavy or Ray was too tired. The light was increasing and he saw a line attached to the railing above the bow. He thought maybe he could get it and at least tie Gerardo to something so he wouldn't wash overboard.

He scooted to the railing and grabbed the cold metal and hoisted himself up to grab the line. The rope was moving as he grabbed for it and held tight. The boat heaved hard, pitching him forward and his leg slid over the edge, ramming his stomach into the bow railing. The line was cold and slick but he held it and as the boat rocked down on the other side of the swell he fell back on his butt next to Gerardo's head. The rope had slid through his hand with such force that he could see that it was bleeding. Gerardo appeared to be sort of jammed in against the pointy part of the bow and that was why he hadn't moved much.

Ray looked over the edge into the distance and could see the pale yellows and pinks of sunrise. Then the sun itself emerged from the sea. The swells were moving the boat to the left of the direction of the sun, so he guessed north. He looked in that direction and saw rocky cliffs. He wondered if it was Japan, Hawaii, or Mexico. North didn't seem right, but he was so disoriented, he hadn't a clue. One thing he was sure of though, was that he could see that in not very long this boat was going to be wrecked on the rocks. He stared at land for a minute. He could see no lights or buildings. Nobody would be around to notice them floundering on the rocks.

Still sitting, he unzipped his Levis and tugged them off little by little. He took off his Carl Perkins shoes, his socks and rolled them up enchilada-style in his pants. He pulled Gerardo's head up as high as he could get it and stuck the enchilada thing under his neck and head to get him a little higher out of the water. He took the wet rope and tied it to Gerardo's arm. He wasn't sure if it was a good idea or not, but he remembered that Odysseus had his crew tie him to the mast so he wouldn't succumb to the song of the sirens. Maybe this would keep Gerardo from going in the water when they hit the rocks.

This boat had no mast for him to tie himself to, but if he crawled past the big lump of the man along the narrow deck that ran along the side, he'd reach that steep aluminum ladder that led to the very top of the boat. Ray lay face down and crawled to his right. When he reached the lump he touched it and knew he could no longer pretend he didn't know who the lump was. He kept crawling, feeling a little safer after passing his unconscious kidnapper. He proceeded into the narrow passage with boat on one side and rail on the other. At the end of the passage, he inched around the corner and grabbed the steep aluminum sides of the ladder. He pulled himself upright, but another swell hit and he lost his grip. He could feel pain through the cold, but crawled back to the base of the ladder and pulled himself up once again, bracing himself with his feet under the bottom rung this time.

He looked to the north and he could see the boat was moving much closer to the rocks. It wouldn't be much longer now. He hauled himself up the ladder and holding tight, crawled on to the top deck. There was a yellow inflatable raft up here, and if he could just get in it, he might survive. He crawled to the yellow raft, but the sides looked slick and insurmountable. He couldn't get a purchase on it. He waited till the next swell subsided and stood up. The down side of the swell helped him tumble into the raft. He lay there spent and thought about the lump.

Then he thought about words with the suffix of 'cide.' Funny sounding ones like fungicide, spermicide, insecticide, herbicide; then not so funny ones like infanticide, suicide and genocide. There were others too, like homicide, patricide and matricide. He figured these were all Latin prefixes, but they all weren't cognates with Spanish words. He thought about the lump and wondered what he should call what he had done. *Avuncularcide*? No, not that. Maybe he could call it, '*taco-tio-cide.*' He tried to make it sound funny, but he knew it wasn't.

Just then he heard the thrumming of the Sirens. Their song

sounded different than he had imagined it would. He looked up and above him. Against the dawning blue sky he saw a radiant orange dragonfly. It was the whirring of its wings he had heard, not the song of the Sirens. As it came closer the noise became a deafening *thwocking* sound. Fascinated, Ray saw something on a web emerging from the dragonfly's belly and descend towards him.

It was a man. It wasn't a dragonfly at all. He could read "U.S. Coast Guard" on the side of the helicopter. He was saved. But he couldn't stop thinking about the lump and what his mother would say when she found out he had killed her brother.

Orange Jello

His hospital room was afloat with gaudy silver mylar balloons, abundantly festooned with dangling curly ribbons wishing him 'Get well' and 'We love you.' Ray thought it looked like some stupid kind of birthday party was about to happen at any second. The story of his kidnapping, rescue, and courage had hit the *Long Beach Press Telegram*, the *L.A. Times* and all the local T.V. channels. He was the boy of the hour. He wasn't happy about it.

His mother and aunt had been keeping vigil over his hospital bed, never taking their eyes off him. Other than the doctors and nurses, the only other visitor allowed to see him had been the short cop who had made the sheriffs arrest Dev. He could see the guy was trying to put the moves on his aunt, but she was avoiding him. The little shit tried to be all buddy-buddy with him too and acted all self-important like he'd saved Ray's life. Ray couldn't believe his family had faith in this creep. He told his mom and his aunt he thought the guy was a real phony and sort of a dickhead—and that he couldn't believe they were taken in by him. His aunt told him he was right and then she cried a lot. So he didn't say anymore about the guy, but apparently Ray would have to put up with him again when the police came to question him.

All the hospital had given him were tests, IV liquids, a few bandages and orange jello in a little plastic cup with a foil lid. He hated orange jello and this stuff wasn't even real jello. The police were going to interview him soon. That seemed worse than the bad jello. He was glad to know that Gerardo would probably survive, but his uncle Vic was in an induced coma. His mom had asked Jay to act as Ray's attorney when the cops came. He wondered if they would charge him with attempted murder or something. He was very nervous about the whole thing. Jay was supposed to arrive before the cops. He wished he'd get here soon. It was all so screwed up. What he hated most was that Dev was in jail because his mom and *tia* had believed he was a bad guy.

Jay came in looking tall and important in a three piece suit. He held out a brown plastic grocery bag to Ray and said, "I have never been so glad to see anyone in my whole life." Jay lightly touched the boy's arm and said, "Here, your mother said you might like these."

Ray opened the bag and it was full of red jellos, the real kind. He pulled them out of the bag and said, "Wow this is so cool, look there's raspberry, cherry, and strawberry." He put the bag on the bed, grabbed a spoon from his table tray and tore open a raspberry and dug in. "Oh Dude, this is delicious. Thanks!"

Jay leaned over and kissed the top of his head. Then he walked over to Paloma who was crying and he put his arms around her, which made her sob. Ray had never heard such terrible noises come out of his mother. Jay was rocking her back and forth like she was a baby. He looked at his aunt who was sitting by the window in a chair. She looked really tired, sort of sallow and not so hot. A nurse came in and pulled the curtain thing around his bed and started taking his vital signs. He hated the stupid blood pressure cuff; it blew up so hard he thought if it kept going his arm would explode. He was relieved to hear the release of air as the dumb thing deflated. The nurse left and reopened the curtain; in the doorway stood Dev.

His aunt stood up from the chair, but didn't say a thing. Dev came in and went straight over to Ray and laid a white gift bag on the bed. He started kissing him on the top of his head. Ray got out of the bed, his little butt cheeks hanging out of the back of the hospital gown and wrapped his arms around the man and they held each other tight. They released each other a little awkwardly and Ray grabbed his gown, holding the back of it together. He said to Adri, "Sorry Auntie, I didn't realize I was going *commando* on you!"

"No worries Mijo, your hiney hasn't changed that much since I changed your diapers," Adri said, while still staring at Dev.

Ray sat on the bed and said to Dev, "Thank you for saving my life, Man. You said you would always be there for me if I needed you and it was true. I even dreamed about you and the *Dos Equis* Man. We were surfing and I knew you were helping me even in my dreams. How did you get out of jail? Are you out on bail or something?"

"No, I'm out. No charges, just some pending immigration issues. Jay knows an excellent immigration attorney. So it'll be fine."

"You should sue that stupid short cop for false arrest or something."

"It's okay, jail was fine. The Cerritos jail is practically a palace, except for the food. Did you know that they have your peanut butter and jelly sandwiches sent all the way down from Men's Central Jail in L.A. to Cerritos? It seems like a waste of taxpayer's money to me. The Lakewood jail was less palatial, a little more of a dungeon atmosphere, but I wasn't there long."

Jay laughed and said, "He wouldn't let me bail him out. He said it would be a waste of money and that jail was okay, because it had very good air-conditioning."

Adri was still standing and hadn't said a word. Dev hadn't looked at her. She surprised herself when she spoke, and softly asked him, "What is the immigration issue about?"

His gray eyes met hers and fixed her in its gaze. He said, "I had been using a false passport and an imaginary identity.

Officer Dracos was correct about that. That was the only thing he was right about though. Jay brought the police my legitimate passport and I explained the reason I had been using the other one. The judge listened and made some phone calls and let me go. I'll probably get a fine or something and have to do a ream of paperwork."

Dev turned back to the boy and said, "Hey Ray, I heard you had an unusual trip to Catalina!"

"Oh man, I thought I was in Mexico or Hawaii or somewhere really far away. It seemed like I was on that boat forever. I never saw any other boats after the first day. The Coast Guard guys told me there were small craft warnings because the swells were so huge. They said it was amazing the boat didn't capsize or break up or something. I couldn't believe it when they said I ended up on the back side of the west end of Catalina. There was nothing there but rocks and cliffs."

Dev said, "Yeah, the news said the hurricane off Baja was huge, it was only the second Category 5 Pacific hurricane to ever make landfall in Mexico. The waves damaged places all the way up our coast. You know on the south side of the Seal Beach Pier, they built up berms to protect the houses, but there still was severe flooding. My house is up the cliff so it didn't have a problem. I heard there were a lot of crazies out there trying to surf those huge waves. Jay told me you did some big wave surfing of your own!"

Ray said, "Yeah, the boat slipped and slammed around so much I thought it was going to flip over." Ray yawned, "Excuse me, I'm still *really* tired."

Dev looked at the boy's cracked lips and said, "I bet you are—and Buddy you need a bunch of some heavy duty Chapstick. So I'll be going in a minute. I'll come back tomorrow if you want. But I wanted to give you this. I stopped at the bookstore and bought you a book I thought you might like."

"A mystery?"

"Well, not exactly, but maybe a little I guess, in some ways."

Ray opened the bag and pulled out a book with a dark blue

glossy cover and what looked like a golden ship's wheel on the cover. Ray looked at it. He didn't want to be rude and say that he hoped it wasn't about boats. The title was, *Awakening the Dream Walker.* "Cool! What's it about?"

Dev said, "Open it up to the back fly leaf and read that. I think that will explain it better."

The boy opened the back cover and read aloud:

> *As a six year old living in Brussels, Tulku Palden Norbu Rinpoche was recognized as the 26th incarnation of a consciously reborn Bodhisattva. His soul embodies a thousand years of the collective consciousness and wisdom of those incarnations. He is the internationally renowned author of* ***Buddhism—the Bridge between East and West****;* ***Now and Zen****;* ***Don't Mind the Gap!****;* ***Happiness is Your Shadow****; and most recently, the best-selling* ***OM means Human: the eternal expression of the universe is within your breath****. A linguist who is conversant with ten languages, Tulku Palden Norbu Rinpoche has also translated more than a dozen poetic yet highly readable versions of various Buddhist holy texts.*

Then Ray said, "And it goes on and on about how amazing and holy this guy is. I'm sorry that sounded kinda rude. I'm pretty tired and cranky I guess. So Dev, you think this is a good book and this Rintintinpoachey dude is pretty wise, huh?"

Dev laughed and said, "Well I'm not altogether sure about that, but he probably has a good heart. One thing I know for sure is that he would like you."

"Is that a ship's wheel on the cover?"

"No, it's called a Buddhist Wheel, but I can understand your confusion. They look almost exactly the same."

Adri looked at Dev hard and said, "Who the hell are you?"

He looked back at her, his eyes dark and more serious than she had ever seen them, shrugged his shoulders and said, "The trouble is, I don't know."

Jay unwrapped Paloma from his embrace and cleared his

throat, "Well, I guess I should introduce you to my friend who I have called 'Pinocchio' since we were little boys. I don't know his real name, nor does he. When we were little his last name was Smith, then he became the *Venerable Tulku Palden Norbu Rinpoche*, but for the last couple of years here in California he has called himself Dev Tagore. My friend believes that none of these are his true identity. He has been hiding in plain sight avoiding those who would want to cash in on him, be enlightened by him, worship him, and generally have ridiculously unreasonable expectations of him. Like the puppet Pinocchio, all he really wants is to find the real boy within. Which I guess might be a catchy title for his next book."

The entire group was staring at Dev. He said, "No, the next book is a comparative analysis of the *Koran* in light of Buddhist teachings. By the way I hate those clever titles; my publisher came up with those."

Ray looked back at the photo on the flyleaf of the book and recognized Dev, a little younger, his head shaved, dressed in saffron robes. He laughed aloud, "No shit! *Tia*, Mom, come here and get a load of this picture of Dev!"

The women crowded around the boy's bedside and scrutinized the photo of the monk. Ray laughed gleefully and said, "Ma I *told* you he was a *saint* or something. I could just tell!"

They were silent for a while, still looking at the photo. Then Paloma said, "I still don't get it."

Dev said, "Well, it's pretty confusing but my mother had what I will characterize as a somewhat unusual problem with hallucinogens, and kidnapped me from my grandmother and father, who I assume had custody. My mother had disappeared from the picture for a long while, so by the time she came back and kidnapped me, I hardly remembered who she was. I don't remember my father at all. Just that I had one. I remember an older lady with white hair and blue eyes who I loved completely before I was taken away. We lived in a beach house that I assume was somewhere in Southern California. I bought my house because it reminded me of the one I lived in. I know it was close to the sand in one of the beach cities, but I don't know my real name or which town the house was in."

Ray said, "Why can't you ask your mother? Is she dead?"

Jay's voice boomed out and he said, "She's batshit crazy, is what she is, that's why. The manipulative bitch refuses to tell him his real name. She profits by her relationship to him. She infers that he is the reincarnation of Gautama Buddha himself. Because of that thousands of people started seeking him out thinking he's divine. He had to have guards and hide out; then he decided to blow it off because of all that ridiculous bullshit!"

Now the entire group was staring at Jay. His outburst was so unexpected that it seemed comical coming from his usually distinguished-looking countenance.

Just then they heard a quiet knock on the door frame. Jay blushed deeply as a man in a navy blue suit introduced himself as Senior Special Agent Jack Arbuthnot of the FBI.

He said, "Mr. Tagore and I are acquainted, and for those of you who don't know him, this is Officer James Dracos of Homeland Security. I came in at the end of the case because it was incorrectly assumed to be a matter which would come under the jurisdiction of the Patriot Act. I am here primarily to wish young Ray a speedy recovery." The shorter man, also in a dark suit, said hello. Muscles in his jaw contracted and the line of his mouth was hard.

Dev smiled and said, "It is gratifying to finally meet you in person, Officer Dracos. When you first followed me it was in a red muscle car, then I guess you thought you would be less noticeable in the beige Camry but you're a pretty memorable guy. Did you enjoy your *baklava* while I lunched with my friend, Mansour? Isn't that little restaurant near my friend's mosque delightful?"

Dev's steady gaze focused on Dracos, whose face was a study in ill-concealed rage. He continued, "Mansour has been my tutor in Arabic orthography and has helped me to learn the script referred to as *arabesque*. He has asked me to be best man at his wedding, which is to be held at the Disneyland Hotel next month. I am honored and was happy to give him a small token of my appreciation in the form of a diamond I owned to be set in an engagement ring for his betrothed. Oh, by the way, I took the tracking device off my car. Would you like it back?"

Special Agent Arbuthnot shook his head back and forth and let out a loud exasperated sigh. Dracos stared coldly at Dev and said nothing.

Jay said, looking at Dracos, "You're right Pinoch. He does smell of ripe *kathal*."

Dracos' jaw worked harder and he stepped forward ready to throw a punch and said, "I beg your pardon, what did you say?"

Dev replied, "Oh, he means no offense. The word *kathal* means jackfruit. In southern India they call it *chakka*. You're probably unfamiliar with it, but jackfruit is a favorite in the tropics. It's a very large fruit that blends the tastes of bananas, pineapple and mangoes. It smells rather like the Juicy Fruit gum you chew."

Dracos' jaw quit moving and he held the gum in the side of his cheek and glared at Dev.

Suddenly Adri, still standing, cried out, "Oh no!"

Dev looked surprised and said, "What's the matter?"

"The cat! I haven't fed your cat in a couple of days!"

"Well," he said, "then we better go feed him. I think Special Agent Arbuthnot and Ray will get along just fine without us." Dev walked over to Adri and took her hand and led her out of the room.

As they walked through the doorway, Adri asked, "So just who is this Tara?"

Abuelita con Marshmallows

Dev knelt, urging the kindling to take the flame. As the fire sprang to life, it lit little gems in the gaudy fireplace the sisters had created. Dev got up and switched on the tiny seed lights they had strung across the mantle. Purple, golden and bittersweet orange twinkles compounded the phantasmagoric effect of the fireplace, revealing little scenarios of dolls' heads, Lego temples and miniature fruit stands, all interspersed with vintage bottle tops. The lavender couch was drawn close to the fire and the sisters had pretty much dog-piled on top of Ray. They seemed to need to touch as much of him as possible, after having nearly lost him.

Jay was on the phone in the kitchen. He had been taking charge of everything, attending Dev's legal issues, as well as follow-up with the police, FBI and Coast Guard. Dev knew that Jay could handle everything better than any of them. The boy looked fine, but he was worried about the women.

"Mom, I hate to tell you this, but you're kind of smothering me a little bit too much."

"Sorry, baby." Paloma looked like she was going to start to cry again.

"You know what I would really like? If you went and made

hot cocoa for everybody and maybe cinnamon toast too. I'm sort of hungry and that sounds good to me."

"Can I help you, Pal?" Adri asked.

"No honey, I think it will be good for me to have something to do." Paloma disentwined herself from her boy and went to the kitchen.

"Tia?"

"What Ray?"

"My Carl Perkins shoes were on the boat. They were really special to me. I wrapped them up to try to raise Gerardo's head up. Did the boat sink?"

"I don't know. I bet Jay will know. We can ask him. I can buy you another pair like those if you want."

"No thanks, I think I'll be moving on from my 'rockabilly' look anyway. Maybe I'll get my head shaved tomorrow. But I'm afraid I might look even geekier."

Dev said, "Don't do it, Dude, your head will get sunburned or cold, or have some gnarly looking lumps and moles you aren't expecting. I shaved my head for years when I was a monk and I never liked it. Hairiness feels freeing to me. I don't have much of a beard, but I think I'll quit shaving too."

Ray said, "I have about seven moustache hairs I shave sometimes. I think my mom has more, but don't let her know I said that."

Adri mock punched her nephew and said, "Listen Buster, some things are absolutely off limits when speaking about women, hirsuteness being primary among them!"

Dev looked at Ray, shrugged his shoulders, and said, "Who knew?"

Ray sat up a little more on the couch and said to Dev, "I looked up this *tulku* thing you are. It's pretty weird because Wikipedia says that Steven Seagal is a *tulku* too. Try saying that three times real fast. Tulkutoo, tulkutoo, tulkutoo."

Adri giggled and punched him again."You're kidding right, that martial arts movie guy who always puts his hands together and bows like he's from India or something?"

"Yeah, that's the one. He has some reality show where he's

some kinda-sorta for-real sheriff in Louisiana. The internet says he plowed a tank into some guy's house, killed a puppy, and a whole bunch of chickens died. I bet he even claims he's a vegetarian after that—and have you ever seen any of his movies? He seems like a real douche bag to me. The internet also says he's good friends with Vladimir Putin and supported the invasion of the Ukraine. Plus he has the pointy fake looking hairline with a ponytail. Dev, maybe Jay's right and you should lose the ponytail!"

Dev said, "Oh Man, you're killing me. You should grow one. I'll give you some of my rubber bands! I don't know about the puppy, or Putin, but some monks did recognize him as a *terton* which is not the same as a *tulku*. The Tibetan Buddhist community was pretty upset about it because they believed the monks might have been influenced by donations to their monastery. I don't know for sure, but that kind of *quid pro quo* corruption happens in politics, religious and other kinds of institutions everywhere. But *tertons* are often considered to be pretty whacky and unpredictable guys anyhow. They're supposed to be the reincarnation of somebody who was a 'treasure revealer.' It's like a *terton* is a spiritual Indiana Jones who has come back from the dead and then is supposed to remember he hid some powerful spiritual treasures here and there. It's his job in this lifetime to remember where and what he hid and then reveal it. *Voila*! It could be a symbol on a mountainside, a statue, or a scroll. Think of it as a kind of reincarnation Easter Egg Hunt. So far I haven't heard that Steven Seagal has revealed any treasures or the Golden Egg. Maybe he just has a bad memory."

"Oh Dude! Can't you just picture Steven Seagal in a bunny suit? You're not supposed to be a *terton* guy are you?"

"Nope, I wasn't recognized as a *terton*. So sorry, no hidden treasures to reveal. I remember my mother got some monks to come and check me out. They recognized me because I was a little kid who apparently understood Sanskrit and recognized some ancient Tibetan writing. Well that and some other stuff like they had certain kinds of dreams that made them believe I am the reincarnation of an ancient adept, probably someone close to Siddhartha. They made a very big deal about me and were very kind. Nothing was spared in my training or education. I do have this savant ability to learn language. When I was little my fascination with foreign languages encompassed my being. I think I was very different from most children. Jay and his uncle kind of socialized me and brought me out of my shell."

Ray asked, "So like did you have to take vows and stuff like a Catholic monk does? You know, like to not have sex?" His aunt gave him a very dirty look. "Sorry, I'm pretty curious."

"Yep, you and I are probably the only virgins around."

Ray giggled, "Well, speak for yourself; you shouldn't be all that sure about me. But I'm confused. Do you believe you are who or what they thought you were? Don't you believe in all that stuff anymore? Is that why you went away?"

Dev smiled. "Wow, you sure get right to the point! I bet Adrianna is glad you're asking me these things, because she hasn't summoned up the courage to ask me them yet." He reached over and touched her hand and continued. "I began to feel like I was *faking* it. I was full of a kind of yearning that I couldn't satisfy through prayer and meditation. I wanted to unravel my real history. Also things were getting out of hand at the monastery. Pilgrims were seeking me out, wanting to touch me and treating me like a demigod. It caused disorder and created dissension among the monks. Some thought it disturbed the harmony of the religious life, while others thought it would enrich the monastery and spread its teachings. I decided that things would be better for everybody if I just disappeared. I came here to establish a different identity. But it wasn't as easy to vanish as I had hoped. My mother sent her people out to look for me. I know that others were looking for me too. They even set up a website with supposed sightings and doctored photos of me dead and risen. My favorite was of me levitating."

Ray said, "Oh, it would be so neat if you could actually do that!"

Dev laughed. "It is such an easy trick! Just notice in photos of *fakirs* who are 'levitating' that they always have a walking stick or a big cane. I'll let you figure it out for yourself. You could make a fortune on the boardwalk in Venice."

Adri laughed, "Yeah, then you could put yourself through college!"

"So," Dev continued, "I realized I was *faking* it here too. You see much of the *tulku* stuff is probably about guaranteeing lineages and keeping what is essentially a medieval religious system continuing. It seems very romantic here in the West. But you don't have to live in a monastery to lead a life of contemplation. And to answer your questions, I *often* feel like I have lived before. But I bet you have certain deep affinities and have experienced *déjà vu* yourself. Right?"

"Yeah, and I have some very spooky but beautiful dreams too, like the one with you and the *Dos Equis* Guy."

"Well Ray, maybe you're an unrecognized *tulku* too. And no, I will not try to say that three times really fast! But some of the *tulku* stuff is not outside the realm of possibility. Anyway, I flew back and talked to the lamas who I was close to and told them I wanted to live here, where I was born. I gave the monastery all the rights to the income of my existing books, took care of some legal business and said my goodbyes. I know I don't want the responsibility of people thinking I have all the answers and also I don't want to live in the monastery anymore. But my way of thinking is still very Buddhist and I doubt that will change. Right now though, I want to be here with you guys."

Adri said, "Speaking of hidden treasures, I forgot to tell you I found a bunch of rubies and emeralds when Pabu knocked over your *hibachi*. What was that about?"

"Oh, I didn't remember to put them back in the safe deposit box. I took them out because I wanted to have a piece of jewelry made up for you. I was leaning toward the two pigeon blood rubies set in earrings. But I started to think it wasn't such a hot idea and so, when I left I just shoved them in the hibachi."

"A ring."

"What?"

"I'd rather have a ring please."

Dev blushed and said, "Okay. Sure."

Ray said, "Did she just propose to you?"

"Beats me! I'll have to ask her sometime." He looked over at Adri and said, "But first I want to know something about when you let Jimmy Dracos in my house."

She exhaled deeply and looking pitiful said, "I'm pretty sure I told you all the nauseatingly embarrassing details."

"Yeah, but do you think Dracos could have gotten into that fancy little box with the jeweled swastika on it that was on my bookshelf?"

Both Ray and Addri looked at Dev and said at the same time, "Swastika!"

"No, no, it's not that kind. I inherited it from Uncle Rakesh. It's an eigheenth century Buddhist antique. The symbol is auspicious to Hindus, Buddhists and Jains. The word comes fromt the Sanskrit, *svastika,* which means it is, well-being, or permanent . . ."

Dev's explanation was inturruped by snorty giggles coming from Adri and Ray. Adri tried to stifle her laughter, and shook her head, looking at Dev.

Perplexed, he said, "What?"

She smiled. "Sorry. We are really tired, but you know the etymology of every word and they all come from Sanskrit!" She paused a while, catching her breath, and said, "I don't know anything about the box but Jimmy would have had time to look around while I was feeding the cat and making coffee. Why?"

"I had only taken one diamond out of that box to give to Mansour. There should have been nine left. Now there are only the two smallest ones, nothing over three carats. I think Dracos probably took the rest."

Ray said, "Auntie, I told you that guy was a total dickwad! How can you prove he did that, Dev, cause in case you hadn't noticed, I don't like that guy at all!"

"When Jay's uncle died, he left me all the stones. Jay needed to insure them and keep them safe for me, so he had them graded and certified and had them laser-engraved with identifying marks. That makes them unique and identifiable. But what I began to wonder is if Jimmy Dracos was involved with your uncle on your kidnapping. They were old friends right? So Jay has been talking to the cops and the FBI about this possibility and they are investigating. Maybe at the very least they can get a warrant to search the guy's house for the diamonds. Unfortunately there were no fingerprints on the box that the diamonds were in. Maybe when your uncle wakes up he can provide more information."

Ray said, "If he wakes up."

His aunt wrapped her arms around the boy and said, "Don't worry about that right now *Mijo*. Please, for me. Okay?"

He kissed her cheek, and said, "I'll try—for you." And then to Dev, "I have an idea I want you to know about. I think I might be able to help unravel a mystery for you. But first I want to see how my mom is doing with the hot chocolate." He could hear his mother sobbing in the kitchen. When he went in he saw Jay hugging her and kind of rocking her. His lips were pressed to the top of Paloma's head. Ray was a little embarrassed but stayed in the doorway.

Jay took her chin and lifted it up to look at him, and said, "Paloma, I'll always be there for you. I promise I'll keep you and Ray safe and never hurt you. I want to marry you but I'll be there for you always even if I can be nothing more than your friend."

Paloma noticed that Ray was in the doorway. She said, "Honey, I know how worried you've been about your father because he hadn't called you before all this happened. Well, I have good news. He arranged to turn himself in to the authorities at the border in *San Ysidro*. He decided he wanted to face up to his mistakes and come home so he could earn your respect. He will face trial here in the U.S. Jay has hired a criminal attorney to advise him. We will try to get him to a prison close enough so that you can visit him."

Ray went to his mom and she embraced him. He began to cry. Eventually he patted her back as if to soothe her and turned to Jay. Laughing and hiccupping simultaneously he said, "Crap, I guess I may be visiting *three* guys in prison. When will I have time to do anything else?"

Jay reached over and, smiling, patted the boy on his cheek. Then Ray said, "Thanks Jay. You've helped my mom and me so much. You're a good guy. If Mom wants to marry you, I think it would be very cool. But I feel pretty wiped out and will be so glad when all this weeping and misery is over. So before you guys make wedding plans, how's the cocoa coming?"

He walked to the stove and saw that the triangles had been cut from the disks of delicious Mexican chocolate—his favorite kind—*Abuelita*, with a bespectacled grandma on the front of the yellow carton. It had cinnamon and ground nuts in the chocolate and he could see the triangles had almost melted in the hot milk. From the big open jar of wooden spoons by the stove, he grabbed an old *molinillo* that had belonged to the grandmother he'd never known. The long wooden wand had a series of ingenious loose rings of various sizes on the end. The entire device was rather ornately carved and studded with bits of inlaid mother of pearl. It looked more like a scepter than a kitchen tool. Ray placed the *molinillo* in the hot milk and rubbed the stick back and forth quickly between his palms, its rings whipping the cocoa into a froth. His mom and Jay watched him silently, a little astonished, but happy.

Ray said, "Jay, this is an Aztec blender. As you know we Mexicans invented hot chocolate and apparently the blender, also chewing gum and popcorn as well as some other cool things that I can't think of right now. Pretty amazing huh? Now all we need to do is find the miniature marshmallows. Where did you put them, Mom?"

Ray carried the tray of mugs carefully back to the living room. He set them down on the coin-covered coffee table. His aunt and Dev were holding hands.

He said to Dev, "I think you'll like Mexican hot chocolate. I like the miniature marshmallows – lots of 'em. I don't know if they have marshmallows in Mexico or even what or if there is a word for them in Spanish."

His aunt said quietly, "*Malavisco* or *bombo'n*."

"Maloviscous – like bad slimy thing?" He giggled. "What the heck do they make marshmallows out of anyway? They're like a weird science experiment that turned out great. Here dude, give it a try but don't burn your lips." Ray handed Dev a cup and said, "Dev, you ever heard about kids on the side of milk cartons?"

"No, I don't know what that is."

"Well, way back in the day, when a kid got kidnapped or went missing, dairies put the kid's picture on the side of the milk carton."

Adri looked at Ray and said, "Yeah, my Dad's dairy did that until they started using plastic bottles instead of waxed paper cartons."

"The picture of the *Abuela* lady on the hot chocolate box got me thinking about grandmas. And if Dev is from the U.S., I bet his grandma made sure he was one of the kids on the side of a milk carton."

Adri said, "You know the thing you said about your moustache?"

"Yeah, sorry about that. My bad."

"Well, you've a big marshmallow moustache right now. You might want to lick it off."

He licked his upper lip, and then turned to Dev and said, "I never met my grandma. Let's get online and see if we can find yours, maybe you can share her with me." He took his aunt's hand and she and Dev followed him down the hall to his bedroom. When they got to his door, Ray turned to Dev and said, "If I buy you a big bunny suit will you wear it for Halloween?"

Dev laughed, "Sure if you dress up like the Tooth Fairy with a wand and a tutu. But I want to wear a little waistcoat and carry a carrot."

Adri laughed and said, "I'll gladly make both of your costumes, but Ray's outfit will have to be a *tulku* tutu. Yeah, I know, say that three times fast."

Sand Tarts

Ray had quickly located the website for the National Center for Missing and Exploited Children. Then all that was required was to click on the *Quick Search for Missing Children*, then a few more boxes to click. male, select state; click CA, missing within; click 25 years. Before they knew it, there was a photo of Dev as a child. They clicked on see poster, and there were three photos. On the left, Michael S. O'Keefe, Date of Birth. 5/29/80, missing Date. 9/14/84. In the center of the page was an age progressed photo of Dev, which looked remarkably like him. On the right side of the page a photo of Tara entitled Companion Type. Mother, with the name Mary Spirisko O'Keefe, possible aliases. Tara, Mary Smith, Green Tara. Michael has an identifying scar resembling a smile on his left knee. Below the photos, it stated that Michael had been abducted from the home he lived in with his father and grandmother in Hermosa Beach. He was last seen in blue and red Superman pajamas.

Dev was astonished at how in just a few minutes his identity was established. To prove to himself that he was that boy—Michael—he pulled up the left leg of his Levis and flexed his knee revealing a smiling scar to Adri and Ray. From there all they had to do was contact the 1-800 number for the L.A.

County Sheriff's Office of Missing Persons. And before Dev could wonder why he hadn't thought of this simple way to find his missing family, he knew their names, phone numbers and addresses. The woman at Missing Persons he spoke to said she would initiate the contacts with his family for him.

It was so stunningly quick he wondered why he had never considered contacting Missing Persons. Perhaps he simply needed more time and distance before he was ready to know. During his first year in the States, he had wandered beaches in Florida, Texas and all over California looking for just the right kind of beach with the right kind of houses. He'd narrowed things down to a Southern California beach town, but he realized much had changed in over twenty-five years. What early memory he had was narrow and exclusive consisting more of smells, touch and tastes than of a wider visual panorama. He remembered only details such as digging pinkish gray wiggly sand crabs, and when the waves departed, bubbles appearing in their wake. He also remembered a big wooden wheel that he could turn—which Dev had thought for years was the symbol of a Buddhist wheel—but now realized was a helm, a ship's wheel. He remembered a cat that would sometimes sleep at the foot of his bed and a small stuffed bunny dressed in a waistcoat. He remembered nobody's face or name, but in his dreams he was safe with her. Her face was revealed to him while dreaming, but so elusive, that it escaped his memory immediately upon wakening. The thing he most wanted in the world was to see her face again.

His father, Steven O'Keefe, contacted Dev by phone the next day. He was a professor of historical linguistics currently working with the Hill *Miri* Tribe in the northeastern tip of India, documenting their language which was quickly becoming extinct. Dev shared that he too was a linguist. He asked his father if he had taught him any Sanskrit or Tibetan before he was abducted. His father said that he had taught him some Sanskrit and that as a tiny boy Dev loved to spend hours in his father's office looking at copies of ancient texts. His father said he wasn't surprised that Dev had become a linguist because, like musical talent, the ability to learn language was a talent that seemed to run in certain families. But no, he hadn't taught him to read or speak any Tibetan. He didn't even own any Tibetan texts back then. So if Dev knew some, he must have learned it elsewhere from someone else. Dev shared that the monastery in Nepal was about 1,000 kilometers west of where his father was currently working. Ironically his father even knew of the monastery where Dev had lived.

Dev learned that his step-mother was a photographer and had gone along to India on this trip, because his twenty year old half-sister Micaela was studying in Seattle. His grandmother, Peg O'Keefe, lived in Long Beach. She had a stroke a few years before, but other than some personality changes, impulsiveness and over-emotionality, she was doing well. Dev was concerned that his presence might upset his grandmother. His father said he would call her immediately to share the happy news, and that Dev better arrive at the crack of dawn, because she had been waiting twenty-five years to see him!

And so this morning he found himself outside The Breakers, once a landmark hotel on Ocean Avenue in Long Beach, now an assisted living and retirement residence. He walked through the magnificent old lobby, with massive archways and chandeliers and took the elevator to the fifth floor. Her apartment was at the end of the hallway. He knocked and the door opened immediately. She was tiny, supported by a walker, but he would have known her blue eyes anywhere. He took her hand, still tanned and freckled, and kissed it. She led him to a couch and he sat close to her and she said, "Please let me look at you, Michael." She held his face between her hands and they looked at each other for a long time. He put his head on her lap and her tears dropped on his hair. She began to stroke his face with her fingertips.

They wept and held each other until his grandmother spoke again. "Honey, my leg has gone to sleep." He lifted his head from her lap and looked at her. "We need to talk. I have to explain something to you. It was entirely my fault. I should have never done what I did to your mother."

"What in the world are you talking about? She kidnapped me and kept me from my family and the only home I knew!"

"That's true, but I'm ashamed to say I forced her hand. I loved Mary, but I loved you more than anything else. You were named after your father's little brother who died of leukemia when he was fourteen. When your mother started acting strangely, I couldn't bear the idea of you being hurt or of losing you too."

"So I'm named after my uncle who died as a boy. What is the "S" for?"

"Spiroski, your mother's real name. Her real Romany name is Mara Spiroski, Gypsies often used common names like Mary Smith. I loved your mother and I know she loved me, your father, and of course, you. But then the mushrooms brought that demon Tara. When she thought she was channeling that horseshit goddess I could do nothing but listen to her prattle on about her experiences." She smiled at her grandson and said, "Excuse my language. The doctors say that I have had personality changes since my stroke, but now I just finally say what I want to and use profanity which I enjoy greatly. But my behavior is the prerogative of a brain-damaged old lady while the changes in your mother made her unrecognizable!"

Dev said, "She's always been the Goddess Tara with me, self-centered, manipulative and narcissistic. That must have always been there and was just revealed by her use of hallucinogens."

"Your mother and I lived in the same house for three years. She was kind, sweet and a wonderful mother to you."

"I can't even imagine that person. How could you believe that what happened was your fault?"

"After the mushrooms, she was convinced she was actually the Goddess Tara. Then when you began chanting in weird languages I was certain she was feeding you the mushrooms too."

He held his grandmother's hand and asked, "What weird languages?"

"You hummed. Then said these unintelligible words and

would fall into these trance-like fugues. Eventually you didn't speak English at all, maybe for a year and a half."

"Wow! Really, I had no idea. Go on."

"I accused her of feeding you the mushrooms – *amanita muscaria-* those red and white polka-dotted ones. She swore she hadn't. I thought you were drugged. Eating the mushrooms wasn't illegal, but feeding them to your child certainly would be considered child abuse. By this time she had changed her name to Tara and completely believed she was a goddess. Your father was in India and he told me to have Mary evaluated and you as well. Rather than do it gently, I called the police and they took her away. It was absolutely horrible. She screamed and begged and bit one of the policemen. They put her in Metropolitan State Psychiatric Hospital in Norwalk. She ended up staying for a few months. They said she had a schizoid break and might even be exhibiting multiple personality syndrome. Meanwhile I had you evaluated and you were diagnosed with autism. They ran various drug panels on you, but no psychedelic alkaloids showed up in your system."

"You all went through hell even before she kidnapped me. I am so sorry that you suffered so much. The autism diagnosis never even occurred to me, but it does make some sense. I need to find out more about it, maybe see my medical records. It's a lot to take in."

His grandmother looked at him and said, "But Michael dear, you seem fine now." She held his hand and continued, "When your father came home, we tried to bring Mary home and get her to take anti-psychotics and give her the support she needed. She was not compliant. The drugs would quell the Tara stuff a little, but then the bitch goddess would come out in all her terrible glory. We woke up one Christmas morning and she had disappeared. We hired a private detective, the same one we had search for you later, but he couldn't find her. Your father and I filed for custody and had protective orders entered against her. I had you for almost two years before she took you. She loved you too, and she was your mother. If I hadn't been so cruel and shamed her so terribly, none of this would have happened. I was unfair to her and disloyal."

Dev said, "You had to protect me. I'm sorry you feel so awful about it. I think you made the right decision. I don't remember her taking me. I do remember we moved from place to place all the time. At the time she took me from you, I don't think that I remembered her at all. I just withdrew into myself as completely as I could. I don't remember if I could talk at all then."

"We hired the same private detective again, but he could find neither hide nor hair of you and your mother. Three months later we got a postcard from Vancouver B.C. saying you were fine, and that she would always let me know that you were safe."

Peg put her hands on her head and began to sob. Dev went to the tiny kitchen to get her a glass of water. As he pulled a glass from the cupboard, he recognized it. It had red polka dots and he remembered having milk and cookies before bed. Suddenly he could see the kitchen table in his grandmother's house, the cat sleeping on the chair next to him. He said, "You kept the cookies in a round wooden container with a fitted lid." He had begun to remember. Images of the house in Hermosa Beach flew through his head.

He handed her the water, and she began again. "We didn't know where you were except abroad. The letters came from different countries, but she always assured us of your safety and good health. I have a photo she sent." Using her walker, she went over to the side table and picked up a silver frame. "Come see this."

In the photograph Dev was sitting on the brick edging of the reflecting pond in the courtyard of Uncle Rakesh's house in Belgium. His legs were skinny in short pants and socks and oxfords made him look even more delicate. He had the most tentative of smiles.

Dev explained, "This is just before they took me away to the monastery."

His grandmother said, "This is so damn hard. I think I need to eat something. I was too nervous to have anything this morning."

He followed her back to the tiny kitchenette and sat at a little round table. "I baked you cookies last night after your father called me." She pointed to a wooden Shaker style container on the sideboard. "It would be easier for me if you poured us some milk in the little polka-dot glasses. They were your favorites too."

He pulled out a chair for her, poured them both milk and brought down the container of cookies. He found two small plates and placed a couple cookies on each plate. They were sprinkled with fine sugar and had three slices of almond forming a triad on the cookie.

"What are these called?"

"Sand Tarts. They were your favorites. Do you remember them?" He dunked his cookie in the milk and she smiled. "Just like when you were little."

He said, "They look just like sand dollars. I remember digging in the sand. Is the house still there?"

"Not like you remember it, but I have photographs."

"I remember the ship's wheel on the deck and were there blue life preservers?"

She smiled, "I still have all of those in storage. I could never get rid of anything that was special to you. You may have them."

"Where was the house?"

"On the Strand, right near the boundary between Manhattan Beach and Hermosa Beach. We used to walk between the lifeguard station at Neptune in Manhattan and the one at Longfellow in Hermosa. The house is different but the beach and the Strand are the same. We can go tomorrow if you like and dig for sand crabs again."

She finished her milk and put down the glass. "Your mother gave me these glasses. I kept them because you always wanted to drink out of them. I hated them because the stupid red polka dots reminded me of her goddamned mushrooms."

Peg looked into her grandson's eyes, held his gaze and said, "Your mother called me last night. She says that Tara flew the coop. That she is just Mary again. Do you think it's possible that she was actually possessed by a demon? It seemed she was fully inhabited by Tara. It's the only thing that made any sense to me. And isn't it an absolutely bizarre coincidence that she called right before your father called me about you? Uncanny huh? Shit! It seems like more than happenstance to me. Oh dear, I think I'm really tired. I better rest for a little bit. When I get tired a blizzard of profanity comes out. Son of a bitch! See? Oh yeah, I forgot to tell you, your mother said she's coming to California. I invited her to stay with me."

Tres Leches Cake and Mexican Wedding Cookies, an Epilogue

The wedding had been lovely, short and sweet. The bride, noticeably pregnant, wore turquoise, her sister shocking pink. Both carried bouquets of roses and bougainvillea they picked from their garden where the ceremony took place. Dev officiated and asked Jay and Paloma if they promised to love each other? They agreed.

Mary was in attendance, but not Tara. So were Dev's father, stepmother and half-sister. Vic, suffering retrograde amnesia, was still hospitalized at the Men's Central jail and of course wasn't invited to the celebration. Both Gerardo and Ray's dad were locked up too. Jimmy Dracos had lit out with the diamonds and left his family high and dry. The Feds were looking for him. Ray was hoping his uncle Vic would get his memory back; they all wanted to know for sure if Dracos was part of the kidnapping plot. All of the jailbirds would have to wait for a visit though, because a group honeymoon had been planned to India and Nepal.

There was a taco lady fixing *quesadillas* and *carne asada* over an open grill. On the other side of the yard a man on another grill was making thin crispy *dosas* and spooning out vegetable curry. Champagne circulated freely, the good stuff, and Peg had already had a couple. Peg and Ray sat together in the first row. They had held hands all the way through the ceremony.

A dance floor had been set up on the other side of the yard with colored lights stretched across it. Musicians were busily plugging in amplifiers and stretching cords across a makeshift bandstand. Ray pointed to the dance floor and said to Peg, "One of the bands my mom produces will play tonight. It's 'Sweet Stevie and Monkey Junk.' She will probably sit-in on keyboards and sing. She has a great voice. Maybe you'd like to dance with me."

Peg patted the boy's hand and said, "That sounds quite lovely. I'm honored. Nobody has asked me to dance in a very long time, but you may have to hold me up because of all the champagne, not to mention having a third partner, my walker. Speaking of champagne, could you grab me another?"

Ray brought her another glass and a couple of Mexican Wedding Cookies. Peg swallowed some more champagne and took a bite of the powdered sugar covered cookie. Like snow, the powdered sugar rained down on her chest and lap. She said, "Oh balls! My new dress is all covered with white powder. Do you think they'll think I've been snorting cocaine or that I'm just a sloppy old lady?"

Ray took a napkin and started to brush her off. "You really cuss a lot."

She said, "Thanks, I do, and more power to me! Hey, I understand you're a top notch detective and a courageous young fellow."

"I was scared shitless the whole time I was on the boat."

"Well that was entirely reasonable on your part. Life is a scary bugger. But listen, my grandson saved your life, and you solved the mystery that gave him back to me. I think that from now on we are inextricably bound."

"That sounds nice. I would always like to be your friend."

"We will be great friends for a while."

"Why just a while?"

"Cause I'm old as dirt."

Ray leaned over closer to Peg and whispered, "Well then maybe we will meet again in our next life. That would be so nice. You know, I *still* think he could be the real deal—some kind of holy guy."

She took his hand in hers, "Maybe."

"Was Dev—Michael—always mysterious?"

"Yes dear, I think he was. He still has a big mystery doesn't he? How is it that he knew ancient Tibetan when nobody taught him?"

"Yeah, that is really mysterious, maybe mystical or at least spooky." Then Ray hummed the theme to 'The Twilight Zone,' "*do-de-do-do*."

She smiled and said, "But you're a solver of mysteries. You helped him discover his identity, perhaps you can help him figure out the Tibetan thing too."

He looked seriously into her blue eyes. "That wasn't a very hard mystery to solve. He's so smart. I don't know why he didn't figure that out way sooner."

"He wasn't ready yet. You were there to help him with the answer when the time was right. Listen Ray, I have a first edition Dashiell Hammet I want to give you as a wedding present."

"That's so nice, but I'm not getting married."

"Oh of course you are. We are all sort of marrying each other. I have a lot of mystery books you can read and I can re-read and then we can talk about them. That would make me very happy."

He said, "Me too. Do you think Dev and Aunt Adri will get married?"

"I don't have a clue. I'm 82 and pretty much I don't know shit. I'm still pretty clueless."

"I have to tell you, it's a little weird, your cussing so much."

"Do you mind?"

"No, I think I like it."

"Good, because since we will be honeymooning together, I don't want to make you uncomfortable. After all, we will be roomies. Could you get me some of that *tres leches* cake? And where is the guy with the champagne?"

Ray got up to get her some cake. When he returned she had a glass of champagne in either hand. She handed him one and said, "This is for you."

"I'm only fourteen."

"Yes, but I have it on good authority that you and the *Dos Equis* Man are already intimates. Besides, this is your mother's wedding." She looked at the cake which was balanced on her lap. "I understand your aunt made the bride and groom on the top of the cake. She even put on your mom's tattoos and she captured Jay's very serious and grown up expression perfectly. Quite charming!"

He said, "We're going to stick it on our fireplace. We have the whole history of our family glued up there. I'll show it to you later. Maybe you and I can add something special to it together."

The sun had nearly set, and in the low light, she could see the silky beginnings of a dark moustache on his upper lip. He asked, "Why do you say you're clueless?"

"Well, I'm only sure of one thing. I believe in love. You know how physicists think there may be multiple universes popping up all the time? Well I think love is like that, just bubbling up more love all the time. You know, limitless. That, my friend, is as deep as I get."

Ray took a swig of champagne and his face puckered up. "Shit! This stuff is sour!"

She laughed. "Well let's try some of the *tres leches* cake. What is it exactly?"

He said, "Well, it's made with three kinds of milk. One of them is that sticky sweetened condensed kind." He lifted the piece of cake up for her to examine. "It's a kinda wet cake. See how it makes like puddles around the bottom, but the cake part is not really soggy. It's a mystery to me. Here try a bite." He held up a big forkful of cake for Peg to try.

She took a bite and closed one eye and frowned. "Holy crap that's sweet!"

The End

Appendix

Instant Mystic, A Reader's Guide

1. What does the title, *Instant Mystic*, suggest about the story?

2. One of the symbols of Buddhism is the Buddhist Wheel. In the book this symbol is sometimes confused with a ship's wheel. Is the ship's wheel a common symbol in American culture? Why do you suppose the author chose to have young Dev confused about the difference between the two?

3. Traditionally in literature, Gypsies are depicted in two contrasting ways. Mary's (Tara's) early recollections engender the feeling of the romantic, mysterious notion of Gypsies traveling the countryside in beautiful *vardo* wagons. Gypsies are *also* represented as pickpockets, con-artists and scammers. Dev seems to characterize his mother's behavior as Tara, as a Gypsy scam. Do you think that Tara (Mary) believed she was being a con-artist by channeling the 'goddess'? The author used these cultural prejudices as part of the story. Did you grow up with any preconceived notions about Gypsies?

4. Did the author effectively use language to create visual images of various people, places and events in the story? Is

there any particular description that resonated strongly with you? Did the story make you want to visit any of the places in the story?

5. Food is used in the title of every chapter of *Instant Mystic,* and that food then appears in the chapter. Currently there is a sub-genre of mystery stories that include terrific recipes. But here, the author was trying to do something different in choosing to use food chapter titles. Why do you think she chose to name each chapter after a food? Was it an effective device? Was there a particular chapter title that amused you, or perhaps even offended you?

6. The story has a comic element. Did you enjoy that aspect of the story? Was there any part you found particularly amusing?

7. We like life's mysteries to have logical solutions, but they often do not. How did the author try to show that life's mysteries are often just that—mysteries?

8. Ray is a clever and engaging young character. Did you find the scenes when Ray is trying to evade his kidnapper effectively building suspense and leading to a satisfying conclusion?

9. Ray, like most children, prays to God when he is very afraid of a bad outcome. Often such promises are forgotten when the crisis is averted. Do you think that Ray is likely to keep his promises? Why or why not?

10. Three of the characters are seeking to find their identity; Dev, Ray, and Adri. Who among them do you think was most successful in finding out who they are and what their life is about?

11. Dev says he is hiding in plain sight. Were there clues in the

story that were in plain sight that helped you figure out the identity of the kidnapper? What about the identity of Tara? Dev?

12. Dev could be a holy man, someone simply deluded because of the decisions his mother made for him in his childhood, or even a person appropriately diagnosed with high-functioning autism. At the end of the book, Ray says he thinks that Dev is ". . . the real deal—some kind of holy guy." What are your conclusions about Dev?

13. There are two characters in the story that are never *truly* within the action. One is Ray's father who has escaped to Mexico, while the other is an imaginary person, the *Dos Equis Man*. How do these characters help the story in its narrative?

14. Adri is very much in love with Dev. She says at one point she thinks she might recover from this 'lovesickness.' Do you agree with the notion that falling in love is perhaps a temporary malady?

15. In the conversation between Ray and Peg at the wedding, she says, "Well, I'm only sure of one thing. I believe in love. I think it is like the infinite 'multiverse,' just bubbling up more love all the time." Do you agree with the message Peg imparts about the nature of love?

16. Dev thinks to himself about the genetic research that identifies a 'religious' gene which 50 percent of Americans may have. Is there evidence in the story that characterizes the gamut of religious belief and non-belief here in America?

17. The ending of the book was written as an epilogue. Did you find the conclusions of the story satisfying? Would you have preferred a different ending? In what way?

Instant Mystic Glossaries for the Hungry

I hope that most of the foreign words and phrases I have used in writing this book are understandable within the context of the story. But just in case something is confusing, or the reader would like to look back for clarification, I have organized some of the terms in three little glossaries.

The first is a glossary of the foods described in the story. The second lists some of the Spanish words and idioms that occur in the book. The third includes words and places from Tibetan Buddhism, Islam, Hinduism, Romani Gypsy culture, as well as the hallucinogens mentioned in *Instant Mystic*.

Hungry? A Glossary of the Foods in Instant Mystic

Abuelita. Brand of Mexican hot chocolate 'tablets' with cinnamon & nuts, like Grandma made.

Baba ganoush. Middle Eastern eggplant dip, usually olive oil, tahini and lemon.

Baingan Barta. An Indian (often Punjabi) eggplant curry with tomatoes and spices.

Baklava. Middle Eastern sweet pastry consisting of layers of phyllo dough and nuts soaked in honey or syrup.

Barbacoa. Beef brisket (or lamb) cooked until tender and falling apart with chiles and spices.

Bombo'n (Malavisco). Marshmallows.

Calabazas. Winter squash that looks like a flattened pumpkin or perhaps Cinderella's coach.

Carne Asada. Thin marinated beef flank or skirt steak, served as a steak or cut up for tacos.

Carnitas. 'Little meats.' Pork braised/fried. Often used in tacos with onions, salsa, cilantro.

Chai. Spiced tea of India. May include cardamom, ginger, peppercorns, cinnamon, milk, sugar.

Chakka. Jackfruit. Largest tree fruit in the world. Tastes and smells of over-ripe banana or Juicy Fruit gum.

Dosa. Crispy thin pancake made of rice and/or lentil flour. Masala dosa has spicy potato filling.

Dos Equis. Terrific Mexican beer. Others favor Corona, Bohemia, or Pacifico, but sadly none of those are represented by 'the most interesting man in the world.' For more on the Dos Equis guy (not the food, but the man and the meme), find him in the last glossary, Still Hungry?

Dulce de membrillo. Sweet semi-solid quince paste. Served with cream cheese or Manchego cheese.

Escabeche. Marinated vinegary jalapenos, onions, carrots with bay leaf and oregano.

Falafel. Fried balls of chickpeas, parsley, spices. Typically served in pita bread with Tahini.

Gypsy Tart. A dessert made of two ingredients, muscavado sugar and evaporated milk. Beat for 15-20 minutes and baked as a pie filling. Has a dark caramel taste. Origin is Kent in U.K.

Halal. Foods prepared under Islamic dietary restrictions. Similar to Kosher food certification.

Jaggery. Cones of dark brown sugar made from sugarcane and/or palm syrup. Not to be confused with 'jiggery-pokery,' which has pretty much the same meaning as 'hanky panky'!

Joe Gray. A British Gypsy stew made of sausages and/or bacon, potatoes, onions, tomatoes and probably whatever else was left-over.

Lassi. Refreshing yogurt drink. Sweet lassis (mango) have fruit, salted lassis are savory (cumin).

Machaca. Shredded beef, sometimes chuck or dried beef, cooked with onion, garlic, spices.

Merveilleux. Belgian crisp meringue filled with whipped cream or cream Chantilly.

Molinillo. Whisk or hot chocolate frother made of a wooden rod with loose wooden rings.

Mukhwas. Indian breath freshener/digestive. Fennel & anise seeds mixed with sugar pastilles.

Murabba. North Indian fruit preserve of mango, apricot or quince. Resembles marmalade.

Muscavado. Dark brown sugar with high molasses content.

Ropa vieja. Shredded beef and bell peppers and onions. Means 'old clothes.'

Sambar. Vegetarian soup made of lentils, tamarind, chiles, mustard seed, garlic, curry leaves.

Samosas. Triangular hat shaped fried pastry filled with potatoes and spices. Served with chutnies.

Tahini. Paste made of sesame seeds and oil. An essential ingredient in hummus.

Tres Leches Cake. Sponge cake soaked in sweetened condensed, regular, and evaporated milks.

Tzatziki. Greek dip of yogurt, cucumbers, garlic. Similar to Indian 'raita.'

Zigeunerschnitzel. Thin pork cutlets with bell peppers in spicy tomato & paprika sauce.

Hambriento: Hungry for Spanish Definitions?

Calaveras. Skulls-Sugar or clay for Day of the Dead, also etchings of skeletons by Posada.

Chi-chis. Bosoms slang –'boobs.'

Chiapas. Southern state in Mexico on border of Guatemala. Has large Mayan population.

Chivas. Female goat, also a slang term for heroin. The name of a gang in the area around Artesia.

Chones. Underwear. Also in 'Spanglish,' *chonies, choners*.

El Corazon en Fuego. Heart on fire.

Ese. Referring to a fellow homeboy (Mexican). In English homeboys are often called 'Homes.'

Hijo de puta. Literally son of a whore, but used more like 'son of a bitch.'

Guera. White girl. Can be friendly, or mean something akin to 'whitey' or 'honky,' depending on the context.

Lo siento. Sorry.

Maestra. Teacher (female).

Mami. Mom, mommy (affectionate).

Mazatlan. Large port city on west coast of Mexico. Home of *Pacifico* beer for you beer drinkers.

Mijo. Spanish conjunction for 'my son' – affectionate.

Nada. Nothing.

Nicho. Shadow box built of wood or tin. Reminiscent of niches for Catholic Saints in churches.

Puto. Literally man-whore, but used more like 'coward' or 'traitor.'

Quetzal. Long tailed bird of Chiapas. Iridescent from green-gold to blue-violet.

Sinaloa. State in Mexico where Mazatlan is located. Also center of the Sinaloa drug cartel.

Tia. Aunt

Tio. Uncle

Tonto. Dumb, retarded.

Tu sabes?. You understand? You get it?

Vato. Homeboy, used like 'Man' or 'Dude.'

Still Hungry?

A potluck glossary of terms, ideas, and places of Tibetan Buddhism, Islam, and Romani Gypsy Culture as well as the hallucinogens mentioned in ***Instant Mystic****.*

Allah. Arabic name of God, the God of the Abrahamic tradition as revealed to Muhammed. Used throughout the Islamic World.

Amanita Muscaria. 'Fly Agaric,' red and white polka-dotted mushroom. Hallucinogen/poisonous.

Apostille. Certification of a document to foreign countries.

As-salamu alaykum. Arabic greeting, 'peace be upon you'; response is 'and upon you peace.'

Ayurvedic. Ancient system of Hindu medicine.

Bardo. The transitional state between one's earthly death and reincarnation in Tibetan Buddhism.

Bhagavad Gita. Hindu scripture written in Sanskrit, *Song of the Lord*. Part of the epic, *Mahabharata.*

Bhutan. A Buddhist Kingdom on Eastern edge of Himilayas.

Bodhichitta. In Tibetan Buddhism, the awakening mind that strives for enlightenment for all sentient beings.

Carom. Also carrom. A strike and pocket game played on a flat board with nets in the corners.

Dal Lake. Lake about three miles outside 'Little Lhasa' near Dharamsala.

Dancers for God. Sufi worship in dance. 'Whirling Dervishes.'

Datura. Poisonous plant called Angel Trumpet, Moonflower. Its alkaloid causes hallucination/illness.

Dharamsala. Located in District of Kangra, State of Himachal Pradesh, India. The Tibetan government in exile is located there, in the upslope village of McLoedganj.

Dharmachackra. Buddhist symbol/wheel. Representing the wheel of law as well as rebirth.

Diamond Sutra. Buddha speaks to a monk about the nature of perception and the path to enlightenment.

Dos Equis Guy. Referred to in the beer commercials as, 'The most interesting man in the world,' brilliantly played by the actor, Jonathon Goldsmith, in an advertising campaign by the firm, Euro RSCG, representing Cuauhtémoc Brewery. This commercial has taken on a life of its own and become a cultural phenomenon and *meme*. On the internet the phrasal template, "I don't always [X] but when I do, I [X]," is a fun take on the commercial. For example, "I don't always look things up on my smartphone, but when I do, it is to prove people wrong."

Fakirs. Hindu or Muslim wandering mendicant, sometimes magicians. Long hair and beard typical.

Ganesh. Or Ganesha. Elephant-faced deity. Lord of letters and learning. Worshipped by Hindus/Jains.

Hakk'ni'panki. Gypsy con where sleight of hand is used to deceive the 'mark.' The Great Tomato Trick.

Hatchi-witchi. Romany name for 'hedgehog.'

Henna mehndi. Staining tattoo used to decorate Indian and Pakistani women for special occasions.

Hindi. One of the official languages of India. There are 20 officially recognized languages in India, one of which is English.

Imam. Islamic leadership position.

Kaaba. Pre-Islamic cubic building in Mecca housing 'black stone.' Direction Muslims face in prayer.

Koran. Qu'ran. Central holy text of Islam, believed to be revealed by Mohammed.

Kufi. Short brimless pillbox style hat worn by Islamic men and also many West Africans.

Lhasa. City in Tibet (now China). The traditional home of the Dalai Lama, who now lives in exile in Dharamsala, India.

Mandala. Ritual design used in Hinduism and Buddhism. Represents a microcosm of the universe for contemplation.

Mcleodganj. Called 'Little Lhasa.' A village seven miles above Dharamsala, previously the summer residence of Lord Elgin, the viceroy of India in the 1860's. It was acquired by the government of India to house the official residence of the Dalai Lama.

Mevlevi. Order of Sufi 'whirling dervishes, founded by Rumi's son. Outlawed by Attaturk, in Turkey, but allowed to be practiced as a form of historic entertainment.

Misbaha. Islamic prayer beads. Each represents one of the 99 sacred names of Allah.

Pen dukkerin. Gypsy fortune-telling.

Peyote. Small spineless cactus containing hallucinogenic alkaloids, especially mescaline.

Psilocybin. Mushroom with mind altering alkaloids. Its growth is widespread throughout Europe and the Americas. It is the main psychedelic mushroom of choice, referred to as "Shroom.'

Rastafarian Saddhu. The author, dear reader, made this up. A Saddhu is a Hindu holy man often with long locked tendrils of hair. Rastafaris are from Jamaica and believe Haille Selassi was God. I doubt saddhus listen to reggae. Although like Bob Marley, they likely are looking for, *One Love*.

Rig-Veda. A collection of archaic (1500 BCE) Sanskrit 'hymns' of praise to deities as well as about creation. It is one of the four sacred texts of Hinduism. The Rig Veda includes frequent mention of the drug, 'soma.'

Romani. Language of Indo-European origin, spoken by the "Rom' or Gypsies.

Rumi. 13th century Islamic scholar, Sufi mystic, and writer of poems of ecstasy and love.

Sanskrit. Ancient liturgical language of Hinduism and literary language of classical India. Considered a 'dead' language, although 14,000 people still claim it as their 'native' language.

Shiva. Hindu deity associated with the creation, dissolution and recreation of the universe.

Sidpa Bardo. A state between death and rebirth described in the Tibetan Book of the Dead.

Soma. A drink described in the Vedas. Some think it was amanita muscaria, although many anthropologists think some form of the ephedra plant is more likely. Ephedra is known as Mormon tea, which was widely drunk by early western pioneers and also Ma Huang, a Chinese herbal remedy. Ephedra was used in many weight loss concoctions until 2004 when the FDA made it illegal for that purpose. It is still available in cold remedies behind the counter at your local pharmacy, although you have to 'sign' for it. Ephedra is a main ingredient in 'crystal meth.'

Steven Seagal. Martial Artist, Hollywood star in 40+ movies. Everything the character Ray found on the internet on Steven Segal is actually there for you to discover too. On Seagal's own website, you will find that he claims that he is. a great blues guitarist, a Zen teacher and healer, an animal activist, a philanthropist. But most impressively, he is the "*first citizen to be honored for destroying a nuclear device*"! You may also buy T-shirts for the Steven Seagal Blues Band, or if you prefer, Steven Seagal, Sheriff. Discovering Steven Seagal is journey not to be forgotten.

Sufi. Sufism is a mystical sect of Islam seeking knowledge of divine love as a direct experience of God.

Swastika. The swastika has become the most hated symbol of our time, forever linked with the atrocities of the Third Reich. To the Western World it represents Nazi hatred and the resulting extermination of millions. However, in the Eastern World, it is still widely used as an auspicious symbol by Hindus, Buddhists and Jains. It often hangs on a doorway or gate as a good luck symbol. If you travel to Japan and look at maps, you will notice that Shinto Shrines are marked with the symbol of a *Tori* Gate, while Buddhist shrines are marked with a swastika. Not only did the symbol appear globally throughout prehistory, it was adopted in an almost fad-like way at the very beginning of the twentieth century in America and Western Europe. So if you travel to Copenhagen to the Carlsberg Brewery you will see the symbol on the Elephant Gates (1901), and if you thumb through postcards in an antique store, you may see the swastika as a symbol used like a four-leaf clover wishing the recipient good luck. It was also widely used in advertising even including Coca-Cola. The state of Arizona used the ancient Navaho swastika symbol on their state highway signs before the outbreak of World War II. And surprisingly, the swastika was painted on some Allied biplanes during World War I.

Terton. Tibetan Buddhism. A lineage of reincarnated individuals begun around 1,000 A.D. who are supposed transmitters of hidden treasures in the form of teachings, treasures taken from the earth and mind treasures. Interestingly, although most tertons have been men, they are often accompanied by a female companion, because the feminine principle was necessary for the concealment of the spiritual treasures as it is for them to be revealed again.

Tulku. The intentional rebirth in Tibetan Buddhist of a master sufficiently realized to control his own rebirth. The lineages of the Dalai Lamas are the most famous of the tulkus. Today's Dalai Lama is the 14th in his lineage. There are approximately 500 tulku lineages found in Tibet, Nepal, Bhutan, Northern India and Mongolia. A tulku takes up the position, teaching, work and administration of the previous holy man's incarnation, thus maintaining the ongoing stature of a particular monastic group. The 19th century Tibetan master, Jamgon Kongtrol the Great, was the supposed tulku of both a great translator as well as Ananda, Buddha's personal attendant. (Not coincidentally reminiscent of Dev's qualities in this story.) A film was made in 2009 entitled 'Tulku,' which documents the lives of five tulkus who were born in the West, including the filmmaker. I have not seen the film, but have read that some of the tulkus lead active lives as monks while others are married, and have secular jobs. The current Dalai Lama has hinted repeatedly that he may be the last of his lineage. He has stated that perhaps the position could be elected and further, that he would not choose to reincarnate in Tibet if it is not free.

Vardo. A horse-drawn British Romani Gypsy traveling wagon always with a chimney. Beautiful examples of woodworking and usually highly decorated, they could be round topped or flat, with or without a ledge. In the 19th century, the vardo was burned as part of the Gypsy funerary rites. The same style wagon was also used for traveling entertainers and circus people.

Viraaga. Buddhist term for non-attachment to worldly cravings and desires of the senses.

Zazen. Zen Buddhist form of mediation, done sitting on a *zafu* pillow in lotus, or legs crossed.

About the Author

Gail Gray Helm describes herself as a combo-plate of her two grandmothers. One was a fanciful storytelling Broadway actress, the other a keenly analytical editor for Randolph Hearst. Gail's family arrived in California before the Gold Rush, and she grew up with a deep sense of her California-ness. Her parents moved to Manhattan Beach in 1948 and lived a very laid-back beach lifestyle, surrounded by artists, actors, surfers, and a whole lot of sand. California's landscape, its multi-cultural society, its history and the Pacific Ocean formed her sensibilities.

Gail, a Magna cum laude graduate in history, taught World History and Creative Writing in Long Beach and Cerritos, California. She was particularly successful teaching at-risk teens to write poetry. Many of her students received awards for their work both locally and nationally. Her love of history and her insight into the soul of young people is evident in *Instant Mystic*, her first work of fiction.

Gail currently is working on two books in different genres. One is a contemporary comic mystery featuring the characters Ray and Peg who are introduced in *Instant Mystic*. The second is a historically accurate 1947 L.A. Noir crime thriller set at the Theatre Mart, an early Los Angeles landmark and home of the play, "The Drunkard." Helm's father managed the Theatre Mart for thirty years and was referred to by Walter Winchell as the "man who had met every star in Hollywood."

Gail is married with one son. Her husband plays blues guitar and is a fixture on the Long Beach music scene.

CPSIA information can be obtained
at www.ICGtesting.com
Printed in the USA
FSOW04n0550131015
12111FS

9 780996 443005